Bino's Blues

by A.W. Gray

A Novel

SIMON & SCHUSTER
New York   London   Toronto   Sydney   Tokyo   Singapore

SIMON & SCHUSTER
Rockefeller Center
1230 Avenue of the Americas
New York, New York 10020

Copyright © 1995 by A. W. Gray

Designed by Hyun Joo Kim

Manufactured in the United States of America

1 3 5 7 9 10 8 6 4 2

Library of Congress Cataloging-in-Publication Data

Gray, A. W. (Albert William)
Bino's blues: a novel/A. W. Gray
p.   cm.
1. Phillips, Bino (Fictitious character)—Fiction. 2. Lawyers—Texas—
Fiction. I. Title.
PS3557.R2914B53 1995
813'.54—dc20   94–34293 CIP

ISBN: 0-671-88186-8

For Sarah Emily Gray.

Little girl gone.

Young lady comin' up.

1

HARRY STRIPPED OFF HIS DIVING MASK, PUSHED HIS SOPPING black hair out of his eyes, and squatted on his haunches. The balls of his feet sank into cool, wet, canal bank mud as he watched the floating barge set its crane in motion. The chain clanked and straightened, its links rising from the murk in slow but steady progression, as Harry thought, When do we get paid for this, and how'm I going to keep the check away from Doris's fucking lawyer?

Jimmy sat nearby on the bank. "You're crazy for going down in that slop without wearing a wet suit," he said. "You cut yourself once on a busted fender or bumper down there, you're going to need a tetanus shot." Jimmy wore a dark green rubber suit complete with hood. He was skinny as a sick man, his face pasty white, his feet encased in webbed flippers and his ass sinking down in muck.

Harry could have made up a lot of reasons he wasn't wearing a wet suit, but the truth was that he thought he looked pretty beefcake for forty in skimpy racing trunks which he'd stolen during his four-month stint on the U. of Houston swim team, before he'd flunked out of school twenty years ago. He had broad shoulders and just a hint of gut, and his hairpiece was both water-resistant and super-undetectable. Nonetheless, he'd sound pretty silly giving the real reason he wasn't wearing a wet suit, with nobody to hear him but Jimmy and those four Houston cops standing around. No woman would be hanging around this nasty old ship channel, even with the chance of running into a stud like Harry. Harry was afraid that if he leveled with Jimmy, he'd sound like a homo or something.

So he said to Jimmy instead, "How we going to get paid, huh? These *po*-lice act like we ain't even got the right to ask. Christ, two days down here clamping onto these old wrecks and not a word about our money. You got any idea what we supposed to be looking for?"

The barge had hoisted up the fifth old junker of the day, slime and muck running from the auto and slopping noisily back into the water. The crane swiveled like a dinosaur against the gray bayou overcast, bearing its cargo over the inclined concrete channel banks. At the last instant the chain slipped; the car's rear end crashed down, recoiled violently, and settled on creaky springs. Harry looked over the vehicle's outline. Seventy-six T-Bird, Harry thought, a real pussywagon in its heyday.

Jimmy said, "All I know is, it's a co-op deal between the city and Channel Board cops. I finally got up the nerve to ask about getting paid, and get this. They act like I'm *insulting* them asking for my fucking money. Then two of 'em get in an argument about who's responsible for paying us, HPD or the Channel people. Harry, you give a fuck who pays us?"

"Are you kidding?"

"Yeah, me neither. Finally the dude from HPD takes down our address and says we're getting a purchase order. What's that deal?"

"A *purchase order*? Bad as *we* need the money? Hey, I got a purchase order one time, from the U.S Army Corps of Engineers. Assholes acted like that piece of paper was pure gold. Ninety, a hundred and twenty days before I seen a dime." Harry's shoulders ached from the day spent underwater swimming in blackness. Houston summer was a muggy bitch; he was still soaked from the last dive, yet he was sweating. Humidity must be a hundred, Harry thought. "I don't have a hundred and twenty days," he said. "Hundred and twenty days, Doris'll have me in jail for child support. She'd love it, too."

"Well, you ain't alone," Jimmy said. "I'm too broke to pay attention."

A loud tenor voice from behind them said, "Time for one more, men. Come on, the City of Houston's not paying you to sit around on your asses."

Harry turned. One plainclothes cop had come halfway down the incline, a puffy-cheeked guy of around forty, wearing glasses. His weight was shifted slightly back to compensate for his downhill stance, and it tickled Harry that the guy's polished black shoes and navy pants legs showed spatters of mud. The detective wore the standard massa-to-slave expression. Visible over his shoulder, the other three city men watched from their vantage point some thirty yards away, clustered around the pickup, the old Ford with HARRY AND JIMMY'S MARINE SERVICE stenciled on the doors in white script.

Harry scowled at Puffy-cheeks, then climbed to his feet, feeling a slight stiffness in his knees. He stretched out the rubber strap on his diving mask. "Our contract says we get double time after five," Harry said. "Of which we ain't got single time, double time, any fucking time yet, by the way."

Puffy-cheeks checked his watch. "Twenty till. One more dive, men." He took a couple of strides up the incline, then turned back. "And I don't want to hear any more talk about when you're getting paid. You nuts or something? This is the city you're dealing with." He continued on his way.

Harry yelled, "Well, Mr. City, sir, how many more days you going to need us?"

Puffy-cheeks halted and squinted at the barge, its bow tipping up and down in the middle of the hundred-foot-wide canal. "Depends on what you find," he said, then went on up to join the other city guys.

Harry muttered something about the city holding a gun to a working man's head as he clenched his mouthpiece between his teeth and checked his air supply. He picked up his flippers and lugged them down the incline, then walked into filthy warm water up to his waist. He lifted one foot at a time to put the flippers on, then shoved off. After looking guardedly around to be certain no one was watching, Harry pushed the base of his hairpiece back and forth on his shaved scalp. The rug was stuck solid as his own skin. He dog-paddled out near the barge to tread water while he felt for the grappling chain. Finally he cleared his mask and dove, following the chain links downward, hand over grasping hand.

Murky green changed to pitch black before his eyes as the cooler undercurrents pulled the chain this way and that. He couldn't see where the fuck he was going. Jimmy was right about the tetanus, and tomorrow Harry was going to bring his wet suit along, like it or not. These sunken cars were corroded to beat hell, and all it would take was a little cut. Most of the old heaps had been stolen, stripped, and then dumped into the ship channel; that morning, two of the rust-infested junkers had fallen apart before the barge could haul them to the surface. Harry wondered exactly what the police had in mind; stolen cars were as common as mud in these canals, and Harry would bet that the cops weren't even running makes on the ones they'd drug up earlier. Nope, these *po*-lice were looking for something in particular.

His feet touched silty bottom; he grasped the iron hook at the end of the chain and let his legs float into sitting position. His eardrums popped with pressure; he yawned, holding his jaws tensed and apart to ease the discomfort. Towing the hook behind him, he plunged straight ahead, touching bottom with his free hand every ten feet or so, feeling the mud dissolve into silt and drift between his fingers. He hadn't moved over ten or twelve yards when he touched smooth metal.

Harry's pulse quickened. This auto was different from the rest; the image of shiny chrome came to him as he felt his way

along the bumper. It was no old heap, and it hadn't been
down for very long; there wasn't a trace of slime on the fenders. Harry swam underneath to hook the rear axle, then wriggled clear of the car and pulled twice on the chain. The links
jerked instantly upward, losing slack, and Harry got out of the
way and hustled for daylight like Jaws after a succulent female.

The blackness faded into murky green, then transformed
suddenly into sky and shore as he exploded to the surface.
Water beaded on the lens of his mask. Jimmy was on the bank
in his frogman suit, arms folded. The barge's motor chugged
overhead. Harry swam the thirty feet to the incline, then
duckwalked halfway up to the bank. He squatted down on
tilted concrete. His breath came in ragged gasps. He wanted a
cigarette.

The barge motor coughed steadily, punctuated by the
creaking and rattling chain. Harry teetered, almost lost his
balance, then steadied himself as he looked up the embank-
ment to where the city men watched intently. Puffy-cheeks
stood away from the pickup with his lips parted in surprise.
Harry looked back at the barge. A snow white car had now
poked its rear end above the water's surface, visible to its
rocker panels. The barge's motor missed a beat, then resumed its *chug-a-chug.*

Caddy, Harry thought. Twin curved olive branches
gleamed in the bayou afternoon. The bumper was shiny and
unmarked, and Harry guessed that the car couldn't have
been down more than a couple of days. Excited, he hustled
up the incline to stand beside Jimmy, who watched with lips
pursed and hands on hips. Harry thought, Eldo? Seville? Jesus, bring it on up. His mask dangling from his fingers,
Harry led Jimmy toward the section of shore where the bat-
tered hulks stood. Something told Harry to be close by when
they set the Caddy down. The winch groaned as it lifted its
load clear of the water.

Eldo. Its squared-off nose came into view, water dripping
from its fenders and pouring from its trunk and doors. The
crane swiveled and the Caddy swung to and fro in decreasing
arcs as it neared the bank. Wherever it's from, Harry thought,

that sure ain't no Houston Cadillac; anyone living in the bayou country would have the good sense to undercoat the body to keep the corrosion away. Harry squinted at the license number. He knew some of the county call letters by heart—Dallas, San Antone, even Lubbock at the southern edge of the panhandle—but was out of luck with the Caddy because the owner had paid the extra fee for personalized plates. The license read RUSTY'S R, which to Harry meant exactly zero.

Harry watched from twenty yards away as the Caddy's front tires slapped down on the bank, and the sight of the dead woman behind the wheel caused him to forget all about the license number. Her head snapped back from the impact, then rolled forward to bang against the steering wheel as the rear tires came down. Harry had a glimpse of bloated cheeks and red hair which clung to her skull in clumps. He leaned over and retched.

He bent at the waist with his hands on his knees until the revulsion subsided, then walked closer to the Eldo for a better look. Harry had heard that many corpses looked as though they'd fallen asleep. The broad in the Caddy didn't look asleep. No way.

The one eye visible from Harry's profile view was swollen shut, the lid dull gray in color. The woman's neck bulged like a goiter; a plain gold necklace had dug a crease into the swelling flesh. The odor of death assaulted Harry's nostrils. He took one staggering step to the rear. One of the cops said softly, "Son of a bitch, will you . . . ?" Jimmy stood by like Hardy's Laurel.

Before Harry could speak, the city men jumped into action. One detective headed for the Caddy while two others blocked the divers' view. The remaining cop stood off to one side, arms folded, and cleared his throat.

This guy was younger than Puffy-cheeks, but even shorter and rounder. His fleshy neck puffed out over his collar. He wore a coal black suit, white shirt, and narrow black tie. His lips were pinched in a half-smirk; his shiny brown hair gleamed in dull bayou light.

He said, "I'm going to remind you that you have con-
tracted with the Houston Police Department and the Harris
County Channel Board for this job, and that automatically
places you under our jurisdiction. Right here and now I'm
putting you under orders that you are to remain silent. You
aren't to discuss what you've seen here with anyone. If you do
and we find out about it, you are subject to arrest and deten-
tion for security purposes." He sounded like a recording. He
pursed his lips even tighter and glared.

Harry jammed his mask under his arm, put his hands on
his waist, and looked down past his bare legs at his feet.
Hunks of mud clung to his flippers. He raised his head to
sneak a look at the Caddy, and once more read the license
plate. RUSTY'S R. Must be something big, Harry thought. An
idea came to him and he stifled a grin.

"I guess we can keep our mouths shut," Harry said.
" 'Course, if we was to start talking you couldn't arrest us 'fore
the word was out what you found down here. So I was wondering. Any way we could get paid for this job right now, without
fucking around with a purchase order? Like in cash, maybe?"

Three of the law enforcement men exchanged glances
while the other stood guard over the Caddy. One, a tall,
square-shouldered guy with eyes like flints, nodded to the detective doing the talking. "Up to you Channel Board people,"
he said.

The Channel Board guy licked his lips. "Well," he said,
"this is unusual. But I think we can arrange it. I'll have to give
you an address, and a woman's name to talk to about the
money. But, yeah. You play ball with us, we'll play ball with
you."

Harry grinned and nudged Jimmy with his elbow.

"Now, this is a pretty nice lady you're going to see," the
cop continued, looking Harry up and down. "So how 'bout
you guys cleaning up your act some before you go calling on
her. Goddam, man, that's the goofiest-looking hairpiece I ever
saw."

2

BINO PHILLIPS WAS GOING TO KEEP HIS HEAD DOWN OR BUST A gut trying. He glared down the fairway with the look of eagles; Rusty Benson's ball was alongside Barney Dalton's, both two-sixty down the middle of Crooked River's lush, green eighteenth like twin dust motes. Bino spat on his palms, rubbing his hands together as he took his stance, then gave his Big Bertha driver two professional waggles. He started with a smooth forward press to begin his one-piece takeaway, forcing his movements to be slow and deliberate all the way to the top, then kept his hands extra low on the downswing to compensate for his six-foot-six height. The clubhead made sweet, solid contact. Bino kept his gaze riveted on the spot where his ball had been for a full count of two. Finally he let his head come up and looked down the fairway, his hands held high in a Nicklaus-like follow-through. Man, he thought, did I ever nail that one. Then he waited patiently for his Titleist to come to rest somewhere in the vicinity of the other balls.

And waited.

And waited.

His ball didn't land in the fairway, or anywhere else in his line of vision. Bino frowned.

From behind him, Barney Dalton said, "My *god*, Bino. Where you trying to hit the fucking ball?"

Bino looked left and right, toward the tall green forests on either edge of the fairway. He stepped back from the tee and glared over his shoulder. Barney and Rusty stood side by side with their eyes trained on the right-hand woods.

Bino said, "Where'd it go, Barn?"

"It . . ." Barney lifted his Crooked River cap to mop sweat from his brow with a damp towel. His thick dark hair was tousled. He put the hat on and tilted it back. "I been the pro at this club nine years. Nine, count 'em. I've played this hole maybe a thousand times, and I never seen a ball hit where you just hit that one. How 'bout it, Rusty, you ever seen anybody drive the ball there before?"

Rusty Benson's tanned handsome face broke out in a grin. "Can't say that I have." Northern accent, faded some during Rusty's years in Texas.

Now Bino was really mad. He ran his fingers through his own short, snow white hair. "Well? Where the hell is it?"

Barney stroked his thick rust mustache as he strode in the direction of the E-Z Go electric cart, parked on the asphalt path east of the teebox. Barney's red leather bag was strapped behind the driver's seat with Bino's clubs encased in turquoise lizard and riding shotgun. "Come on," Barney said. "I can drive you there easier than I can tell you where it is. I damn sure hope there's no cannibals in those woods. We're dead if there are." Then, to Rusty: "How you want your money? Cash? Check? MasterCard?"

Rusty continued to smile as he went to his own cart, taking short confident steps, his shoulders square and his hands swinging easily. Amazing, Bino thought, the guy doesn't even look like he's sweating. Bino's own white golf shirt was drenched with perspiration. He watched Rusty climb aboard the cart, kick off the brake, and wheel away. The cart gave out a high-pitched whine as it rolled away down the path with Rusty's foot propped up on the dashboard. With Rusty's looks, Bino thought, no wonder I've lost clients to him in the past year, most of them women.

Bino trudged over to climb into the E-Z Go, and Barney pressed the accelerator to head off in the direction of the forest. Bino narrowed his eyes against the sun's glare; it was hot as the blazes. Not muggy-hot like Houston and the bayou country; Dallas heat was more of a dry blast furnace. Bino had grown up not fifteen miles from Dallas and had baked in the sun every summer of his life, but the heat still got to him at times. He could imagine how Texas weather must have felt to a guy like Rusty Benson, who'd moved down from Michigan awhile back to practice law. So, Bino thought, why doesn't Rusty sweat?

As the cart rolled along, Barney said, "Look, Bino, you know I'm the pro around here. I got an image to maintain. The members sort of look up to me, and I can't afford to let them know I'm gambling. So tell you what. Next time maybe you better find yourself another partner, okay?" He steered off the fairway and entered the shadow of the fifty-foot elm and pecan trees.

"Shut up and drive, Barney," Bino said.

Rusty took cash. Bino counted the money out in twenties and fifties as he and Rusty stood in front of the lavatories in the shit 'n' shower area behind Crooked River's locker room. Rusty's expression was mild as he eyed the stack of bills, then the tight muscles in his face relaxed into a smile. "You had an off day, buddy." He pocketed the money in his pressed gray slacks. "Better luck next time."

"No way it's luck," Bino said, "and there's not going to be any next time. Unless I get strokes. Hundreds of 'em." He selected a red Sonofagun dryer from among the half dozen or so on the counter, and blew his hair dry as he watched the jewelry show.

And quite a show it was. Rusty spread out a towel to hold his rings, then lovingly slipped the gold expansion band around his wrist and clenched his hand to look his Rolex over. There were fifteen twenty-point diamonds encircling the face, and on Rusty's big, muscular forearm the watch was right at home.

Next came the rings. There were two, both for pinkies, and Rusty held his hands palms down to model each one in turn. When he'd finished, jade gleamed dully from Rusty's left pinky while a sparkler which Bino figured for two carats, minimum, glinted on the other hand. The pale line on Rusty's wedding ring finger was darkening and blending with the rest of his tan, Rusty and Rhonda having split the blankets. Rusty hadn't mentioned his problems on the home front; Bino figured it was none of his business and had kept his nose where it belonged.

Rusty looked at the top of Bino's head. "Careful, buddy, you'll burn your hair up." He had deep brown eyes framed by dark lashes and brows.

Bino winced; he'd been standing with the dryer trained on one spot. He punched the OFF switch, laid the Sonofagun on the counter, and rubbed his head where his scalp still burned. So I was starstruck, Bino thought. Hell, Rusty *is* a star. Star at everything. Swings a golf club like a Masters champ, plays poker like Amarillo Slim. Handles himself around the courthouse like the reincarnation of Clarence Darrow, perhaps even more Hollywood than Racehorse Haynes himself.

Rusty walked to the opening which led from the showers, then paused and turned. From behind him came the soft click of poker chips. A loud but muffled voice said from the card room, "Fifty-two cards in the deck and I got to catch the fucking queen." The voice sounded like Barney Dalton's.

Rusty said casually, "Look, I don't like taking your money, so how about I buy you dinner at Arthur's? Maybe after then we make a few spots."

Bino thought it over. "Well, we do need to talk about the trial next week."

Rusty's gaze shifted slightly. "Okay, that, too. But first I've got a client I want you to meet."

Bino leaned his shoulder against the wall between the two gleaming white urinals, disinfectant tablets in the bowls like dull green pucks. "Well . . . sure. A client?"

Rusty smiled. "White collar guy. You'll like him."

"I don't guess I . . . Sure, a white collar guy. No holdup men or anything. But we do need to visit about the trial."

"No problem," Rusty said, checking his watch. "What time you want to meet?"

"I'm going to get belly-up in the poker game awhile, get my money back," Bino said. "Up to you, after that."

"Say eight, then." Rusty looked thoughtful, then said, "I'm baching it now, in case you haven't heard."

"I've heard," Bino said.

Rusty motioned as if batting mosquitoes. "Yeah, just one of those things. See you at eight, buddy." Rusty left.

Bino took long, determined strides through the drifting card room smoke, then flopped into the one open seat in the Texas Hold 'Em game. Nine tanned faces turned in his direction. "Deal me in," Bino said.

Bino made it to Arthur's fifteen minutes late and with a buck eighty-five in his pocket, wondering if perhaps there were a couple of bets he shouldn't have called. No way, he thought, it's just bad luck, nothing wrong with my poker playing. Slight possibility he shouldn't have drawn for inside straights a couple of times, but other than that . . .

Arthur's was the restaurant on the ground floor of Campbell Centre, a gold-tinted, mirror-walled tower rammed twenty stories above the intersection of Northwest Highway and Central Expressway, and definitely catered to the big-buck crowd. Bino slowed his white Lincoln Town Car to wheel into the parking lot, and steered between Caddys, Mercedeses, and even one Bentley on his way to the canopied entryway. He did his best to dodge the valet parking attendants but didn't make it; a gold-jacketed teenager jogged from the curb and waited directly in the Linc's path. Bino jammed on the brakes, got out, and accepted a pasteboard ticket. The kid hesitated with the car door open. Bino grinned. The attendant grinned back, but didn't move. Finally, Bino dug out his last dollar and handed it over. The kid drove away with a squeal of rubber. Bino entered Arthur's. Cocktail hour music soothed his eardrums, accompanied by the clink of glasses and the hubbub of muted conversation.

Just inside the entryway was a long horseshoe bar. Three men in gold vests and black bow ties hustled about behind the counter, freepouring from spout-corked bottles, whipping margaritas into a frothy pink in electric blenders, and mixing martinis in chrome cocktail shakers. Daylight savings time was hell on happy hour; though it was after eight, sunlight filtered in through the stained-glass windows and only about half of the seats at the bar were occupied. Green ferns protruded from hanging baskets at intervals around the bar and over the windows. The customers were businessmen—guys with razored hair dressed in suits—and women in everything from cocktail dresses to shorts and halters. Bino touched the Crooked River Country Club emblem knitted on his shirt as he sat on a barstool near the front. He fingered the three quarters and a dime in his pocket and hoped like hell to spot Rusty before anyone asked him what he wanted to drink. Jesus Christ, he didn't even have his credit cards.

Alongside a tiny dance floor at the far end of the room, a three-piece combo played. The young lady singing with the group wasn't bad at all. Her strapless green dress was cut from some kind of shiny spacesuit material which molded to her curves like skin. Luxuriant jet-black hair hung halfway to her waist in back, and there was an almost Oriental slant to her eyes. The number was "Misty," which she sang in a strong closing-time alto, and Bino got the impression that she was trying hard to keep the rock out of her tone and the rhythm in her hips to a minimum because this was Arthur's and not some jive joint on Lower Greenville Avenue. He decided that he'd like to catch her act when she was really letting her hair down.

One bartender, a thin balding guy in his forties, bent over close to where Bino sat. "What'll it be, sir?"

Bino lip-synced the words along with the singer and pretended that he hadn't heard.

The bartender cleared his throat and said, louder this

time, "What'll it be, sir?" From two seats away, a gray-haired man swiveled his head and shot an irritated glance in Bino's direction.

Bino leaned close to the bartender. "How much is a beer?"

Bushy, untrimmed eyebrows lifted in surprise. "Huh?"

Bino glanced to his right. The gray-haired guy was openly staring. Bino said in a now slightly hoarse whisper, "I said, how much is a beer?"

The bartender threw a can-you-believe-this-guy glance at a cocktail waitress, and said to Bino, "In *Arthur's,* you're asking how much a drink costs?"

Warmth crept around Bino's collar and up the side of his neck. He thrust his jaw forward. "That's what I said. How much is a beer?" Visible from the corner of his eye, the gray-haired man said something to the woman seated beside him. Both of them laughed.

The bartender scowled. "It's two bucks, Mac." All of the "sir" was gone from his tone.

Bino managed a weak grin. "Oh." At that instant he spotted Rusty.

Rusty stood near the bend in the horseshoe with his forearms crossed on the leather padding and one foot propped against the rail, listening to a man who talked nonstop from his seat on a barstool. Even white teeth flashed as Rusty nodded and smiled at the man.

Bino said to the bartender, "Excuse me. I see a guy I know down there." He rose.

The bartender's eyes narrowed. "I'm watching you, Mac. You put the touch on one of our customers for a drink and I'll throw you out on your ass. We don't like freeloaders in here." He grabbed a towel and wiped down the counter.

Bino moved along the bar. Customers swiveled in irritation as he said, louder than necessary, "Rusty. It's me. Am I late?" His voice cracked. A woman snatched up her purse and clutched it to her chest as he went by.

Rusty backed off and raised a hand. "Yeah, hey. This is the guy I was telling you about. Pete Kinder, meet Bino Phillips."

Rusty's companion was in his thirties and too fat. He wore a light gray suit, and his throat hung out over his collar in folds. His complexion was an unhealthy red and he looked worried. His handshake was weak, his palm clammy. He said in a flat tone, "Glad to meet you, Beano."

Bino nodded hello. "It's *Bye*-no," he corrected. "Just like Rusty pronounced it." White hackles rose. Bino decided he wasn't going to particularly like this guy.

Rusty said, "Look, there's an open table. Let's carry our drinks over and . . . What're you drinking, Bino? Like I said, buddy, on me." He waved a ten-spot, and Bino's friend the bartender came over.

Bino ordered J&B and soda. The bartender mixed the drink with his gaze riveted on the ten-dollar bill, and didn't slide the glass over until he'd rung the money up in the register and delivered the change. Rusty left a dollar on the bar. The bartender pocketed the tip and seemed happier. Rusty led the way to a rectangular table for four, and sat alone on one side with Bino and Kinder across from him. Onstage, the singer whispered into a dusky rendition of "I Left My Heart in San Francisco." She still seemed to be holding back, but her delivery wasn't bad at all.

"Now this guy," Rusty said, gesturing at Bino, "this guy I got to tell you, Pete. This mild-looking man over here was one of the best basketball players ever to come from these parts. Took his college ball club all the way to the Final Four one year. He's done it all in the federal arena, even got a federal judge acquitted a couple of years back. Bino, Pete's got a problem." Now showing Bino the hopeful, getting-something-for-nothing look. "Since you've got experience, we thought we'd, you know, pick your brain."

Bino sipped his Scotch and soda and did his best to look attentive. "Yeah? What's the problem?"

Kinder suddenly blurted out, "I've just gotten indicted. Me, Pete Kinder, can you believe it?" His hands shook.

Bino chewed an ice cube. No way should Rusty Benson need help from another lawyer in handling a criminal case. What in hell was going on? As Rusty toyed with his drink, Bino said to Kinder, "Sounds like you've got some bad news."

Kinder banged a chubby fist on the table. "It's a bullshit indictment, and old Rusty over there's going to show 'em in court." He gulped liquor as if for emphasis.

Just another innocent guy, Bino thought, the woods are full of 'em. He said to Rusty, "What's this case all about?" Darkness was falling fast outside. The bar's interior was dimmer now, more in keeping with a nightspot. A leggy waitress passed the table carrying a tray.

Rusty sipped whiskey. "This is the type of case I wouldn't ordinarily handle, a federal mail fraud deal. But Pete's a personal friend and . . . well, I wanted some advice from a real expert. Which is you." He showed a wink, really spreading it on thick, verbally backslapping his client and Bino at once.

All of which translated: Kinder is some kind of mail order swindler with a big cash flow, good for one helluva fee. And since Rusty was picking up the tab, Bino was now obligated to help string Kinder along. No such thing as a free lunch, Bino thought. He kept his mouth shut. Rusty went on.

"I've spent quite a bit of time with Pete over the past couple of days, all day yesterday and last night." Here Rusty looked to Kinder, who nodded without taking his gaze away from his drink. "In a nutshell," Rusty said, "Pete's business is telephone solicitations. Vegas packages, a couple of hundred bucks buys you two nights at the Sahara, Dunes, whatever. Hundred dollars' house chips, drinks, two or three shows. The package is sold over an eight hundred line, the guy gives his credit card number and gets billed."

Rusty took a small handful of nuts from a bowl and munched away as he said, "So, anyway. Things were rocking along pretty well for Pete, but . . . well, we think he pissed off a few bureaucrats down the line. He sent out two hundred *thousand* pieces of solicitation mail every week. I couldn't get the post office to give me the exact figures, but there's what, a million and a half population in Dallas? Christ, if everybody sent a letter a week, then Pete's mail would account for better than ten percent of the total volume. On top of which he dumps it all on the post office in one load. Now what I think is, somebody in the U.S. Mail's fine organization started bitching about handling all that mail, called up the postal inspectors and told them, Hey, anybody that's sending this much mail has to be up to no good. Get on this guy.

"So one day out of the blue," Rusty said, "along comes this news team from Channel 8, boom, walks right into Pete's office and starts shooting pictures. They didn't have an appointment, so Pete ran them the hell out of there. Made a great picture for TV, Pete shaking his fist and calling one of the interviewers a moron. What was it you said?"

Kinder perked up. "I told the guy that if he had an IQ greater than one, he'd better haul ass."

"The next thing you know," Rusty said, "there Pete is on *20/20*, John Stossel in person doing the hatchet job. And, friend, when *that* guy smears somebody, they're smeared big-time."

Something stirred in Bino's memory, a *20/20* piece he'd seen one night, a scene inside a posh office with a guy standing behind a desk, snarling and wagging his finger at John Stossel, who'd seemed tickled to death by the insults. Not real good PR. Bino looked sideways at Pete Kinder. Yep, this was the same guy.

"The rest of the story's a first-class nightmare," Rusty said. "The day after two-oh, two-oh airs the piece, Pete's banks all panic and freeze his accounts. They're all credit-card deposit accounts, and the banks say they're afraid everybody's going to want a refund after what they've seen on television. And of course that's exactly what happened, all these people who bought Pete's Vegas package suddenly decide the whole thing's a swindle and demand their money back. Pete's hands were tied. The banks wouldn't release the money to Pete so he could make the refunds, and the sorry bastards at the bank wouldn't refund it directly to the customers, either. Hell, those banks were getting *interest* on that money, what did they care? And, of course, that's exactly what the postal inspectors were trying to achieve when they called up the newspeople and put them on the story to begin with. Bam, next came the indictment."

"What Rusty's telling you," Kinder said, "that's the nuts and bolts of it. There wasn't a single fucking complaint against me, not one, before the *20/20* show. I can prove that. Sure, we're a boiler room operation and that makes me suspect from the get-go. But a *crime?* What a bunch of bullshit. Rusty tells me we might have one helluva lawsuit when this is over. What do you think, Beano?"

"*Bye*-no." Bino's gaze shifted back and forth between Kinder and Rusty, Rusty with a Go-Pete-Go expression, Kinder's look anxious. Onstage the combo was into "Feelin' Groovy." Smooth. Bino lifted his J&B, then paused with the rim of his glass inches from his mouth. "Stop whining," he said, then took a long pull. He set his glass down. "And cop out."

Kinder said, "Huh?"

Bino turned to face the chubby red-faced man with the pugilistic attitude. Bino said, "Cop out. Plead guilty. You'll get two years, maybe three. If you go to trial you'll get seven minimum, maybe as much as fifteen years."

Kinder said, "What the living fuck . . . ?"

Rusty seemed about to choke on the cashews. He coughed and said, "What are you talking about? If there's ever been an innocent man, it's old Pete here."

And, Bino thought, if ever there's been a man about to get taken to the cleaners for a legal fee, that's old Pete as well. He briefly wondered if Rusty was going to kick him in the shins under the table. Bino rocked back, lifting the front legs of his chair off the floor. "What I believe in," Bino said, "is people not bullshitting each other. I represent guys like you all the time, Pete, and do a good job of it. But don't come on innocent with me. A guilty guy's a helluva lot easier to defend. You got guys hustling people on the phone, I'll lay five to one the mooch thinks he's getting a plane ticket when he's not, and that your price is based on space available at the hotel, which most of the time there isn't any. And the money's not refundable, right?"

Kinder's beet red complexion was suddenly pale. "Christ, it says right on the package . . ."

" 'Based on space available,' " Bino said. "In letters about one centimeter high. Plus, aside from the fact you're screwing people, nobody beats a mail fraud case. Nobody. It's the broadest statute there is, and they'll convict you on it."

The cocktail waitress paraded by, and Rusty held up three fingers. She nodded and headed for the bar, her firm behind wiggling and her short skirt popping from side to side. As Kinder watched her go, Rusty nudged Bino under the table. Bino ignored the guy.

"You asked my advice," Bino said. "Okay, here's what I'd do. The U.S. Attorney's not going to drop any charges, but he thinks trying a case like yours is a massive pain in the ass. He'll make a good deal, drop everything down to one count, and you'll get two years. Do it in a country club without a fence around it. With good time and halfway house, you'll be out in thirteen months. If you go to trial you've got rocks in your head."

Kinder pushed back his chair and rose. He was trembling all over. "I appreciate the information," he began, then firmed up his lips and said, "No, hell, I don't, either. I'm not pleading guilty. The feds can shove it up their asses. For that matter, so can you. Thanks for your time . . . *Beano*." He nodded curtly to his lawyer. "Rusty." Then he was gone in the direction of the exit, very nearly colliding with a woman near the bar as he stalked away.

Rusty got up in a hurry. He yelled out, "Pete. Wait. I'll walk out to your car with you." Then, as he took off in hot pursuit of his client, Rusty hissed at Bino, "Thanks a whole heap, pal."

Bino was now alone with three full drinks on the table. He considered chasing Rusty down to remind him that they still hadn't discussed the trial, but changed his mind. He could bring up the subject once Kinder had gone and Rusty had cooled off. If Rusty hadn't already punched him out by then, that is. Jesus, Bino thought, what'd he have to ask me for?

Nightfall had brought the clubbers out in droves. Men and women now stood three-deep around the bar, gesturing and yelling for service. The tables were full as well, couples, unescorted ladies in twos and threes, men who traveled mostly in pairs and shot glances at the ladies. The dining room was now open for business, and Bino looked in at white linen tablecloths, at jacketed waiters hustling to and fro, delivering meals by candlelight—veal or chicken hidden beneath shiny chrome half-spheres. A slim brown-haired girl had set a podium at the restaurant entrance and was taking names for seating purposes. Ten or twelve couples waited in line, men in suits and women in filmy summer dresses.

The combo swung into the crescendo finish to "I Don't Know How to Love Him," and the raven-haired singer got all of Bino's attention as she raised up on the balls of her feet, her breasts thrust proudly forward in the strong-voiced, emotion-packed finale ("What's it all abowwwwwwwt . . ."). The song sent chills galloping up and down his spine. It seemed to him that the singer was looking his way, but he was certain he was imagining things. Probably it seemed to all the other guys in the place that she was watching them as well.

She received a blockbuster of an ovation, some standing to applaud, others cheering at the top of their lungs as she bowed from the waist and uttered a few breathy thank-you's into the mike. Then the band swung into a bouncy take-five theme. She did a little hop-step-prance up to the U-curve in the bar, covering the twenty yards or so with thighs flowing under snug green fabric. The bartender had a drink made for her, ice and clear liquid in a rock glass, likely gin. She picked up her toddy and headed straight for Bino's table, lightly bumping a stool with her hip as she did.

At first Bino thought he was dreaming, but as she drew closer he sat up straighter. The corners of her eyes were crinkled in a smile. Her gaze was fixed on him, no doubt about it. She held the glass in both hands as she bounced along; though she almost collided with a man in the aisle, her hip-swinging gait never missed a beat. As she halted before the table, she bumped lightly into Rusty's empty chair.

She said, "Oops. Rockin', huh? Tomorrow night they'll be bringing in Artie Shaw and having me do 'Accentuate the Positive.' Where's Rusty?" She looked around.

Bino stood, flustered. "He's . . . just stepped away for a minute, he's . . ." He glanced toward the exit. No sign of Rusty.

Her lips parted and she cocked her head. "Wait a minute. You're too tall." Bino decided that if this girl wanted him to shrink a few inches, he'd do his damnedest to oblige.

Tinted glasses in big round frames hung from around her neck. She perched them on her nose and peered at him. "Why, you're not him," she said.

Bino's neck flushed. "I'm not? Excuse me, but I'm not who?"

"My guardian." She giggled the cutest giggle that Bino had heard in a coon's age. "Rusty's friend, the guy he usually sits with. I'm really sorry, but the white hair fooled me. You're not him, you're too tall and you're not old enough. Is your hair bleached? Okay if I sit down?"

Bino said, "No." Then, as she backed away a hesitant step, he stood quickly and said, "I mean, please sit down, but no, my hair's not bleached. I was born with it." She slid gracefully into the empty chair as Bino sat as well. He wondered fleetingly, *What* guy that Rusty usually sits with?

She leaned forward, propping her elbows on the table as she regarded him over the rim of her glass. Her bare upper chest and shoulders were flawless and her skin the color of rich vanilla ice cream. Or, he thought, maybe vanilla with just a touch of dark rum added. The tautness of her upper arms told him that this was a girl who got some exercise. *Indoor* exercise; with that complexion she didn't spend a lot of time baking in the sun.

Bino cleared his throat. "So you're a friend of Rusty's." He did his best to sound casual, but felt he'd put it over about as well as he'd done at the country club playing poker.

She moved her pointed chin a bit sideways, her eyes knowing behind the big round lenses. "You might say that," she said, smiling a secret-keeping smile.

"Oh. So, do you see him often?" He couldn't keep the disappointment from his tone.

"*Weh*-ell. Just when his wife isn't around." She took a slow and deliberate sip of her drink. "Here lately it's every night."

He sagged in his chair.

She laughed, hunching her shoulders, showing a bit more

of the crease between her breasts. "Oh, he's just a customer. Fan, or whatever you want to call it. Rusty's one of our regulars. Sometimes he catches us at this other gig we've got, down on Lower Greenville Avenue. Here at Arthur's we're the Dinner Hour Quartet. Wow-oh. You should see us on Greenville, down there we're Carla and the Creepers. So. I'm Carla. Who are you?" She glanced at his hair. "Please don't tell me you're Whitey. God."

"Well, no, I'm . . . Wendell Phillips," Bino said. She looked as if she wasn't too crazy about that name, either, so he said quickly, "That's my given name. Bino is what everybody calls me. Short for albino. It's . . . sort of like being called Whitey, I guess."

"I suppose it is," she said, "but how can you be an albino when your eyes are blue and you've got a tan?"

"It's just this nickname," Bino explained. "I picked it up when I was playing basketball. Just like some white-haired guys are Cotton. Or Whitey. Same difference." He grinned hopefully.

"Bino," she said, rolling the name over her tongue as if trying it out. "Hmm. Well, it beats Whitey. Or Cotton. So, Mr. Bino, we've got one more set to do. We finish here at nine, then it's down to the Greenville strip. Want to come along and rock with the Creepers?" Just like that.

Bino wasn't sure he'd understood. "Huh?"

"Look," she said. "Just so you'll know, I don't go around walking up to every man I meet and saying, Hey, you want to go someplace with me? Believe it or not, I'm not that hard up. I came over to the table because I thought you were Rusty's other friend, I really did. I'm nearsighted as hell, and that's something I can't help. So now that I'm here, I like what I see." She took off her glasses and let them dangle between her breasts. "So please don't make me feel like a dope by sitting there and saying something dumb like, 'Huh?' "

Bino couldn't believe that she was actually talking to him. From all around the club, jealous male glances came in his direction. Eat your hearts out, boys, Bino thought. He rolled his head around on his neck, Burt Reynolds fashion, as he said to

Carla, "Sure, I guess I could. Just take a couple of minutes for me to tell old Rusty I'll have to see him later, okay?"

She lifted her gaze to the ceiling. "Thanks. The suspense was killing me." The tops of her breasts quivered slightly as she stood. "Last set. We're going to rock the joint with 'Tennessee Waltz.' Don't go 'way." She headed for the bandstand with her bottom jiggling nicely.

Bino thought, Hot damn. Then he looked around in an effort to spot Rusty Benson, wondering if good old Rusty could spare a few bucks until tomorrow. Where was old Rusty when you needed him?

Bino got up and went over to peer through the window into the parking lot. The valet attendants were gathered underneath the awning, chewing the fat, but otherwise Bino didn't see anyone. No sign of Rusty, and no sign of what was his name?—Pete Kinder.

It dawned on Bino that Rusty seemed to have left. He couldn't have, Bino thought, we haven't talked turkey regarding the trial. Surely Rusty couldn't forget something that important. Naw, good old Rusty wouldn't desert a guy.

But it appeared that good old Rusty had.

He headed for the bar, conscious of Carla onstage in the periphery of his vision as she took the mike from its stand. A yellow spot shone on her as the combo played the lead-in to "I'll Never Fall in Love Again." The old Burt Bacharach tune.

His pal the bartender was still on duty, the thin fortyish guy watching suspiciously as Bino approached. Bino put one elbow on the counter and leaned close in a buddy-buddy attitude. "Say, friend. Is there any way I can get a check cashed in here? Say, for our drinks over there and a few extra dollars? Oh, yeah, and for a pretty good tip to boot." He winked.

The bartender was filling a tumbler with soda from a liquor gun, and now froze like a store window dummy. He stood unmoving as the fizzy liquid filled the glass to the brim, then cascaded over the tumbler's edges to drench his cuff and hand. The soda dripped down and puddled on the drainboard. Still he didn't move. His eyes widened. His lips parted.

"A check. A fucking *check?*" the bartender finally said.

• • •

After her final number, Carla showed the clapping, whistling
patrons a couple of extra bows. She wondered if she was making a big mistake. God, what if . . . ? She'd never even *seen* the
guy before. What had gotten into her, coming on like that to a
total stranger? He looked all right. Cute, too, super-tall dude
with snow white hair. Too late to back out now, she thought.
So they find me in a ditch in the morning, I won't be the first
ravaged female to wind up that way. Ha, ha. Big headlines.
Singer conked, whatever. She told the boys in the band that
she'd meet them at the Greenville Avenue gig, then hustled
on her way. Halfway to the bar she froze in her tracks.

Bino stood by the door. A uniformed security guard was
over there as well, his hands folded behind his back, bouncing up and down on the balls of his feet like a middleweight
fighter. Vernon, the night manager/bartender, was on the
phone, saying, "Yeah? Yeah, good. We'll hold him till you get
here."

Carla went up to the counter and said, "What's the trouble, Vern?"

"Just another deadbeat, happens all the time," Vernon
said. "Ordered drinks and then tried to pass a check on us. Jesus Christ, you'd think they'd learn."

Bino shrugged and showed Carla a weak grin.

God, Carla thought. God, God, God, can I ever pick 'em.
She got her purse from underneath the cash register. "He's
with me, Vern," she said. "Here, I've got some money." Then
she said to Bino, "You do have a car, don't you? Or should I
bring cabfare?"

3

"AND I CAN'T REALLY KNOCK IT," CAHLA SAID. "DOING summer road shows was great experience, but . . . let me give you an example. The last job I had was in *Music Man.* I was in the chorus and even had one solo singing line, which is like, you're on your way up, you know? 'A hundred and one clarinets close behind,' or some such, but the main thing was, I was first stand-in for the lead. Never know when the big break's coming in that business. Lana Cantrell, an Aussie yet, plus I thought she was a bit, shall we say, *mature* for the part, but anyway, she was Marian. So like I said, I'm first stand-in and, *boom.* Second night, Cantrell comes down with the flu. There they are, making me up. Ta-*taaa,* instant librarian. So I'm waiting in the wings, the overture's playing. And guess what."

"You were a hit," Bino said. "The director married you."

"Not even close. Right at the last second Cantrell shows

up, smelling like a locker room. Not b.o., Ben-Gay. And would you believe it? They put her on and let her croak through the performance like a frog. So I tell them, Look, if somebody with pneumonia does a better job than I do, well, you can kiss my ass, you know? It's been rock 'n' roll for little Carla ever since." She pursed her lips and smacked off two pantomime kisses. "You're *cute*, baby. What's hap'nin'?"

Bino had a sip of J&B. "He's a fish, Carla. Not a dog. An Oscar fish."

Cecil was getting quite a show. Carla had blown her kisses at the Oscar over her shoulder, wearing black bikini panties, her glasses, and nothing else. Bino thought that Cecil was opening and closing his mouth faster than normal. At any rate, the stupid fish wasn't turning his back on her and swishing his tail, which was Cecil's version of the cold shoulder. Bino should know; Cecil had shown *him* the act often enough. But Carla seemed to have the Oscar's undivided attention.

She came out of her hootchy-koo posture and strutted over to the couch to drop bouncily onto the cushions beside him. She took off her glasses and let them dangle, then crossed her ankles on the coffee table and rocked one foot in rhythm to the music. Bino had put on an old Harry Chapin tape, and heavy guitars moaned over the speakers in the lead-in to "Dog Town." Carla's toenails were painted a bright iridescent pink.

"Our fifties night is Sunday," she said. "You should catch us, the bass player can sing 'Walkin' to New Orleans,' and if you closed your eyes you'd think Fats Domino was up there."

Bino watched her calf muscle bunch and elongate in time to the beat. "Not this week," he said. "I've got work to do." He was clad in white Jockey briefs, and his bare ankles were crossed on the coffee table alongside hers. Her feet, he thought, were less than half the size of his Number 13 clodhoppers.

"I didn't think lawyers did any work," she said. "I thought they just stood around and collected everybody's money and then ran around getting drunk every night. By the way, I'm not forgetting that you owe me. Twenty-two bucks so far, and the interest meter's running." She wrinkled her nose.

"I got it in my bureau drawer," Bino said.

"Why didn't you tell me that when we were in bed?"

"I had other things on my mind. It may not look like we do any work, but the fact is I've got a trial starting a week from today. Next Monday. And the only reason I was out tonight is that I had a hearing scheduled in the morning, but the prosecutor told me he was getting it postponed."

"The prosecutor probably wanted to get drunk tonight himself," she said.

"Not this prosecutor," Bino said. "He doesn't drink anything stronger than a carrot juice cocktail. I don't think this guy even fools around with women. He's so in love with himself there isn't any room for anybody besides him to gaze at his reflection."

"Sounds like Rusty Benson. God."

"I wouldn't touch that one with a fifty-foot pole," Bino said. "Rusty is . . . well, Rusty. Hey, Carla, who's the guy you thought was me? You know, Rusty's friend."

"My guardian? I don't even know his name. Sweetest old guy. He's come into Arthur's with Rusty at least twenty times. I'd sit with him on my breaks. You'd be amazed what sitting with somebody who looks like your dad will do to discourage other guys from hitting on you. He'd get awfully silly sometimes and kind of lonely-sounding. I don't think he's got a family."

"Why not?" Bino said.

"You can just tell. A man his age out on the town every night. The night I met him was also the only time I've ever seen Rusty with his wife. You know her?"

Bino pictured Rhonda Benson, tall, willowy, a lot more body than one noticed at first glance. There'd never been much flash to Rhonda until the past couple of years, when Rusty's success had seemed to make her bloom. The last time Bino had seen Rhonda was the previous spring, in the gallery at the Byron Nelson Golf Classic. She'd been in tight shorts then, and a halter top which bared her midriff, and there'd been a sultry gait in her walk. The lipstick she'd worn had matched her flaming red hair. He remembered thinking at the time of a butterfly hatched from a cocoon. Bino said to Carla, "Yeah."

"Well . . . you see a lot of things when you're working these clubs. First I knew Rusty. Then I knew her. But not together. She came around the rock clubs a lot. Redheads, especially the ones built like her, well, they really stand out. She always came alone, and as far as I know that's the way she left. She was older than most of the Lower Greenville crowd, but God, did she ever have the dance floor moves. The young guys were always trying to hit on her." Carla cut her eyes mischievously. "You know how that works, don't you, Mr. Lawyer? The young guys seem to dig the older stuff and the old guys . . .

"Anyway," Carla went on, "one night I'm playing at Arthur's and all of a sudden there she is, sitting at a table with Rusty. And the older guy, the one I mistook you for. At first I thought Rusty had come with a date, but when I went over at my break Rusty goes, Carla, I'd like you to meet my wife. If you want to know the truth, I'd never figured either of them for married. Usually you can tell."

"Oh? How's that?"

Her purse was on a chair beside the big-screen Mitsubishi TV. Carla boogied some to Harry Chapin as she crossed the room, then fished in her purse. "Easy," she said. "They're always looking around to see if anybody they know is hanging around. Both Rusty and his wife walked around those clubs like they owned them. Like neither of them cared if the other knew what they were up to. Kind of a strange relationship, if you know what I mean." She came up with a Virginia Slim and a disposable lighter, set her purse down, and headed back for the sofa.

"To each his own," Bino said.

She curled up her legs and sat on her ankles, hooking her elbow over the back of the sofa. "That's what I say," she said. She started to light her cigarette, then paused. "So how 'bout it, big fella? Ready for a rematch?"

Bino decided that he was really going downhill in a hurry. He was a respected member of the Bar and pretty well known around Dallas, especially by those who remembered his Final Four basketball days at S.M.U. But Christ, was he ever slipping, hanging around Crooked River Country Club with Barney Dalton and gambling on golf and poker and doing a lot of drinking. And now here he was, really scraping bottom, a milk-skinned girl in her twenties who sang like Barbra Streisand or Janis Joplin, depending on the mood she happened to be in, running around his apartment in black bikini panties and saying, Hey, you ready for another roll in the hay?

He stood. "Sure, if you are."

She winked and let the lighter dangle by her side, removed the cigarette from between her lips, stood beside him and stuck one hip out at a saucy angle. "About the twenty-two bucks, buster," she said. "I'm not forgetting it, in case you were wondering."

4

CARLA LIVED IN DUNCANVILLE, IN FAR SOUTH DALLAS COUNTY, and Bino made the drive at seven in the morning with a hangover. She stood alongside her driveway and waved, then pranced to the front door of her duplex as he thought, I'm too old for this. He stopped in a 7-Eleven, bought a couple of Alka-Seltzers, bummed a glass of water in which to mix the fizzy stuff, then climbed into the Linc and fought stop-and-go traffic all the way downtown.

He trudged through the crosswalk at Akard and Main with the honking horns pounding in his ears like drums. Inside the Davis Building he entered the elevator and pressed the sixth-floor button, then steadied himself against the wall as the car ascended. On the way down the corridor to the door marked W. A. PHILLIPS, LAWYER the floor seemed to tilt.

As he came in, Dodie Peterson said, "You're early. *Eek!* Wow, you look like death warmed over." Crystal blue eyes softened in pity.

"I'm a little under the weather, Dode. Something going around, I think." He went through the reception room, entered his own spacious office, and sank into his chair thinking about an ice pack.

For long moments he just sat and stared at the picture hanging above his imitation leather couch. The twenty-year-old photo featured a jubilantly celebrating basketball team, young men with upraised clenched fists and block letter S.M.U.'s stitched across the fronts of their jerseys. The Bino of the sixties was in the top row, giant Southwest Conference trophy held aloft over his flattop haircut. Bino thought, They look too happy. I've *never* been that happy. And Dodie, yeah, she's punishing me, too. She's found out about last night, and she's giving me hell by banging all those drawers around out there. He just didn't have the strength to reflect on his sometimes-lovers, sometimes-friends relationship with his secretary. In fact he didn't have the strength for anything but a nap. He considered stretching out on his desktop and copping a few z's.

Dodie came in grinning cheerfully. She wore a sleeveless peach-colored blouse over a pale green skirt, had file folders stacked in the crook of one arm, and carried a cup of coffee. She placed the steaming black liquid before him, then sat in a straight-backed visitor's chair. Her blond bangs were carefully tousled, and normally just the sight of her brightened his day. Bino groaned.

"Drink it, boss," she said, opening a file on her lap. "You're going to need it. I need to ask you a few things so I can get the motion ready."

Bino raised the Styrofoam cup to his lips, sipped and swallowed. The blistering hot liquid scorched his tongue. "Wha," he croaked, then cleared his throat and said, "What motion?"

"The motion for continuance. You're in no condition for a hearing. Besides, I think you'd probably want to put the hearing off even if you weren't . . . sick. There's another nasty story on page one this morning and a big picture of Lieutenant Clinger, and I don't know how the papers manage to make him look so mean." She readied a pencil. "So what do you want the motion to say? It had better be good, I don't think Judge Sanderson's going to want to put this one off. Too much publicity, and with the trial starting Monday she's going to want to get the preliminaries out of the way." Visible through the window, the morning sun glinted from the mirror-walled skyscraper next door. The day was going to be another scorcher.

Bino pinched his nose. "The story's only about Tommy Clinger? Just *my* client? What about Rusty Benson's guy? And what about all those other cops going to trial? Nothing about them?"

Dodie shook her head. "The entire piece is quotes from Mr. Goldman. He says he's going to prove all sorts of bribes and things on Lieutenant Clinger, but doesn't say a word about anybody else."

Bino closed his eyes and murmured, "Shit," softly under his breath. No wonder Rusty had vanished last night, he'd already known about the newspaper story. Bino said, "I'm sure we've got big problems, then, but don't worry about filing any continuance motion. I already talked to Goldman yesterday. He's cancelling this morning's hearing and setting it for Monday, just before the trial begins. Goldman told me something new had come up, and now that you've told me what's in the paper, I got a pretty good idea what the something new is. My client's neck in a noose and Rusty's boy as a federal witness. Anyhow, there's not going to be any hearing."

Dodie chewed her lower lip. "Are you sure about that?"

Bino lifted his cup and blew on the coffee's surface. Slowly but surely, his head was clearing. "Yeah. Goldman told me himself."

Dodie frowned. "I don't think you heard him right, boss. Mr. Goldman's office called a few minutes ago, wanting to know if you'd like to meet with him before the hearing. His secretary said he's already on his way upstairs to court."

Bino sipped the cooled-down liquid. It was better. "That can't be, Dode. Goldman said he was getting Judge Sanderson to postpone while he investigated these other matters. Hell, it was Marv Goldman that suggested since we weren't having the hearing today, maybe I should get together with Rusty and play some golf. Blow off a little . . ." Bino paused in midsentence as it dawned on him. He gave a long disgusted sigh as he finally said, "Steam."

He had a sudden mental image of Goldman, thin lips in an evil smirk over his black goatee, his ear flattened against the receiver, throwing broad winks at a grinning FBI agent across his desk while he fed Bino a line of shit about putting the hearing off. Probably giving the agent the old thumb-and-forefinger circle sign as he told Bino to go play some golf and blow off a little steam. The picture in Bino's mind rolled on, now shifting to Goldman calling Rusty Benson, telling Rusty that if he'd be sure the white-haired lawyer stayed out really late, there'd be some extra perks in it for Rusty's client come plea bargain time.

Bino stood quickly, ignoring the throbbing in his temples. "Get Tommy Clinger on the phone, Dodie, and fast." He grabbed his attaché case and opened the snaps, taking the files one by one from Dodie's lap, reading the labels, shoving some of the folders into the satchel and stacking the others up on his desk. "It's a good thing I told Tommy to hang loose, just in case. Tell him to beat it down to the courthouse, that the hearing's on. Also tell him that I'm afraid Nolby's going to testify for the feds. Jesus, Goldman's done it again."

Dodie's jaw slacked, her gaze darting back and forth between Bino and the stack of files. "But the motion, boss, I can get it ready in time. Surely the judge won't go ahead with the hearing if—"

"No good, Dode." He shook his head vigorously. "That's why Goldman's already sneaked down to Judge Hazel B.'s office. Probably took the old heifer some coffee and doughnuts. Five'll get you ten he's going to have her sitting there with her gavel raised, ready to bang it down and deny the motion for continuance she expects us to file. Well, we're not going to give them the satisfaction. Hell, Rusty Benson knew we were going ahead with the hearing last night, it's another reason he ducked out on me. What does *he* care? He knows his client is going to be the snitch, and he's probably already got a signed deal from Goldman giving *his* frigging client immunity. Hustle, Dode. Get Tommy on the phone." He snapped the loaded attaché case closed.

Dodie got it in gear, practically running in her high heels back to her desk. Bino grabbed up his coffee and drained the cup as he strode into the outer office with his navy coattails flying and his satchel swinging at his side. He glanced toward the closed door to Half-a-Point Harrison's cubbyhole, wondering if Half was having a good time in Vegas and wishing he was out there with Half, shooting a little craps and playing some poker. After marching to the hallway door Bino paused and snapped his fingers. He turned back. "Uh, say, Dode."

She looked up. "Yes?"

"Listen, could you spare ten bucks? Just until the banks open and I can cash a check. I'm running a little short."

She put down the phone and rummaged in her purse, yanking out car keys, lipstick, and rouge, dropping them in a pile on her desktop. "Seven-fifty's all I've got, but you can have it. Robert's buying my lunch." She held out three bills and a couple of quarters.

Bino scratched his forehead as he took the money. Yesterday she'd said Robert was "coming by." Before that she'd told him that Robert was "in the cement business." Bino wondered who this Robert could be, but it was really none of his business; his friend-secretary-lover relationship with Dodie was confusing enough as it was. Besides, she'd never ask him about the other women in his life. Would she? Naw, whoever Robert happened to be, it was none of his . . .

"Who the hell is Robert?" Bino said, slipping the seven-fifty into his pocket.

"Oh," she said with a secretive smile, "no one. Just a friend." She picked up the phone and punched Tommy Clinger's number in. "No one important, boss."

Bino mumbled to himself as he headed down the hall toward the elevators, his temples throbbing with every step. It was starting out to be one helluva day.

5

THE TROUBLE HAD BEGUN FOR LIEUTENANT TOMMY CLINGER
two years earlier, when Darius Grant Fontaine made an illegal left turn off Pacific Avenue. The unpredictable ma-
neuver carried Mr. Fontaine directly into the path of a Dallas
Area Rapid Transit Authority Park 'n' Ride commuter bus in
five o'clock traffic, causing the jam-packed DART vehicle to
jump the curb—scattering sidewalk pedestrians like fleas
while miraculously failing to run anyone down—and slam
into the side of the old Republic Bank Tower. The collision
shook the historic structure to its foundations and sent four
bricks clattering from the building's face onto the sidewalk,
there later to be claimed by souvenir hunters.

Darius Fontaine was a light-skinned black youth of nineteen. He had the misfortune to make his illegal turn in full
view of a Dallas Police cruiser which was stopped at the north-
bound traffic light on Harwood Street, catty-cornered across

the street from the Republic Bank Tower. Patrolman Waddy Meyers, a white two-year veteran known by his black and Hispanic peers as a wild-eyed bigot, was at the wheel of the squad car. His partner was a thickset black officer named Whit Whitley, whose regular patrol compadre was out sick, and who was more than a little pissed at having to buddy around with Patrolman Meyers to begin with. As Darius Fontaine fishtailed his way north on Harwood, Patrolman Meyers remarked, "Lookit that stupid nigger," causing Patrolman Whitley nearly to choke on his chicken-fried steak sandwich. The police car's radio was operational at the time, and the tape reel at Main Headquarters recorded Patrolman Meyers's untimely remark. Patrolman Meyers then switched on the bubblegum flashers and siren, floorboarded the accelerator, and burned rubber through the intersection in hot pursuit of Mr. Fontaine.

Inasmuch as Darius Fontaine was piloting a black 1991 Buick LeSabre he'd stolen from a West End parking lot, and inasmuch as the skinful of pop he'd injected earlier had played some havoc with his senses, Mr. Fontaine wasn't about to surrender peacefully to no motherfuckin' laws. He careened to his left, jumped the curb to pass a line of moseying homebound commuters, whipped to his right against one-way traffic onto Bryan Street, and left the policemen behind in a wake of exhaust fumes. With Patrolman Meyers driving and Patrolman Whitley reporting details to the higher-ups via radio, the chase was on. The duty officer responsible for coordinating police activity in cornering the suspect was Lieutenant Tommy Clinger.

What followed was to become a bone of contention in court, but it is undisputed that Darius Fontaine led quite a parade in his twisty, zigzag path through near East Dallas. The pursuit vehicles eventually numbered four, and the chase came to an end in the middle of the block on Fitzhugh Street between Ross Avenue and San Jacinto Boulevard. Seeing his forward path blocked by two police cars, and desperately aware of Patrolman Meyers's twisted features in the side-view mirror as Meyers pursued relentlessly in his own black-and-white, Darius Fontaine slammed on the brakes, threw open the door, and took off on foot. Mr. Fontaine was a former star running back for the South Oak Cliff High Golden Bears, but was no match for the anger-crazed Patrolman Meyers. Meyers sprang from the front seat of the cop car, charged across the asphalt, and hit Darius Fontaine with a flying tackle. At that instant, police tape reels recorded someone shouting, "Whip his black fuckin' ass for him," such words later alleged by federal prosecutors to have originated from Tommy Clinger.

Seated on his front porch a stone's throw from the action was a white unemployed bricklayer named Wilfred Creech. Mr. Creech had been out of work for three months, having injured his back carrying a hod up a ladder, and was in convalescence on the advice of his attorney, who was negotiating settlement with Mr. Creech's employer's workers' compensation insurance carrier. When Officer Meyers brought Darius Fontaine down in full view of Mr. Creech, Mr. Creech had just been thinking of his Magnavox CVR 325 video recorder, which lay in a closet inside Mr. Creech's rented house. He'd been thinking of the recorder with the idea of carrying it down to the nearest pawnshop on Bryan Street, but as the fight broke out before his eyes Wilfred Creech got other ideas. Up he sprang from his rocker and dashed into the house, returning in a few seconds with the recorder to preserve the incident between the cops and Darius Fontaine forever on videotape. Unfortunately for Mr. Creech, insurance company investigators had their own video camera going in an upstairs room across the street, and Mr. Creech's agile retrieval of the Magnavox was to seriously reduce the size of his workers' compensation benefits.

Nonetheless, mercilessly recorded by Wilfred Creech, Patrolman Waddy Meyers and several other officers proceeded to beat the living hell out of Darius Fontaine. Mr. Creech sold his videotape to Channel 8 News for a hundred and fifty dollars, thus saving his Magnavox from the pawnbroker's clutches, and the entire incident was the lead story on that night's ten o'clock newscast. The Police Internal Affairs Division investigated the attack on Darius Fontaine and—influenced in no small part by claims that Darius Fontaine was

drawing a pistol when tackled by Officer Meyers—ruled the
beating justified, thus incensing the black community into a
series of riots. Within weeks the FBI had interviewed all involved to determine whether the officers had, under color of
law, violated Darius Fontaine's constitutional rights by reason
of race, color, or creed. The feds determined that Mr.
Fontaine's rights had indeed been sullied. Indictments came
down in short order against Patrolman Waddy Meyers, two
cops from another pursuing squad car, and Lieutenant
Tommy Clinger for the instructional racist remark leading to
the beating of the motorist. Patrolman Whit Whitley resigned
from the force to become the U.S. Attorney's key witness
against his fellow officers, and soon found employment as a
GS-9 transporting federal prisoners on behalf of the U.S. Marshals Service. Auto theft, unlawful flight, and heroin posses
sion charges against Darius Fontaine simply disappeared into
the sunset. Assistant United States Attorney Marvin Goldman
headed up the federal prosecution team.

Enter Bino. The big white-haired galoot of a lawyer under-
took to defend Tommy Clinger after an interview in his Davis
Building office. The hour spent with the steady-eyed police
lieutenant, accompanied by his pretty, concerned, and
equally steady-eyed wife, Molly, convinced Bino that his new
client was getting the royal shaft, and the thought of facing
Goldman in court—particularly in a case where public pressure had brought the indictments and the evidence wasn't
likely to be up to snuff—was absolutely mouth-watering.

Law enforcement malignment of Half-a-Point Harrison's
dual role as Bino's private investigator and one of the leading
bookmakers in the area aside, Half's pretrial work on the case
uncovered quite a bag of worms. Much of the ammunition
which Bino used in questioning government witnesses—the
fact, for example, that Wilfred Creech's Magnavox bore the
same serial number as one stolen during a burglary at Ralph's
Camera Shop—was nothing but a smoke screen, but the real
bombshell he reserved for his questioning of Whit Whitley,
the black officer–turned–U.S. marshal who was the feds' star
witness. It seemed that voice prints of the racial slur con-

tained on police tapes indicated that Tommy Clinger hadn't spoken the words at all, and that the voice on the tape was then-Patrolman Whitley's. The jury convicted Patrolman Waddy Meyers and two other officers, but quickly acquitted Lieutenant Tommy Clinger on all charges. As Tommy and Molly tearfully hugged each other, and then threw their arms around Bino's neck after the verdict came in, Bino himself had a cold warning chill as he caught Marvin Goldman's glare from across the courtroom. Bino accepted his client's thanks, then returned to his normal duties while waiting for the next shoe to fall. He didn't have the heart to tell Tommy at that point, but the expression on Goldman's face had told him that the feds weren't through with Lieutenant Clinger by a long shot. Anyone who beat Goldman once in the courtroom was likely to have the chance to whip old Marv a second time.

Bino didn't have long to wait. Ever since he'd been practicing law—eighteen years, though it was hard for him to believe it had been that long—rumors had floated around about corruption in the city police's Vice Division. Since most of the stories about cops looking for handouts in return for keeping the heat off of certain illegal businesses had come from his clients, and since most of the clients had themselves been looking at serious time in TDC when they suddenly remembered the bribe solicitations, Bino hadn't paid the stories much heed. He had his own deep convictions about victimless crimes, and knew that cornered pimps, hookers, and two-bit gamblers were likely to say anything to make things easier on themselves. For the past two years, Tommy Clinger had headed up the Vice and Patrol Divisions. His boss was a ferret-faced police captain named Terry Nolby.

About a month after Clinger's acquittal in the Darius Fontaine matter, Bino began to hear from his jailed clients that Goldman had been visiting certain inmates in the Lew Sterrett Justice Center. The fact that old Marv was showing interest in the welfare of pimps and prostitutes made the white-haired lawyer's antennae stand erect, and Bino was just about to tip off Tommy Clinger that more trouble was afoot when Goldman saved him the effort. After making the usual leaks to his media stooges—and giving the local channels a week to air their stories of corruption in the police department—the federal prosecutor brought indictments against Nolby, Tommy Clinger, and a fistful of lesser-ranked cops, alleging a bottom-to-top funneling of bribe money from gambling businesses and whorehouses.

Bino had a call in to Tommy Clinger for about a week before the indictments, but Clinger was on vacation and out of town. Goldman knew about Clinger's trip, of course, and got plenty of mileage out of having the police lieutenant arrested as he and his wife stepped off a flight from Albuquerque at DFW Airport. With newsfolk taking notes like mad and mini-cams grinding, FBI agents cuffed Tommy Clinger in front of Molly and hauled him off for a night in the cooler. Captain Terry Nolby's arrest as he returned to his office from lunch drew equal media coverage. Bino's next contact with his client came the following morning at the arraignment and bond hearing in front of Judge Hazel Burke Sanderson. As Bino, Clinger, Terry Nolby, Rusty Benson, and the other cops along with their lawyers stood in a cluster before the bench, old Hazel listened in rapture to a series of we-the-people speeches from Goldman, then set bond for all of the policemen at ten grand apiece. Bino had already made arrangements with a bondsman, and Tommy Clinger was free in short order. Clinger then accompanied Bino back to the Davis Building. There occurred the first in a series of meetings which were to convince the big lawyer that keeping Tommy's chestnuts out of the fire this time was going to be a real bitch of an assignment.

At first Bino had thought that the rather vacant expression on Clinger's face was the result of the night spent in jail. Tommy looked like a former tackle who'd let the groceries get out of hand once his football days were over, a thick strong body with an extra layer of fat, a round pleasant face over a once-firm chin beginning to sag. His five o'clock shadow had lengthened overnight into the beginnings of a full-blown beard. He sat on the sofa beneath Bino's old basketball photo. Bino tilted his swivel chair and crossed his ankles on the corner of his desk.

"There's going to be a big difference between this deal and the other case, the beating charges," Bino began.

"How's that?" Clinger's tone was dull, his expression disinterested. Somewhere in Bino's mind, a warning bell sounded.

"Because in your first trial we had some evidence. Now it's just going to be your word against a bunch of pimps and whores that Goldman's going to drag over from the county jail."

"Those shitheels are liable to say anything," Clinger said.

"Right on," Bino said. "The main thing we've got going for us is that our skirts are clean. Witnesses that are full of bullshit generally trip themselves up, one way or the other."

Clinger studied his knees and didn't say anything.

Bino's head tilted. "Tommy?"

Clinger pulled out a wadded handkerchief and blew his nose.

"Our skirts *are* clean, aren't they?" Bino said.

Clinger folded the handkerchief into a rectangle, then into a square. "Well, there were a couple of deals."

Bino looked at the ceiling. "Uh-oh."

Clinger put up the handkerchief. "Now, I didn't get any money."

"Since you've got a wife, please don't tell me you opted for a free piece of ass from one of the hookers," Bino said. "Goldman would really get his jollies over that."

Clinger's lips tightened. "I haven't gotten a free anything. No money, not a dime." He scratched his cheek. "It's control."

"Oh? Control of what?"

"If you're going to know what's going on in a neighborhood, you've got to have information. Any cop will tell you that. Without cooperation from somebody, you can't catch a cold. So we . . ."

Bino folded his arms.

"Look," Clinger said. "Say there's a guy been hitting

liquor stores. Every one of these holdup artists is into drugs, and ninety-nine percent of 'em run with whores. They want to brag to somebody, and their main audience is a broad they're screwing."

Bino grinned. "That's been *my* main bragging place, okay."

"So you just . . ." Clinger said. "You make deals. So a guy's running a bar, maybe operating a few poker machines and paying off under the counter. You bust the guy, he gets a two-hundred-dollar fine and he's out of business. You leave him alone, he tells you who blew two clerks away in a holdup. Which is better?"

"I wouldn't touch the answer to that one," Bino said. "But I'm getting your point."

"Same with the hookers," Clinger said. "You drag in a carload, they get a blood test and a fine, big deal. Those girls got the inside scoop on murderers, robbers, you name it. So you go easy on them and learn a lot, or really let the hammer down and know zilch about the real serious beefs coming down." He lowered sleepy-lidded eyes. "I didn't create the world, Bino. I just live in it."

Bino took his feet down and thumbed through some papers on his desk. "So nobody's actually taken any bribes, huh?"

Clinger rested his forearms on his thighs, interlocked his fingers, and regarded the floor.

"Tommy?" Bino said.

Clinger rubbed his eyes. "I said *I* hadn't taken any money."

"Meaning, somebody else has?" Bino said.

"Now, I don't talk about other people," Clinger said, "even if it means going to jail."

"Goddammit, Tommy, I'm not the FBI," Bino said. "I'm your lawyer. If you don't want to level with me, find yourself another guy."

Clinger's cheek twitched. "You're working for me. Not the other way around."

Bino intertwined his fingers behind his head. "No, I'm not, Tommy. I'm *representing* you, and that means exactly what it says. When we get in the courtroom, I *am* you, and if I don't know everything that's going on I'm going to do a fucked-up job. So fill me in, right now, or tomorrow I'm filing a motion to withdraw."

Clinger's jaw slacked. "You'd do that?"

Bino blinked. "You betcha. I've represented everything from paperhangers to pedophiles, and I tell 'em all, You don't want to let me in on the details, then fuck you."

Clinger licked his lips. Finally, he said, "Anything I tell you is between us."

"Like I said, I'm your lawyer."

Clinger sighed. "I didn't start this. It's been going on long before I even thought about being a cop."

"Most things have," Bino said.

"There's some beat guys that do make a little money on the side. I couldn't testify to that. I've never seen a cent changing hands."

Bino couldn't say anything for a moment, then said, "Jesus H. Christ, don't you see what's going to happen? Goldman's already cut deals with the hookers, he's going to have them telling who they paid what. Once he gets them to finger the cop that took the money, he'll cut a deal with the cop to say he passed the money along to you. The bottom line is that you're probably fucked."

"They didn't pass it to me," Clinger said. "Not a quarter."

"But they did pass it to somebody," Bino said. "Come on, Tommy, give me a break."

"I already told you, I've never seen a dime changing hands."

"No," Bino said, "but you know about it."

Clinger expelled air, accepting the fact that he was in a world of hurt. "There are certain cops," he said. "Officially they report to me, but they really don't. Some doors upstairs are always open to them."

"Whose door?" Bino said. "Terry Nolby's?"

"You said that," Clinger said. "I didn't."

Bino cocked his head, getting it now. "Sure. Vice was Nolby's, before he moved up the ladder."

"I said I'm not talking about anybody."

"So what've we got?" Bino said. "We got you, the guy in the middle, that's going to claim his skirts are clean while all this shit's been going on around him."

Clinger's face softened. "Just don't throw me to the wolves."

"I won't do that," Bino said. "I've never done that to a client in my life. Christ, Tommy, how could you let all that go on?"

Clinger shrugged. "I wanted to be lieutenant. Right now I wish I'd never heard of the job. But it meant a lot to me, you know?"

That had been eight months ago, and the closer the case moved to trial, the more Bino felt up the creek without a paddle. Instead of his usual leaking of information to the media every week or so, Goldman had kept his battle plan under wraps until just a few days earlier when the series of articles smearing Tommy Clinger had begun. This morning's newspaper hatchet job pretty well cleared things up: Rusty and his client were joining up with the feds and throwing Tommy Clinger to the dogs. As he made his grim and determined way to court, Bino did his best to shake the sinking feeling in the pit of his stomach. It wasn't going to be easy.

6

HE APPROACHED THE EARLE CABELL FEDERAL BUILDING FROM the east, walking on the south side of Commerce Street against the flow of noisy one-way traffic. The sky was a hazy blue dotted with wispy cloud banks; though it wasn't yet nine in the morning and he was in shade, Bino's forehead was damp and his collar stuck to his neck. Directly ahead, the mammoth glistening ball atop Reunion Tower crowned the skyline. He reached the federal building and did a column-left through the revolving door into the lobby. Sudden refrigerated air raised goose pimples along his jaw. His head throbbed like a thousand beating tom-toms.

He rode the elevator up to the courtroom level, set his briefcase on the conveyor, and passed through the security arch as the U.S. marshal on guard yawned and looked away. The plush-carpeted hallway was a subdued madhouse, lawyers and clients conversing on corridor benches, minicam opera-

tors standing ready for the action to start. Bino dodged
around a gang of newspeople—three young guys in sport
coats and two young women in calf-length skirts, all with pads
and ballpoints in hand—and took two long strides toward the
courtroom entry before halting in his tracks.

Three corridor benches were jam-full of what looked like
a Quaker convention, women in long gray dresses with white
starched collars and men with Abe Lincoln beards and
stovepipe hats. Bino turned around and said to the reporters
in general, "Who's the Pilgrim's Progress bunch?"

"Mountainites," a big-nosed newsman said. "Big Preacher
Daniel goes to trial today, right across from you guys. Good
for us, we can kill two birds with one stone. If nothing's going
on in the cop trial, we can skip across the hall and check up
on the Mountainites."

"Good thinking," Bino said. "Just don't get my client con-
fused with the Big Preacher, okay?" He shuddered as he
looked at the stone-faced religious nuts. At closer glance the
men were younger than they appeared; the beards could fool
you. The women's mouths were set in rigid lines.

Mountainites, huh? Bino thought. Repent, brother, or
we'll blow your ass off. Big Preacher Daniel had drawn a
pretty firm judge, Edgar Bryson, quite a Bible-banger in his
own right. Bryson was strictly dunk 'em to save 'em and Peace
on Earth, Brother, right up until he strapped the thirty or
forty years on unsuspecting defendants. Bino wondered who
would win in a Scripture-quoting contest, Big Preacher Daniel
or the judge. He edged away from the newspeople and
treaded lightly toward Hazel Sanderson's courtroom.

He came abreast of the Mountainites, watching them
from the corner of his eye and recalling what he knew about
them. A synagogue bombed. A Jewish reporter cut down by
machine gun bullets. Blacks dragged screaming from their
homes in the middle of the night, the men castrated and then
executed firing squad style. The latest episode in the Mountainites' East Texas reign of terror had to do with the burning
of a church rumored to admit homosexual members. Bino
whistled nonchalantly as the Mountainites glared at him. He
supposed that they glared at everybody.

From down the hall a deep male voice said loudly, "Stand back. Back up, please." Bino turned.

Coming off the elevator was Judge Edgar Bryson, surrounded fore and aft by U.S. marshals in Stetsons and western boots. Judge Bryson was only a couple of inches shorter than Bino's six-six, had thick silver hair, razored and combed, and wore glasses in dark plastic frames. The jurist walked erect among his escorts, wearing a dove gray suit and red tie, and he returned the stares from the Mountainites like Samson about to raise some hell among the Philistines. As the envoy drew near the benches, the Mountainites rose as one.

The largest of the cultists, a broad-shouldered man with flecks of gray in his beard, began a basso, singsong chant: "The Lord is my shepherd, I shall not want . . ." One by one his brothers and sisters joined in, and by the time he got to "He maketh me to lie down in green pastures," he led a full-fledged chorus.

Bino thought that Edgar Bryson did a marvelous job of not letting the cultists buffalo him. Bryson ignored the chanting as he nodded and smiled in Bino's direction. The judge's lower lip trembled slightly, but otherwise Bryson looked as calm as if he were on a stroll through the park. "Morning, Mr. Phillips," Bryson boomed, and Bino squeaked back, "Hi, Judge." Then the judge and his escorts did an abrupt right turn to enter Bryson's courtroom. As the Mountainites joined hands to sing "Amazing Grace," Bino went on into Hazel Sanderson's court.

Bino spotted Marvin Goldman beyond the rail on the prosecution side. The Assistant U.S.D.A. had close-cropped black hair—*too* black of late, and Bino suspected that old Marv was using Grecian Formula—and was hunched over talking a mile a minute to Terry Nolby. The police captain was dressed in a brown suit, had a pointed nose and receding chin, and his head was cocked in a listening attitude. Rusty Benson sat on the other side of his client, and Rusty had on a pale blue iridescent which contrasted nicely with his tan. Involuntarily, Bino's lip curled.

He passed through the gate and neared the prosecution's table on his way to the defense side. Rusty looked up, half smiled, and raised a hand in greeting; Bino shot the handsome lawyer a look that would wilt roses. Rusty dropped his gaze, and suddenly was very interested in whatever Goldman was saying to Nolby. Goldman showed Bino a happy grin. Bino ignored the prosecutor, went straight to the defense table, and set down his attaché case with a solid thump. Screw Goldman, screw Rusty, screw Nolby, and screw the horses they all rode in on.

Bino pretended to go through his file—which he already had committed to memory—as he watched Goldman from the corner of his eye. The prosecutor rose, took a couple of steps in the direction of the defense side—Son of a bitch is going to rub it in, Bino thought—then came to a screeching halt. The courtroom bailiff, a wheezy older guy who walked with a limp, hobbled out to stand at attention before the bench and bellow, "Awwl rise."

Clothing rustled and papers rattled as the spectators stood. There were muted clanks and snaps as lawyers put away the briefs and motions—or more likely, Bino thought, the sports pages—which they'd been studying. Judge Hazel Burke Sanderson strode majestically in from her private entry, favored one and all with a scalding glare, and ascended to her throne.

Hazel the Horrible was in rare form. She was a blocky, square-shouldered woman of about sixty with steel-gray hair the consistency of papier-mâché. Martha Washington glasses rode the hump in her broad nose. She wore no makeup, her lips firmly pursed to show that if anybody intended to give her any guff they'd better think twice about it. Hazel Sanderson didn't like Bino Phillips for shit; Bino knew it and didn't particularly care. She looked first at Goldman, and, fleetingly and contemptuously, at Bino, then swept the courtroom at large with her fearsome gaze. She said, "Be seated," in a voice like doom, then sank grandly into her chair. Bino sat, thinking, Come on, Tommy Clinger. Get here, and fast.

The judge cleared her throat. "There's a hearing this morning which is going to take quite a bit of time." Her raspy voice reminded Bino of the Wicked Witch of the West just as the old broad was about to put the screws to Dorothy and Toto. "In view of this hearing," she said, "all other matters before this court are hereby suspended until further notice. Emergencies, writs of habeas corpus and whatnot, will be heard at the court's discretion. This means that anyone may . . ."

Bino tuned old Hazel out as she droned on, explaining to the other lawyers in court that they now had an excuse to fuck off for a couple of weeks, and turned his attention to Terry Nolby. The police captain resembled a damp rat. Bino had made it a point in recent weeks to learn everything he could about Nolby—though he hadn't told Tommy Clinger, Bino had suspected the captain all along as a potential rollover artist—and every time he looked at Nolby, the white-haired lawyer couldn't help picturing damp, stinky underarms. According to Clinger, Nolby's perspiration problem caused him to go through as many as four shirts in a single day. Another tidbit on the captain: None of the detectives liked to go to lunch with Nolby because, even though he made more money than anyone else in the unit, the captain was too cheap to leave a tip. Neither his stinky underarms nor his tightness with the dollar provided any defense ammunition, but Nolby's Ebenezer Scrooge tendencies brought something else to mind.

While Tommy and Molly Clinger were putting themselves in a serious bind in trying to pay Bino's fee, Nolby's legal expense was next to nothing. Rusty Benson made it a practice to handle any policeman's divorce for free, and any other legal matter for a cop at a reduced rate. The deal was tit for tat. The divorce rate among Dallas's Finest was astronomical, and if Rusty helped out in marital problems the odds were good that the cops would go easier on Rusty's criminal clients. Rusty had been handling a divorce, Nolby's fourth or fifth, when the indictments had come down. It was possible that Nolby's having a free lawyer could work to Tommy Clinger's advantage. Nobody, but nobody, Bino thought, worshipped the almighty dollar as did Rusty Benson. With paying clients waiting in the wings, Rusty was likely to be less than enthused over Nolby's case, and somewhere down the line could miss a detail or two that could help Tommy Clinger. At least, that's what Bino hoped. It wasn't much, but any port in a storm.

And something else Tommy had said about Nolby was beginning to fit. Sure, Bino thought, Nolby was one of the cops who'd been through the FBI's training school in Quantico, Virginia, and his nifty FBI certificate was something for Nolby to point at when promotion time came around. Being a Quantico grad gave a policeman some status, okay, but those in the know suspected that the main reason the FBI invited so many local cops to their school was to give the feds stool pigeons in every major department in the country. Just an occasional phone call was all it would take: Say, old school chum, what's your little police force been up to lately? Hell, Bino thought, Nolby and Rusty might have been working with Goldman all along. Tommy Clinger had been the feds' main target ever since the Darius Fontaine incident, and bringing a phony indictment against Nolby to put Tommy's defense off guard would be right in line with Goldman's way of doing things.

Hazel Sanderson said loudly, "Is there something wrong with your hearing, Mr. Phillips?"

Bino jolted back from dreamworld. "I beg your pardon?"

Old Hazel laid down her pencil, leaned back and regarded Bino with her eyelids at half-mast. "Mr. Phillips and his client have something in common," she said. "Neither one of them is with us. Please repeat yourself, Mr. Goldman."

Goldman was on his feet at the defense table, strutting in place. "I merely remarked, Your Honor, that the co-defendant in this case isn't anywhere in sight. The government has gone along with two delays, but we're now primed and ready. And would point out that his absence is a violation of the conditions of his release on bond."

"Thank you," the judge said. She arched an eyebrow. "Mr. Phillips?"

Bino very nearly bit his tongue to keep from popping off. Yeah, there'd been two delays in the case. Both requested by Goldman. Bino turned and searched the gallery. No sign of

Tommy. Bino faced the judge. "My client's been notified, Your Honor. I'm sure he's on his way." He looked pointedly at Goldman, then said, "We didn't think we were having this proceeding this morning."

"Now, that's strange," Hazel the Horrible said. "It's right here on my calendar. The other defendants had their pretrial motions heard last week, and they were all here. Yours was set separately because of your own motion, Mr. Phillips, to sever Lieutenant Clinger's case from the others. Isn't that right?"

"That's what *my* calendar says," Goldman said. Bino didn't like Marvin Goldman much to begin with. Right now he hated the guy.

The judge's glasses slid a hair closer to the end of her nose. "Mr. Phillips, this matter has been docketed for sixty days, and I see no reason for your client not to be here. Bailiff." The bailiff had been lounging in the jury box. He rose. "Bailiff," the judge repeated, "go to the courtroom entrance and call for Mr. Thomas Allen Clinger three times. If he doesn't answer I'll issue a warrant for him." Bino studied his shoes. They needed polishing.

The bailiff showed an apologetic smile as he stumped through the gate and made his painful way up the aisle. He'd gotten halfway to the courtroom exit when Tommy Clinger came in, huffing and puffing.

Tommy's round face was slightly redder than normal, as if he'd been coming at a dead run. His hair was in wind-whipped disarray. As he paused and looked around, Goldman's shoulders slumped.

Bino waved like a third base coach. Tommy hustled down the aisle to take his seat at the defense table. As Clinger sat down, Bino whispered, "Perfect timing. We got trouble." He jerked his head and eyes toward Terry Nolby. Clinger's features sagged.

Hazel the Horrible's tone showed her disappointment. "Court convenes at nine sharp, Mr. Clinger." Bino made a show of checking his watch. It had been nine-thirty before the old heifer had made her own appearance, and she damn well knew it. "For the balance of these proceedings," she said, "you are to be on time. If you aren't you'll be in trouble." She cleared her throat. "Now, gentlemen, we can proceed with the motion hearing. I'm going to . . . yes, Mr. Goldman?"

Goldman was standing. He scratched his goatee. "I'm afraid the government is going to have to request a delay, Your Honor. Something's come up. One of the defendants has come to us with a plea bargain offer that we're going to accept. We need time to structure the plea." Tommy Clinger gasped out loud.

The judge beamed. "Oh?" old Hazel said. "How long of a delay, Mr. Goldman?"

"Sixty days," Goldman said.

She lifted her gavel and brought it down with a bang. "Granted. Draft the order, Mr. Goldman. I'll sign it." Just like that.

Bino was livid. Hell, they'd never intended to have the hearing to begin with. The whole performance this morning was in hopes that Bino, Tommy Clinger, or both, wouldn't show up. Then they could have revoked Tommy's bond and held him in jail until the trial was over. Jesus Christ, Bino thought, the judge would have to . . . He looked at Hazel Sanderson with his jaw slack in astonishment. She dropped her gaze. Yep, the old heifer had been in on it.

"I'm afraid it's our night in the barrel, Tommy," Bino said softly.

At the prosecution table Nolby said something to Rusty Benson. Then he listened to Rusty's reply, nodded, then went past the defense table on his way out. He left with both Clinger and Bino staring holes in his backside.

"Tell me this isn't happening," Clinger said. "Hell, he's the one that's been fattening his wallet, not me. Now he's going to be their *witness?* Jesus Christ. Up to now I'd halfway thought this was all a joke."

"Nothing funny about it," Bino said. "Anybody with a federal beef has their tit in a big wringer."

He led his client out in the hall for a quick goodbye. "We've got sixty days, Tommy," Bino said. "I'm going to come up with something. For what it's worth, I'm about to go in there and give Mr. Nolby's lawyer a piece of my mind." Clinger hung his head. As Bino turned to reenter the courtroom, he gave Tommy's arm a parting affectionate squeeze.

Goldman and Rusty stood down front near the jury box, along with a third man whom Bino had never seen before. Bino stopped in his hell-bent-for-leather trip down the aisle. Who the hell was *this* guy?

The newcomer talked a mile a minute while Goldman stood with his arms folded in an attentive attitude, and Rusty tugged nervously at his own lapel. The stranger was a stocky, square-headed guy with shaggy, untrimmed eyebrows which joined above his nose. He wore a checkered sport coat and accompanied his dialogue with hand signals. Cop, Bino thought. Be they tall or short, fat or skinny, policemen stood a certain way and viewed the world with a certain cant to their mouths, and this new guy had John Q. Law written all over him. He's either a city or county cop, Bino thought, no way would an FBI or DEA agent come to court dressed in that getup. He went quietly through the rail, approached the trio, and stood off to one side.

The newcomer was saying, "There's a Southwest Airlines flight every half hour, all day. We should be able to catch the one, say, one-thirty or two." He looked at his cheap fabric-banded watch.

Rusty nodded morosely, then glanced at Bino and did a double take. "Bino. I'm glad you're here. I may need a friend."

Bino thought, *Friend?* Why, you double-crossing son of a bitch. He almost said as much, but Rusty went on. "This is Detective Fuller," Rusty said, "from Harris County. Houston. He wants me to fly down there with him to identify . . . It's Rhonda. I think she's dead."

7

THE HARRIS COUNTY COP TOLD RUSTY TO MEET HIM AT LOVE
Field airport in three hours, then left the courtroom with
Marvin Goldman. The detective and the prosecutor went
up the aisle talking in normal tones, Goldman laughing at
something the detective said, the cop holding the door and
ushering Goldman into the hallway like the pair were old buddies. What the hell is going on? Bino thought. Goldman, an
Assistant U.S. Attorney, shouldn't have anything to do with a
state case in Harris County, but it was as if Goldman and the
cop had a prearranged appointment. Maybe they liked the
same restaurant and just were going to lunch together, but
Bino doubted it.

Bino followed Rusty out in the hall, where they sat on a
bench across the corridor from a gang of wild-eyed Mountainites. Rusty bent forward, rested his forearms on his thighs,
and touched his fingertips together. "About last night," Rusty

said. "Look, I owe you one. Pete Kinder kind of flew off the handle, and to tell you the truth, by the time I got him calmed down I completely forgot about you. I didn't leave you in a bind, did I?"

Bino thought, The guy just found out his wife is dead, and all he wants to talk about is . . . He said merely, "Nothing I couldn't handle."

"Well, what I need," Rusty said, "is for you to stand by. The way they found Rhonda, her death wasn't any accident. And that detective's not just here to play games. I don't have to tell you the husband, especially the *estranged* husband, is the first suspect in something like this. I've got most of the past few days accounted for. I spent most of the time with Pete Kinder, and yesterday and last night you know where I was."

Only part of last night, Bino thought. Still no sign of grief from Rusty, only a concerned look as he carefully considered his alibi. Bino hooked an arm over the back of the bench. "Are you talking about me representing you or something?"

"It's a thought," Rusty said.

Bino chewed his lower lip. "I don't think I'm the right lawyer, Rusty. We're on opposite sides of the fence in the cop case now, and I'd be lying if I didn't tell you I don't like that worth a damn. There's no connection between that case and whatever happened to Rhonda, but I might not be able to work up a gung-ho attitude in trying to defend you, if it came down to that."

Rusty spread his hands, palms facing. "Hey, you're pissed, and I don't blame you. When Terry Nolby came to me with the deal this morning—"

"Look." Bino pointed a finger. "Just don't bullshit me, okay? Snitch deals aren't worked out overnight, and you already knew your client was rolling over yesterday while you were grinning at me on the golf course. That's all I got to say about the Clinger case, because from now on I'm treating you just like you were one of Goldman's prosecution team. See you in court, and all that shit."

Rusty's features tensed in a measuring look. "Okay. All that aside, you do practice law for a living, don't you?"

"Last time I checked," Bino said.

"Right. What I'm offering you is strictly a business proposition, fee paid. Hey, I couldn't ask you to represent me in any murder trial. If it came to that I'd need you to testify where I was yesterday and last night. I've only got three hours until I'm supposed to meet that cop at the airport, and sorry, but that doesn't give me time to conduct a lot of interviews with prospective defense attorneys. All I want, in case I get arrested, is for you to jump in at the start until I can get a full-time guy to defend me. Getting somebody like that, that would take some thinking."

"Jesus Christ, Rusty, nobody's even charged you with anything. What makes you think they're going to?"

Rusty studied the floor between his feet. "The way that detective talked is the main thing. The way he said, 'I'd like for you to fly down with me to identify the body,' but meaning if I didn't, he'd bust my ass right then and there. I think he'd love for me not to show up at the airport, so he could proceed with the manhunt."

"I can't argue with that," Bino said. "If you're a suspect, I'll lay odds they've got somebody following you until you meet that plane. If you take off for Mexico, I doubt you'll get very far."

"My thinking exactly," Rusty said. "If they just wanted me for ID purposes they'd have called me on the phone. No, that guy was wanting a nose-to-nose look at me, to check out my reactions."

"Well, I hope you did a better job with him than you're doing with me," Bino said. "I got to tell you you don't look really overcome with grief."

"Well, let's just say," Rusty said, straightening, "that it hurts a lot more than I'm letting on. Hey, it's no big secret that Rhonda and I were splitting the blankets. Nobody's talked to her since Saturday, and I thought she'd gone to stay with her sister in Austin. Pam, that's her sister, Pam called my office yesterday to ask if I'd heard from her. I say, 'Heard from who? Rhonda? I thought she was at your place.' Hell, Pam hadn't even been expecting her. Tell you the truth, I

thought Rhonda was off on a toot or shacked up someplace. I
sure didn't expect anything like this."

Across the hall a third Mountainite came out of the courtroom and talked excitedly to the other two. The newcomer
was the same man who'd earlier led the group in the Twenty-
third Psalm. The three cultists stalked away toward the elevators like holy gunslingers.

Bino watched the Mountainites go, then said to Rusty,
"Like you said, I got a living to make. I'll agree to represent you
if you get indicted, for a fee. Two grand will do as a retainer,
and then we'll take it from there. I'm in for the ride only on
preliminary matters, arranging for bond and whatnot."

Rusty looked relieved. He reached in his breast pocket
and produced a checkbook. "Hey, great," he said.

"I don't know if it's so fucking great or not, Rusty," Bino
said. "I'm not going to ask you if you know what happened to
Rhonda, 'cause if I turn out being a witness in some kind of
murder trial, the less I know the better."

Rusty showed a pleading look. "As God is my witness, I
didn't—"

"You're wasting your breath," Bino said. "And no matter
what you told me, I wouldn't know whether to believe it or
not. From now on until I finish whatever I do for you, you're
just like any other client, buster. If it turns out you're just over-
reacting, and that nobody's going to charge you with anything, then your retainer's refundable. Something else.
Tommy Clinger's still my main client. If I find out something
while I'm representing you that'll help Tommy's case, I'll re-
sign as your lawyer and use it. Cash talks and bullshit walks,
baby, when I'm dealing with you."

Wick, Hamill & Co., with a seat on the New York Stock Exchange and hotlines to London brokers, had swanky picture-
book offices. The reception area contained four plush sofas,
visitor's phones on two low mahogany tables, and an eight-
foot-high transparent world atlas as its centerpiece. A pleas-
antly round young woman with smooth cheeks and gazooms

that wouldn't quit sat behind a half-moon counter, pressing flashing buttons and routing calls. She had a tiny receiver plugged into one ear, and a silver rod curved from her ear around in front of her full lush mouth. She glanced up as Pete Kinder entered, then sat stiffly erect. "Hello, Pete," she said.

Kinder grinned. He considered some good-natured banter to thaw her out, but her look said she wasn't having any. His smile faded quickly. "What about Larry? He in?" Kinder said.

Her tone was impersonal and just a bit on the haughty side. "Mr. Murphy is tied up. You can wait if you like."

"Okay, Bobbi. I think I will." He sat on one of the sofas; air whooshed out of the cushion as his fanny sank down. He rested his elbow on the armrest and crossed his legs. He's tied up, Kinder thought. You can wait if you like. Things change. Do they ever.

He tried not to look at Bobbi but couldn't help watching her. He pictured her a few weeks earlier in his own office (Christ, was it only weeks?), squealing in delight as she rubbed those super-big, super-soft bosoms all over him while they watched the video.

Larry Murphy had brought her by and had been watching the tape as well, taking pulls from a tall bourbon and water as he'd said, "I toleya, Pete. Look at that *dong*, man. It's got to be a fake. Shove it to her, Johnny Wadd. Goddam, Pete, he gets it up higher'n them Avco options are gonna go, don't he? How 'bout that, Bobbi girl? That's some pork, ain't it?"

Later, with Bobbi's panty-covered bottom resting on his desk while she swung a plump bare leg, Kinder had written a check. Murphy had sat beside him on a cushioned footrest, puffing on a cigar as he'd said, "Helluva buy, Pete-boy. Them Avco's goin' right through the fuckin' roof."

That had been three days before the *20/20* show featuring Pete Kinder and his company, Pleasures of Vegas, and four days before Kinder's banks had frozen his accounts. The following week Kinder's wife had had the divorce papers served. And one month to the day after he'd watched the video, the indictment had come down.

Kinder closed his eyes and rubbed his lids. The past month was like a whirlwind. Divorce court. Lawsuits. Finally his arraignment on criminal charges, lawyer after lawyer draining what reserve he had left. And now last night the tall white-haired attorney in Arthur's telling him he ought to plead guilty. Too much. Too, too much. Right now Pete Kinder was running on bourbon, speed, and desperation, and the thought that he might actually go to prison made his stomach do flip-flops.

But somehow, through all the porno tapes, booze, and bullshit, Murphy had been right. Not on purpose, not by a long shot; Kinder was certain that Murphy hadn't given a hoot whether the price on the Avco options went up or not, so long as he received his commish on the deal. But an early summer merger had brought about a two-for-one split, and Pete Kinder's fifty-grand investment was now worth a quarter of a million. It was his only remaining asset except for a checking account that now contained six hundred bucks. Six hundred, that is, if the condo owners did their usual farting around with Kinder's two-thousand-dollar check and didn't deposit it for a month or so. If the condo people tried to negotiate the check anytime soon, Pete Kinder was going to be living in the street.

A man came out of Wick, Hamill & Co.'s inner offices. He looked Middle Eastern, with pinched features and olive-complexioned skin, and wore a dark three-piece Armani suit. He hurried through the reception area with his briefcase banging against his leg, and didn't glance in Kinder's direction. Bobbi watched the visitor leave as if she was sizing up his bankroll, then pressed a button on the switchboard. In a few seconds she said, "Mr. Kinder to see you." Then, in hushed tones loud enough for Kinder to hear, she said, "No, there's no one. Come *on*, Larry, that's not my *job*." She pressed another button and said to Kinder, "You can go on in," then pointedly ignored him. Kinder avoided looking at her as he went on in.

•   •   •

Larry Murphy kept his ankles crossed on the corner of his desk as he considered his choices. The toe of one of his gray lizard boots was scuffed; he rubbed the marred spot on the back of his pants leg. He cradled the phone between his neck and shoulder and trimmed his nails with a silver clipper.

"Anybody with him, Bobbi?" Murphy said. He brushed a quarter moon of fingernail from his dove gray slacks.

"No, there's no one," Bobbi said.

"Well, find out what he wants. Shake your ass at him, he'll follow you anywhere."

"Come *on,* Larry, that's not my *job.*"

Murphy punched the keys on his computer terminal and pressed the ENTER button. He frowned. Damn, that Avco was up another point, which would make Kinder's stash around two and a half. Lessee, five percent of that . . . Touchy situation, Larry-boy, too many players sweating indictments for any smart broker to let the word get around he's swinging with Pete Kinder. Still, shit on a stick, five percent of . . .

"Send him on in, Bobbi," Murphy said. A man with broad shoulders, a narrow waist, jutting cheekbones, and a pointed chin, he hung up, stood, and packed his tapered shirttail deeper beneath his waistband. On his wall were two ornate silver picture frames. One enclosed a certificate for his lifetime endowment membership in the S.M.U. Mustang Booster Club; in the other frame was a color photo of Murphy himself in a foursome at the Byron Nelson Classic Pro-Am, along with Lee Trevino, Mickey Mantle, and Bino Phillips. Murphy sat down and folded his hands on his desk in a businesslike posture. His brows knitted as he reached down to rattle his bottom drawer. Locked. There were videotapes of *Deep Throat* and *The Devil in Miss Jones* in the drawer along with some recorded conversations with investors who hadn't known they were being taped. Tools of the trade. Visible through his picture window, sunlight filtered through the light Dallas smog. The spire on top of the old Mercantile Bank Tower was blurred in haze. The door swung open and Pete Kinder came in. He looks like death warmed over, Murphy thought. He flashed a grin, stood, and extended a hand. "Come in this house, old *podnuh.*"

Kinder's grip was fish-limp. He sank into a padded arm-chair.

"Oil's down to eleven a barrel," Murphy said, sitting. "Got 'em jumping out windows. Fuckin' Ann Richards, if that woman's elected governor come November the oilmen are all dead meat. But that's not your problem, Pete-boy, your Avco's solid as a rock. What'd I tell you when you bought it, huh?"

Kinder's eyes were hay fever watery. "I've got to get right to the point, Larry. The shitstorm I've gotten into is draining me. I need to dump everything. I'm at bedrock and I need cash."

"Gosh amighty, Pete, I sure hate to hear that. Damn those feds, it's getting to where a man can't make an honest buck any more." Murphy frowned. "You know, what's in your name, it's not all yours."

"I'm not talking what I've got invested for other guys. Just mine. Just that Avco. The other stuff, I'll let it lay."

"With Rusty's okay I'd—"

"Nope," Kinder said. "The Avco, that's all."

Murphy produced a form and a gold ballpoint. "Sure, Pete. You know how it works, old podnuh. Just gimme your John Henry on this sell order and it's a done deal. Getcha a check, less commish, in four working days." He slid the form over in front of Kinder.

"Well, there's a problem." Kinder's voice wavered slightly. "The four days isn't soon enough. I need some sort of advance, Larry. Not much, a couple of thou to tide me over till the big check comes. The bail bondsman got damn near my last nickel."

Murphy tilted back and clasped his hands behind his head. "That's a tough one, podnuh. It's flat-out against SEC regs for us to . . ."

"I'll pay interest." Kinder licked his lips.

Murphy sat forward. Kinder's problems, he thought, were nothing short of tough shit. Play with the big boys . . . "You checked this out with Rusty?" Murphy said.

"Nope. Five hundred. Two grand gets twenty-five hundred."

Murphy relaxed as he thought it over. Haste makes shrinking bankrolls. The money would come to Murphy's office, and there was no way for Kinder to cash the check and make the dodge without paying him. "I guess I could do it personally, Pete," Murphy said.

"Done," Kinder said.

While Kinder signed the sell order, Murphy took a Dallas Cowboys money clip bulging with currency from his pocket. He counted out twenty crisp new hundreds, popping each one in turn, and shoved the money over in front of Kinder. The soft round guy's gaze was on the Pro-Am photo. As he shoved the bills into his pocket without counting them, Kinder said, "I saw that guy last night."

Murphy felt a twinge of panic. "Mickey Mantle? You talked to the Mick?" Shit on a stick, Mantle was into the options, and doing business with Pete Kinder could easily queer deals with guys like Mickey Mantle.

"Not him," Kinder said. "The tall guy."

Murphy's forehead softened in relief. "Oh, Bino. Bino Phillips, I went to college with the guy. He's a lawyer."

"Of course he's a lawyer," Kinder said. "All I've met lately is lawyers. The guy told me to cop a plea, Larry, he's the only one that's told me that. The other guys all want to try the case, at four million dollars an hour or some shit. What do you know about the guy?" He squinted at the photo.

Murphy studied Bino's image as well, the slightly jutted jaw with a determined set about it, the steady blue eyes under a hank of white short-cut hair. Murphy scratched his chin. "Well, I'll tell you, podnuh," he said seriously. "If Bino Phillips told me something, I'd put a lot of stock in it. Not many lawyers would I say that about. But that guy, yeah."

8

INO STOPPED AND CASHED A CHECK. THEN HE HAD LUNCH AT Bek's, a cafeteria-style catery in the tunnel beneath One Main Place featuring greasy hamburgers dripping with chili, and finally headed on to the Davis Building. An old woman in a ragged dress had set up a display in front of the building entry. Laid out on a rolling cart were bunches of pink and yellow roses wrapped in wax paper, and red and orange azaleas in plastic pots. Bino paid two-fifty for six yellow roses, then rode up on the elevator sniffing the flowers' fragrance until he noticed another passenger—a tall, thin pimply kid in a UPS uniform—giving him funny looks. Bino let the roses hang down by his side and riveted his gaze on the far wall. The kid snickered as Bino exited the car.

Outside his office Bino threw open the door and stayed out in the hall. He thrust the roses inside across the threshold with a flourish as he sang out, "Da-*daa.*" He stood in place for fifteen seconds, waving the flowers around, then peeked around the doorjamb. No Dodie. The reception area was vacant.

Bino thought, Oh. Then, feeling sort of stupid, he dropped the roses on her desk and went on inside to flop down in his swivel chair. To hell with her, she could find water for the damned flowers on her own. The walk to and from the federal building, coupled with the double-meat cheeseburger he'd eaten, had done a lot to clear the cobwebs from his brain. Nonetheless his head throbbed just enough for him to feel sorry for himself, so he sat for a while and did so.

He considered checking the machine for call messages, mainly because he suspected that Half-a-Point Harrison might be trying to get in touch, but just thinking about Half out there in Vegas with all those showgirls and galloping dominoes caused a sharp pang of jealousy. Nope, to hell with the messages. Right now Bino wanted Dodie and no one else; wanted her to tell him how great he was as a lawyer, and to nod agreement while he sounded off about what a horse's ass Goldman was for trying to put the screws to Tommy Clinger. That's what Bino needed, a sounding board. Where the hell was Dodie when he needed her?

Dodie's soft voice now drifted in from the reception area. "Wow, it was delicious. Call me later, huh?" Honey literally dripped from her tone. Seconds later she said, "Whee, flowers. Bino, did you . . . ?" She came in sniffing the roses, carrying the wax paper bundle in both hands. "They're beautiful. Thanks, boss."

Bino folded his hands and put on his most serious look. "Sit, Dode. We need to have a talk."

She sat across from him and blinked expectantly. "Okay."

"It's these lunch periods," he said. "They seem pretty lengthy."

Her grip on the flowers tightened. "It was only an hour, and it takes fifteen minutes of that to walk all the way to the West End. The new crabmeat and oyster bar. I made Robert hustle through his meal so fast that the poor thing's probably got indigestion, because I was in such a hurry to get back here and hold down the fort while you were in Lieutenant Clinger's hearing. Which, by the way, why aren't you?"

"They put the case off, and that's a long story," he said. "But that's not what's under discussion here. It's you leaving in the middle of the day with God-knows-who and—"

"Now hold on, Mr. Phillips. I'm not neglectful."

"And what about this Robert? Who the hell is this guy?"

She looked down at her lap. When she raised her head she showed an impish grin. "So *that's* it. Wow, I didn't know you were so interested in my private life. Most of the time I'd have to get down on all fours and trip you before you'd notice I was around."

He folded his arms. "Well, I *am* interested."

"Well, why don't you start showing it, then?" There was a flush in her cheeks, visible through her light makeup.

"I *do* show it," Bino said. "I'm . . . well, sure, I'm interested, Dodie. I've got a lot invested in you."

Her smile faded. "*Invested?* I'm not some piece of property, sir. Away from this office I'll do what I want." The roses were taking a beating as she drummed them angrily against her thigh.

"I don't mean that you're a piece of property, Dodie, I just—" He stopped in midsentence as the phone rang. "Let the machine take it. I'm not through," Bino said.

"Oh, yes you are." She reached across his desk to snatch his receiver up. Her tone a bit huffy, she said into the mouthpiece, "Lawyer's office," and then listened and placed her clenched hand on her hip and said stiffly, "May I ask who's calling?" Her eyebrow arched. She thrust the phone at him. As if each word were snipped off with scissors, she said, "It's Carla something-or-other."

The look on Dodie's face gave Bino a real charge. Robert, huh? Into the phone he cooed, "Yes?"

"Toodle-ooo," Carla said. "Have you recovered?" Dammit, Bino thought, where does she get her energy?

He said, a little too loudly, reveling in satisfaction as he watched Dodie's backside twitch as she stalked back to her desk, "Carla? Great, great. Yeah, I'm fine."

"Is there something wrong with your phone?" Carla said. "You're about to puncture my eardrum."

"No, the phone's all right. What's new?" Bino said.

"I just called to tell you you must be my lucky charm. We've got a new gig."

"A what? Has somebody filed a complaint?"

"No, silly," she said. "Gig. Job. Four nights at the Hyatt Regency Skyroom in Houston. Not just hard rock, either, show tunes and dance music. You wouldn't be-*lieve* the money. We start tonight."

Bino thought, Houston? Small world, half of the people he knew seemed to be going to Houston. He said, "Well, it could be that I'll have some business down in the bayou."

"And it could be that I'll shanghai you down there even if you don't," Carla said. "Two-thirty flight, Southwest Airlines?"

He pictured her panty-covered rump as she'd boogied across his living room floor to Harry Chapin. "I'll be there," he said.

"I'll be waiting," Carla said. She hung up.

He sat there for a moment with a dumb-looking grin on his face, then went out into the reception room and said to Dodie, "I'll be out of town a few days. Listen, call Rusty Benson's office for me. Leave him a message that if he needs me I'll be at the Hyatt Regency, downtown Houston."

"I wouldn't take my briefcase if I were you," Dodie said. "It might have a bomb in it that'll blow you all to hell." She looked through her Rolodex, found Rusty's number, and furiously punched the buttons on the phone. Bino hoped that she didn't break a finger.

It was straight-up two o'clock when he made the curve off Mockingbird Lane and entered the Love Field access road, rolling along between billboards announcing that Southwest Airlines loved you, that Hertz gave you a better deal than Avis, and that Budget had *both* competitors nailed to the wall. In the long-term parking area he nestled the Linc in between a Dodge Caravan and a green Mazda. He strolled into the terminal with his suitbag over his shoulder like William Holden in *Picnic*. All at once he spotted Carla. She looked fit to be tied.

In the middle of the terminal's marble-tiled floor was a

world map the size of a handball court. Carla had her feet planted somewhere in the vicinity of Topeka, Kansas. Her hands were balled into little fists and resting on her hips. Her lips were pouty and her almond-shaped eyes were narrowed. Beside her were three suitcases the size of dressers, and at her feet sat a round leather cosmetics case with a strap attached.

She said, "You took your time. Smokes."

He eyed the suitcases. "Did you say four nights at the Hyatt Regency, or four months? Jesus Christ . . ."

"Ha, ha. They're costumes, mostly. And it's going to be *zero* nights if we don't get a move on. Come on, hurry. The boys are already at the gate. Dondi thinks you're a narc."

He wondered if he could lift any one of the suitcases, much less all three. Backache City, he thought. Then he grabbed a dolly and breathed heavily as he tugged her luggage aboard. Between huffs and puffs he said, "Well, why didn't the boys load this stuff? There's four of the boys and only one of me. Who thinks I'm a narc?"

"They had plenty to do," she said, "loading all those drums and bass guitars and amps and whatnot. Dondi. You know, the Elton John type with the big rose-colored glasses. The drummer, does the vocals with me. It's *five after*, Bino. God." She wore jeans with puffed legs and six-inch stitched cuffs.

"Yeah, okay, I'm going," he said, pushing the cart toward the ticket counter. Behind the counter were chic young women in orange and yellow Southwest Airlines uniforms, selling tickets, tagging luggage, and pointing directions to the proper gates with manicured nails. Carla jiggled along beside him, taking two steps to his one in an effort to keep pace. Bino said, "I got to tell you that hurts my feelings. Hell, a narc doesn't *look* like a narc. If he did he'd never get to bust anybody. A narc looks like Serpico. You ever see *Serpico?*"

She giggled. "Tell Dondi that. I even told him you liked to toot some yourself once in a while, just to set him at ease. He goes, 'Yeah? Anybody see him?' I'm like, 'No,' and he goes, 'See? Get him on the witness stand and he'll lie about it.' He wants me to feel you up to see if you're wearing a body mike."

"Jesus Christ, Carla, you told him *I* like to toot? How do you know *he's* not a narc?"

They checked the luggage—the Southwest Airlines lady almost lost her smile when she got a load of Carla's suitcases—then charged up the ramp, through the security checkpoint, and reached the gate just as the passengers were starting to board. The Creepers, minus Carla, were already in line waving their boarding passes. All four musicians wore blue blazers. Now Bino remembered Dondi, a short, pink-cheeked guy with shoulder-length hair, wearing rose-tinted glasses with lenses the size of dinner plates. Visible through the huge plate-glass window, a tractor hauled loaded-down baggage carts alongside a waiting jet. The outer shell of the Boeing Stretch 737 was painted into a caricature likeness of Shamu the Killer Whale.

Carla said to the musicians, "I told you we'd make it. You guys remember Bino, huh? From last night."

Dondi eyed Bino head to toe. "Yeah," Dondi said. "I talk to him, I'm gonna have witnesses."

9

POLICE CAPTAIN TERRY NOLBY HELD THE PHOTO AT ARM'S length, closed one eye and squinted through the other.

"What's Bino Phillips got to do with anything?"

"We don't know, Terry," an FBI agent said. "We were kind of hoping you'd tell us."

Nolby stood from behind his desk and yanked the pull cord; the drapes parted with a rasping sound and waved in reflex from the curtain rod. Sudden additional light flooded the office. Three floors below, a huge sign featured a man parachuting out of a jail window underneath the caption "EASY OUT BAIL BONDS." Next door to the bond office was another sign announcing that JOHN P. LOVELADY, ATTORNEY specialized in drunk driving and burglary cases. Fucking bloodsucker, Nolby thought. "Phillips and Rusty Benson are lawyers," he said. "Maybe the other guy's a lawyer, too. Three shysters out on the town. So what?"

"You're not helping, Terry," a second agent said. "The other guy we already know. Kinder. He's under federal indictment."

"So? Half the world's under federal indictment. He's joined the crowd." Nolby wore a long-sleeve white shirt and pale yellow tie along with an empty shoulder holster. His underarms were soaked with perspiration.

"We thought that's why we were having this talk," the first agent said, "because you wanted *out* of the crowd."

"Look, Mr. Federal," Nolby said, "you told me you wanted to talk about Tommy Clinger. So okay, I'll talk Clinger. What's that got to do with Bino Phillips having a drink with Rusty and some other asshole?" Beneath Nolby's pointed nose, his lips twitched nervously.

One agent, tall and thin, sat in a chair before Nolby's desk. His partner, short with a thick head and wavy blond hair, rested one hip on the table which held the coffeepot. The tall agent fished in his inside breast pocket and produced another photo. "Look this one over, Terry," he said. "Call it family album day."

Nolby stroked his underarm. The short agent wrinkled his nose and averted his gaze. Nolby picked up and studied the photo. Then he went back to his desk, retrieved the other picture, and held the two glossies side by side. "That's the same table, isn't it?" Nolby said. "In both pictures?"

"Right on," the thin agent said. "The second was taken just a few minutes after Benson left with Kinder. You know the woman?"

Nolby shook his head. "I mean, you said this was Arthur's. Didn't you? The fuck I know about Arthur's? Two bucks for a beer, I never even been inside the joint. You want to talk bars, talk to me about one of the beer joints over on Columbia Street, what I can afford. So maybe Bino Phillips was trying to get a little pussy. Who knows?" He handed both photos back to the agent. "Couple of massage parlors, maybe a poker game or two, yeah. That I can give you. But *Arthur's*, for God's sake . . ."

"Terry, you're beginning to sound awfully stupid." The short agent raised his navy blue coattails and shoved his hands into his back pockets. His hair was parted on the left and he wore glasses with clear plastic frames. "You think we're giving you all this immunity and getting you reinstated on this police force so we can get Tommy Fucking Clinger? We got him already, Terry, and you, too. Listen, you know what happens to cops in the federal prison system?"

Nolby pinched his lower lip. "Protection, I heard."

"Right. From guys in their own neighborhood, that might have a hard-on. You know how it's done?"

Nolby shrugged. "Move them?"

The agent grinned. "You've been studying. Sure, as far from home as possible. In your case, you know where?"

Nolby expelled breath through his nose. "California someplace?"

"Duluth, Minnesota, Terry, you and Clinger both. So cold in the winter your nuts might crack in two. You want to try for Duluth, Minnesota, you just keep fucking with us."

Nolby flopped into his chair, showing a weak grin. "Hey, I already said I was going to cooperate. What the plea agreement says is that I'm going to furnish information about Tommy Clinger, that's all. You're throwing a load at me I'm not ready for."

"You don't read too good, Brother Nolby," the thin agent said. "That agreement says you'll cooperate wherever and whenever the Attorney General of this fair land designates." He leaned closer to Nolby and said in a near-whisper, "Hell, man, aren't you curious? Don't you even want to know how she wound up in Houston?"

"Who? Who you talking about in Houston?" Nolby said.

The stocky agent leaned on Nolby's desk. "That's one for Houdini, isn't it?" the agent said. "Broad's getting a divorce and wants to see us about her old man. First thing you know she gets popped and has the inconsideracy to wind up in a ship channel two hundred and fifty miles from here. I'd wonder about that if I was you."

Nolby's voice went up an octave. "I don't know what you're talking about, any broad. Hey, I need my lawyer to sit in on this?"

"Yeah, Terry," the thin agent said. "Your lawyer. Only he doesn't happen to be in town at the moment. Now, we're going to give you a couple of days. For starters. You know nothing about that woman talking to Bino Phillips, right?"

"I already told you."

"Strictly zero."

"Not shit."

"Okay," the short agent said. "Assume we buy that. That means you're going to tell us twice as much about Rusty Benson."

Nolby sat down. "Rusty?"

"Yeah, Rusty. Your lawyer. Also your close buddy for the past couple of years."

"What about him?" Nolby said.

"If you should remember something about old Rusty, then we're going to have some more things to discuss. Oh yeah. If you don't, that plea bargain agreement goes straight in the shitcan."

Nolby found a paper towel in his desk and mopped sweat from his forehead.

"Couple of days," the thin agent said. "That's Thursday. We'll be calling you." He motioned to his partner, and the two agents walked to the door. "Talk to you Thursday, Terry. You think hard, okay?"

10

BINO LICKED THE SALT-FROSTED RIM OF HIS GLASS, THEN SIPPED some of the bittersweet margarita to mix and mingle with the salt. Red vinyl-covered foam padding vibrated beneath his elbows to the *dum-dum-brrmmm*, followed by the clash of baton on cymbals. He had a perfect seat near the entrance to the jam-packed Hyatt Regency Skyroom, Carla shim-shimmying in gold lamé that moved and flowed with her hips and sparkled like sequins in the spotlight. A picture window ran the length of the far wall, and visible in the distance was the faint outline of Cullen Center. On beyond the center were the double rows of lights along Southwest Freeway. The bayou sky was a starless black.

Being far from home gave Bino a little tremor, a sort of *not-quite* feeling as though something was wrong, or was about to go wrong in a hurry. The *not-quite* feeling had begun as the Southwest Airlines jet dipped underneath the ever-present bayou cloud bank, then rode muggy currents of air over marshland, over subdivisions dotted with crystal blue pools, golf courses, and finally over downtown skyscrapers to make a bumpy landing on Hobby Airport's tar-veined runway. The nearer the plane had come to landing, the more the *not-quite* feeling had grown. Bino couldn't have explained it in a hundred years, but every time he left his Dallas turf something bad seemed to happen.

As the band played their take-five theme and Carla sashayed center stage, Bino plucked a call-message slip from his pocket. The message from Rusty had been waiting for him when he'd checked in, and created a nagging sensation at the back of his mind to mix with the *not-quite* feeling. There was nothing ominous about the message itself, merely a request to contact Rusty across town at the Inn-at-the-Park, but Bino had made five attempts to return the call without finding Rusty in.

He came back to reality as Carla slid her pert bottom onto the stool beside him and said, "Socko. Strong set, huh? Well, *you're* really with it, where's my drink?"

He passed a ten-spot across the bar and ordered her a Tanqueray on the rocks, folded Rusty's message and put it away, then said to her, "You bet it was strong. You guys are blowing the doors off."

"Okay," Carla said. "Name the last three numbers."

"Well . . . there's the Elton John number you and Dondi just sang, and before that . . . I'm not too good on titles, just the tunes."

"And aside from being someplace in dreamland you just don't remember," Carla said. The bartender delivered her drink. She picked up the glass, sipped, and made a face. "I don't know about you, Phillips. Every other man in the joint is salivating for my body, of course, but not old Bino. From you I get reaction zero, unless you want to count a couple of grunts last night while you were screwing me. So what's the deal?"

Jesus but she was cute. Bino was conscious of men looking his way as if thinking, Who's the dumb-looking bozo talking to the singer? "Tell you the truth, I was thinking about Rusty

Benson," Bino said. "I got a message to call him."

"Let me guess what he wants. You told him you scored with the singer last night, and he's calling up wanting to know if it's any good? God, Bino. Gross."

A fat man wearing a gray suit came by and asked her to sing "What's Love Got to Do with It?" during the next set. She nodded and smiled. The man moved on. Carla crossed her legs, propped her elbows up on the foam padding, interlocked her fingers, and said, "So?"

"So what?"

"So Rusty's in town. And so are you. You going to see him, or what?"

"Maybe tomorrow," Bino said, "but not for long. I told him I'd stand by in case he needs me."

"Well, he'd better not need you tonight," Carla said. "We're going to Gilley's."

"Gilley's? What's wrong with this place?"

"Nothing," Carla said. "But we're through here at eleven, and there's nothing going on downtown after that unless you'd like to get mugged. You see the two women over there?" She swiveled on her stool and looked toward the bandstand.

Bino followed her gaze. Dondi was seated at a table with two women, a blond with short permed hair and a brunette with hair to her waist. They were no spring chickens but looked trim and fit, and were groomed like pages from *Cosmo*. Dondi sipped a draft beer; as he bent his head, light reflected from his plate-size lenses. The brunette reached out and pinched Dondi's leg. He brushed her hand away, deadpan. Bino said to Carla, "I guess you mean them."

"That's the two," Carla said. "They work in a real estate office around here, and they're taking all of us to Gilley's as soon as this place closes."

"Great," Bino said. "You mean, Dondi's letting me come along, narc and all?"

She giggled. "Actually he didn't want to. But I told him maybe he could pawn you off on those two. Dondi likes them younger."

· · ·

Bino slammed hard against the backseat door; Carla's firmness pushed against him, then shifted away as the Seville fishtailed into the middle lane on I-45. The brunette was driving,
her long straight hair draped over the seat, her slim red-
nailed hands gripping the wheel, gold rings on four of her fingers, a martini on the rocks balanced precariously in front of
her on the dash. She picked up the drink and sipped, weaving
all over the road, drawing an angry honk from a Mercury
Sable in the inside lane. She shot the Merc the finger as she
said, "Just 'cause I ain't got a free hand, Bettilu, don't be get-
tin' no designs on that cute thing. Once we get to Gilley's it's
every girl for herself, don'tcha know?" The digital speedometer showed 85 per, the freeway lights zooming past like glow-
ing whippets.

Dondi sat on the front seat console, drinking beer from a
long-neck bottle and looking bored. The blond rode shotgun
with one arm around Dondi, tickling his ear with a fingernail.

"Shee-it, Becky," the blond said. "Let's just blow off
Gilley's and take this cute thing over to my place. I don't mind
sharin' him, long as I get mine." She hugged Dondi.

He shrugged her off. "I'm like, you broads aren't hearing
me. I like, want to see Gilley's, I heard a lot about that place.
But I can't be doing no sex, I'm in training."

"Ain't he *cute?*" the brunette said. She whipped to her left,
floored the accelerator, and the speedometer jumped to 95 as
if by magic.

Jesus, Bino thought, slow the fuck down. He leaned forward. "Say, girls. Let's take a few side streets, whaddya say? I'd
like to see some neighborhood scenery."

Bino thought that he looked out of place dancing western
swing in Gilley's, doing the push in the world's most famous
honky-tonk wearing tan slacks, a knit golf shirt, and brown
Gucci loafers, his mop of white hair bobbing and waving
above the crowd. And he knew good and well that Carla
looked out of place in her gold lamé pants and navy blue
spike-heeled shoes, giggling, bumping, and wriggling. When-

ever they moved in close to push apart, her nose touched his breastbone. The other dancers wore boots and jeans, the men in Levi's and the women in Lady Wrangler's with stitching on the butt pockets, about half of the women sporting sprayed, stand-up beehive hairdos. Probably, Bino thought, everyone else on this freaking dance floor thinks Carla and I are refugees from a circus act.

"What say we sit the next one out?" Bino shouted. "Take a little break." He gasped for breath.

Carla rocked back on one heel, pranced forward, and ducked under his outstretched arm. "What's the matter, hoss? You ready for the glue factory?"

"No. No, this is *great fun,*" Bino said. "I just thought you'd like to go over there and watch the action." He gestured toward the jerking, bucking mechanical bull. A cowpoke was tall in the saddle, one arm waving, loose as Raggedy Andy.

She went on boogying. "I don't picture you riding the bull. *Shooting* the bull, now that's a different story."

"Carla . . . Jesus . . . *Christ.*" He stopped dancing and stood, shoulders drooping and chest heaving. She stuck out her tongue. He grabbed her upper arm and herded her firmly toward the bull riders. "What's happened to Dondi?" he said, peering around the dance floor.

"He hasn't come up for air if that Bettilu has anything to say about it. I think they may have left. God, Bino, please tell me that this time you brought cabfare."

Behind the bull-riding arena was a mile-long stand-up bar, cowboys and cowgirls whooping it up, swigging from longnecks, cheering the riders, groaning loudly whenever someone went ass-over-heels from saddle to sawdust. The mechanical bucking contraption was headless. Handling the controls was a bearded guy whose gut nearly popped the buttons on his western shirt, and every time a rider hit the dirt he cackled in glee. Bino shouldered his way, leading Carla through to lean on the bar. She snuggled into the crook of his arm.

In a few seconds a bartender with a hawk nose and thin features tipped his hat and said, "What'll it be, tall podnuh?"

Bino thought, Now this is carrying the Buffalo Bill shit a little far, but ordered a couple of Lone Stars, trying to get in the spirit of things. On the faraway bandstand the guitars twanged into "Lookin' for Love in All the Wrong Places." Bino halfway wished they'd look someplace else.

The beers arrived; Carla sipped while Bino tilted his head back and swigged. Two burly cowboys came from the bull pen, backslapping and elbowing each other. Both were huge. One had collar-length hair hanging below a light-colored Stetson. His face was craggy, like a rugged Indian's. His partner was only an inch or so under Bino's six-six, had thick red hair, and wore a black cowpoke's hat along with a huge GOLDEN NUGGET—LAS VEGAS belt buckle. The redhead sported a walrus mustache.

Golden Nugget was saying, "That's two you owe me, Billy Ed. Shit, you're easy money."

"I'll give you fuckin' easy money," Indian said. "Git yore ass back in line, Spooky, I'll give you— Hold on there, Spooky, what we got here? A little golden girl. Hidy, darlin'." He showed a crooked grin and leered down at Carla.

Carla smiled vacantly and watched the jerking bull.

The redheaded saddlebuster, Spook, fingered his belt buckle. "Don't guess she heard you, Billy Ed. Looky here, she's got her a feller. A big whitefish."

Now Bino stared at the bull just as Carla was doing. A groan went up around the bar as another rider bit the dust.

Billy Ed stood spraddle-legged in front of Bino, hands on hips. "Damn straight," Billy Ed said. "A whitefish, Spooky, a big 'un."

Bino thought he'd be wise to grab Carla and get the fuck out of there.

Spook egged it on, hooking his thumbs under his belt. " 'Spec' these folks a tad too good to visit with us, huh?"

Billy Ed licked his lips. "Well, they might be. How 'bout it, little gold girl? You too good to talk to Billy Ed an' old Spooky? Coupla tired cowhands, been on the range all day?"

Bullshit, Bino thought. At the bowling alley, maybe. On the range, no way.

Spook's mouth twisted in a mean-looking grimace. "She still ain't talkin', Billy Ed."

"Well, lessee if she can hear this." Billy Ed bent from the waist until his big crooked nose was just inches from Carla's. "Hey, bayy-bee," he yelled. "Seein' as how we're among friends, what would you say to a little fuck?"

Bino'd say this much for Carla, she didn't let it rattle her. She looked up at Billy Ed as though seeing him for the first time. She showed a sweet smile. "My. What would I say to a little fuck? Why, I don't know. I don't see any little fucks around here. I see a *big* fuck, though. You. So why don't you get lost, you big fuck?"

Bino thought, Oh, shit. He stepped forward. "Look, guys," he said. "This has gone about far enough, don't you think?" He grinned.

Spook drew closer and stood beside Billy Ed, the two big cowboys shoulder to shoulder. "Whatcha think, Billy Ed? This here whitefish fixin' to give us some shit?"

Bino stood between Spook and Billy Ed as the Yellow Cab pulled into Gilley's parking lot. The cowpokes had their arms around him like old buddies. Carla stood to one side, looking down at her feet.

Spook held the cab's door open for Carla, then whacked Bino on the shoulder. "You're okay in our book, whitefish," Spook said. "We don't hold no grudges. Next time you're in town, look us up."

Bino nodded and climbed silently in alongside Carla. The two roughnecks whooped it up, nudging each other and hee-hawing as they went back inside the honky-tonk. Carla gave the cabbie the Hyatt Regency's address, then snuggled against Bino as the taxi pulled onto Spencer Highway. "Well, shut mah mouth," Carla said. "Rough day on the trail, huh?"

Bino's lips were swollen and bleeding. "Next time," he said, "why don't you try, 'I don't care to fuck, sir, thank you just the same.' Something like that, Carla, okay?"

• • •

"You see the look the bellman gave you?" Carla said. "God. Hold still, now." She tilted the bottle to soak a cotton ball in rubbing alcohol. She pressed her tongue against one corner of her mouth as she dabbed at Bino's eyebrow.

"*Ow.* Jesus *Christ.*" He jerked away and conked his head on the headboard.

"Big baby. Come on, it's good for you. Concentrate on my boobs, it'll make it easier."

She sat on her haunches, clad in pale blue bikini briefs, bending over him on the king-size bed. He was propped against the headboard, her nipples bobbing in front of his face like inquisitive pink lambs' noses. Bino was shirtless and had taken off his shoes. She moved in closer and dabbed once more at his eye.

He said, "I wish the bastards would've let me take 'em on one at a time."

The lambs' noses moved up and down. "They did, remember? The redheaded guy went first and the other one watched. The Injun Joe type never even got in action."

"Oh," he said. The alcohol stung like hell. He touched his eyebrow.

"But don't let it bother you," she said. "I've never gone for the he-man type, anyway."

"Now wait a minute. I'm not exactly a pansy."

"There." She capped the bottle and bent over him to place it on the nightstand. One nipple brushed his chest. "I didn't say you were a pansy, egomaniac. Men. How's that feel, Nurse Pease got you fit as a fiddle?"

He ran his finger over his swollen lip. "That your last name? It's the first time I've heard it."

"I know. Pretty imaginative way to slip it in, huh? That's so if you have to introduce me to someone you won't be stumped. Besides, if we're going to be screwing regular . . ."

"Please don't make me laugh. It hurts."

She twisted around to sit beside him. "Pease is okay, it's the name I was born with. I had an agent once that wanted me to be Carla Starr, but I go, Nope, that sounds like a stripper. One year in high school they elected me Sweet Potato Queen.

I was coming out of the girls' room and this big dumb football guy, Eddie Fields, he yells, 'Hey, goddam, Queen Carla *pees*.' I thought I'd die."

He held the corners of his mouth to keep from grinning as his shoulders heaved. "Sweet Potato Queen?"

"Some title, huh? Actually, in Kaufman that was a pretty big deal. That's sixty miles east of Dallas, by Cedar Creek Lake."

"I know where it is," Bino said. "I grew up in Mesquite."

"That's the big city compared to Kaufman. We had like two hundred in the whole school." The crease along the inside of her thigh deepened as she hugged one knee. "Actually my name isn't Pease any more. It's Carnes. I got married once."

"I did, too," Bino said. "To a cheerleader, no less. Hey, Carla Carnes isn't bad for a singer. C.C., for short."

"*Two* C.C.'s. He was Chris." She reached to the nightstand for her glasses, then picked up the remote and switched on the TV. On-screen, Alan Ladd leaned against the bar, coolly regarding Jack Palance. Brandon deWilde peered under double barroom doors. Bino knew the lines by heart. Ladd: *What'd he say, Wilson?* Palance: *He said you were a lowdown, yella dog, Shane.* Palance went for his gun; Ladd drilled the bastard before he could clear leather.

Bino said, "Local Kaufman boy?"

"No, I'd left the sticks by then. I met Chris at North Texas U. He had a group, you know, ever since the Eagles got together at North Texas everybody's got a group up there. I was Chris's singer, but what I mainly did was stand around shaking my ass and rattling mariachis. We took off to find the footlights and all that. Found each other for a while. It was neat until Chris got on coke and speed." There was a catch in her voice. It was the first time Bino had seen her in a serious mood. He supposed that everyone had their moments.

"Ever hear from him?" Bino said.

"Not lately. I still toot a line now and then, but I can take it or leave it. Not Chris. He had some real talent, but stuffed most of it up his nose. The last letter I got from him had a

string of numbers after his name. Federal Prison Camp at
Lompoc, California. God, I hope he gets his act together."

Impulsively, Bino squeezed her hand. On TV, Alan Ladd
rode into the distance while the music built to a crescendo
and Brandon deWilde followed at a dead run. The bedside
phone rang.

It took a couple of seconds to register, Bino sitting on a
posh hotel king-size nursing a fat lip, Carla's bare firmness beside him, warmth radiating from her body, the scent of her
perfume in his nostrils like honeysuckle. The theme from
Shane for background, and suddenly the jangling of the
phone. The ringing seemed far away. He checked the digital
clock on the bedside table. Two-thirty in the morning. He
picked up the receiver and said hello.

The television was too loud for him to make out what the
excited female on the line was saying. He said, "Hold on."
Then, swiveling his head, "Turn it off, please, Carla." Carla
pressed the MUTE button. Bino said hello again.

"Turn what off?" Dodie said into his ear. "The vibrator?"

"No, the . . . Hi, Dode."

"Wow, I've called about ten times. Robert thinks I'm
crazy, making all these calls."

"Who the hell is . . . ? We . . . I've been out," Bino said.
Spook had landed a solid haymaker on his right ear, and Bino
winced—picturing Hurricane Calhoun, an ex-pug client who
had a cauliflower ear—as he shifted the phone to the other
side of his head.

"I assumed you were," Dodie said. "Rusty Benson is in the
Harris County Jail. They're holding him without bond. Capital murder."

Bino probably should have been surprised, but wasn't. He
pictured Fuller, the Houston detective, leaving the courtroom
that morning with Marvin Goldman. He said to Dodie, "Did
you talk to him?"

"He called collect from the jail just as I was leaving the
office. It's all over the news. You need to see Rusty early in
the morning, there's some kind of hearing in court down
there at ten."

The television movie was over and a rerun of the ten o'clock news was on. Carla stirred and brushed against his arm. Bino said, "Yeah. It'll be a bail hearing. Let's sign off, Dode. Something's coming up that I want to see."

"Wow, I'll bet." Tone on the line like cracking ice.

"No, Dode, on television. Oh, and Dode. Thanks for keeping after me, I hope it didn't mess up your evening."

"Oh, shut up," she said. She disconnected.

He took the remote from Carla and clicked on the sound. The program lead-in consisted of some aerial shots of downtown Houston, of Intercontinental Airport, and of the Astrodome sitting beside the freeway like a giant upside-down cereal bowl. Then came a commercial, a fast-talking guy in overalls named Honest Fred Homer who wanted to sell a cream puff of a used Toronado. Finally there was the anchorperson, a peppy black female who chanted the story lead-ins like come-hither rock tunes. The first item had to do with Houston Mayor Kathy Whitmire addressing a group of gay libbers. Rusty's arrest was next.

Carla gasped when the video clip of Rusty, handcuffed and hustled along between two burly deputy sheriffs, flashed on the screen. The story was brief, a rehash of what Dodie had already told Bino over the phone. The on-the-spot newsperson was another black female. She closed by saying that she was Karen Porter at the Harris County Jail as Rusty and his escorts disappeared behind sliding, hissing steel doors. The no-bond bullshit will never stand up, Bino thought. A guy like Rusty was a lead-pipe cinch to be granted bail. The Harris County cops would understand that as well, but would want to hold Rusty overnight for a few little chats. Bino was just about to shut off the TV when another item came on, once more riveting his attention. There he was in living color. Bino Phillips in the flesh.

Actually there was only a brief glimpse of the side of his face and his snow white hair as he stood outside federal court, followed instantly by a close-up of the rugged bunch of Mountainites as they chanted the Twenty-third Psalm. Judge Edgar Bryson looked even paler than Bino remembered, the tall, silver-haired man keeping his dignity as best he could as a gang of U.S. marshals escorted him past the Mountainites and hustled him into his chambers.

Carla stiffened abruptly. "I can't believe it. He's a *judge?*"

"Yeah," Bino said absently. "Edgar Bryson. That's Big Preacher Daniel's trial. Didn't you see me? I was—"

"It's *him,* Bino. The guy I mistook you for when I first met you at Arthur's? Gee, that's him."

11

MANCIL ADRIANI HELD UP ONE LEG OF THE RUMPLED KHAKI chinos, aligned the seams, flattened the trouser leg across the padded board, and reached for the iron. Steam hissed as Adriani smoothed the fabric into wrinkle-less perfection, with straight firm creases. "The steam's the secret," he said. "First time I tried it, I used starch. No good, the cloth gets so stiff it'll wrinkle before you got 'em on fifteen minutes."

A man with graying razored hair balding at the temples sat nearby on a kitchen stool. He wore a blue pinstripe Hart Schaffner & Marx along with polished black shoes. He glanced out the window at pairs of headlights going back and forth on Telephone Road. "They will?"

" 'Course they will," Adriani said. "That suit you got, you think the dry cleaner uses starch? Hell, no, the dry cleaner knows better." Adriani moved the smoothed-out leg upward and applied steam to the still-rumpled portion. "You want to know why I'm doing this?"

The man looked Adriani over, burly forearms beneath a cutoff sweatshirt, receding forehead with thinning strands of hair combed back on a glistening scalp. "Doing what?" the man said.

"Ironing these fucking pants, doing what. What else I'm doing?"

"I don't suppose I'd thought about it," the man said.

"Well, you ought to. I got a sixty-thousand-dollar Mercedes parked out there, that stand-up big-screen Magnavox set me back twenty-nine hundred bucks, those sculptured horses on the coffee table cost me four hundred simoleons apiece. I got a maid coming five days a week, and I'm standing here ironing these fucking pants. Don't you want to know why?" Adriani carefully stroked the iron.

The man checked his gold Piaget. "I've got an early meeting."

"Yeah?" Adriani's voice was hoarse, a slightly breaking alto. "Well, now you're having a late meeting. You're going to sit around awhile and shoot the shit, pick up what, couple of thousand? Then you're on a plane back to Sunny Southern, be copping z's beside your old lady out in Westwood tomorrow night. All that shit ain't nothing. This meeting here's what's important, if I'm reading you right."

"I still can't afford to stay all—"

"This ironing's a reminder. About this one fuckup cost me four years federal, you know? Doing the time I got to iron my own clothes. The hack's and the warden's, too, this was in the camp at El Reno, Oklahoma, and kind of laid-back. Wasn't that bad, I keep the warden looking spiffy I get some extra furlough consideration. Point is, that little federal beef I done ruined it for me. Now I can't go home no more. I'm living in this hotass Houston fucking Texas and can't even walk around my old neighborhood. So I iron—"

"The man I want to talk to you about follows pretty much the same routine . . ."

"—these pants . . . shut the fuck up about routines for a

minute. That name on my mailbox, Charles Dorrell? That's a pseudo, case you ain't figured it out. My real name's—"

"Now I don't want to know . . ."

"You're going to know, if we do anything," Adriani said. "Mancil Adriani, that's me, and don't you forget it. And I iron my own pants because it reminds me, no more fuckups." He switched off and laid the iron aside, then got two glasses down from the cabinet. "So you want a drink? Got Chivas, you name it, Perrier or fresh-squeezed OJ. I don't drink alcohol myself. Fucks the head up, but a man thinking about what you're wanting to do might need a buzz on."

The man's thin lips trembled. "Nothing for me."

Adriani raised one eyebrow. "Suit yourself, but I'm the one needs a clear head. You can get blasted if you want to." He opened the refrigerator, poured orange juice, led the way into the living room, and sank down on the sofa. In addition to the sweatshirt he wore army pants with big pockets. The man followed, sat in an easy chair, and wiped his forehead with a monogrammed handkerchief.

"This witness protection program," Adriani said, "is the pure shits, but it's got its advantages. Long as certain people don't see me, you know? So how's the airplane parts business, Whitley?"

The man lowered his head. "Good God."

"Yeah, I know all about you. You're Whitley Morris and your coolies make a quarter of the wing parts sold. Aside from this Houston bank, you're on the board of directors for six other companies. You sit on a guy's board, he sits on yours, right? Allows you people to trade dollars. Your old lady is named Mimi. She's Old Lady Number Two. Did a few commercials for you, right? I like the miniskirt scene where she's riding the wing on the 747 and the wind's blowing her skirt up around her ass. Old Lady Number One lives out in Beverly Hills and ain't too happy about being traded in for some young pussy. This man that referred you to me couldn't testify to shit, 'cause he's not acting as any middleman. But I had him check you A to Z."

Whitley Morris firmed up his posture. "I think I should go."

Adriani took a pull of orange juice and set the glass on a coaster. "Maybe you should. But you go hanging around some sleazebag bar looking for somebody, you'll wind up dealing with John Law. This way you know you're talking to the real thing."

"I hadn't expected it to get so personal."

"Getting somebody offed is personal as shit, Whitley."

Morris vacantly bit a knuckle.

"Where I fucked up," Adriani said, "was in dealing with a bunch of go-betweens. Longer the chain, the weaker the links. What I did was, I arranged to hit this guy—"

"Please," Morris said. "I feel the less I know about you—"

"You can feel that way all you want to," Adriani said. "But that ain't the way it works."

"I thought if you were going to whack someone," Morris said, "you'd prefer to remain anonymous."

"Whack? *Whack?* You been seeing too many picture shows, *Goodfellas* and all that. Nobody ever heard of whack before, but you know what? You're not the only one, there's guys in the business going around talking about whacking people now. The expression catches on."

"Well, murder someone."

Adriani pointed a finger. "That's the first intelligent thing you said. 'Cause that's what it is, murder. I think people going around talking about whacking, they believe they're cool using the lingo, and that don't sound as bad as calling it what it is. You're here because you want a guy murdered. Your partner or something."

Morris bent over and hugged himself. "It's scary as hell."

"You bet it is. This guy I done in Baltimore was going to be a federal witness against some money laundering guys. Guys sort of like you, Whitley, people that screw each other in business deals but ain't got the cods to look at somebody and make them dead.

"So they go," Adriani said, "to the only real convict any of 'em know, guy used to like it up the ass at Joliet prison in Illinois. The guy comes to me and arranges things. The murder goes without a hitch because that's the way I do things. But the fucking go-between, two years later he takes this fall on a dumbass stickup, and first thing you know he's talking to the federals to get his own ass out of a crack.

"So thanks to that asshole I got to take the snitch route my ownself. That stand-up guy bullshit is just that, Whitley, once you got the death penalty staring you in the face. So I testify against those money laundering guys, which serves them right, do my four, and now I'm sitting in this federal witness program. Can't go home. Can't be Mancil Adriani no more, got to be Charles fucking Dorrell."

"Look," Morris said. "Can't we just talk business? I've done everything you said."

"You ain't done everything," Adriani said, "because I ain't finished saying. I know who you are and you know who I am. Now if somebody says something about this, can't be no doubt who's talking, right? Then the talker gets fucking dead himself, which is the best insurance I know to keep people's mouths shut."

A thin dribble of fear ran from the corner of Morris's mouth. He finally said, "Maybe we shouldn't make a deal at all."

"You gone too far for that, Whitley."

Morris shivered. "Good God." Then he murmured "Good God" again, and looked resigned as he said, "You can make the whole thing appear accidental?"

"I can make it appear," Adriani said, "any way you want it to appear. The guy can just vanish. I know ways nobody ever finds the guy. Take 'em on an airplane ride over the ocean, dump that body in the Atlantic and let 'em hunt. That's the safest way."

"But the way this has to happen . . ."

"Relax, Whitley, I was only giving an example. Sometimes, with women, I can make it look like a rapo. That way nobody ever suspects it's a contract murder, you know? You got to collect on a partnership insurance policy. Way you and your partner been getting along, you're lucky it's you talking to me instead of him. Am I right?"

Resignedly, Morris said, "I suppose you are."

Adriani looked at his watch. "I'm going to have to interrupt this little talk. Just like when Mimi interrupts your meeting to give you a blow job. Something on the news I want to see."

Adriani picked up the remote and turned on the big screen, sipped orange juice while Morris fretted in silence. Adriani's pliant features changed from impatience—as the Houston scenes rolled across the screen—to disgust—as the mayor addressed the gays. As the station played the feature on Rusty Benson's arrest, Adriani squinted attentively. As soon as Rusty and his deputy escort disappeared into the jail, Adriani switched off the television.

"I may have fucked up again, Whitley," Adriani said.

"How's that?"

"Didn't you see? Fucking guy's a lawyer. Anytime a lawyer's involved, you're in for a world of hurt." Adriani reached into an end table drawer, came up with a pad and a ballpoint. "Now we're ready for particulars, Whitley. Going in. I don't fly nothing but First Class. Let's have that understood at the outset, okay?"

12

INO CALLED THE HARRIS COUNTY JAIL AT SEVEN IN THE MORNING and learned about what he'd expected. Rusty was on his way to court as part of a prisoner's chain gang. His lawyer could consult with him in the holding cell behind court around eight o'clock, an hour before the bond hearing. The deputy on the phone had slurred speech, as if he was speaking through a jawful of chewing tobacco. Bino asked directions to the felony court where Rusty's case was assigned. The deputy wouldn't say for security reasons, and referred Bino to the Harris County District Attorney. Bino called the D.A.'s office, found out what he wanted to know, and hung up the phone.

He went in to take a shower. He had a tough time adjusting the massager-nozzle so that the Niagara of water wouldn't knock him out of the tub, and an even tougher time squeezing enough shampoo from the tiny complimentary bottle to wash his hair. He somehow shaved without cutting himself, but singed his scalp with the hotel blow dryer. Finally he looked himself over in the mirror. His lips were bruised and the cut over his eye probably could have used some stitches. Well, if he couldn't argue Harris County into granting bail for Rusty, maybe he could scare the judge into action.

He left the bathroom and dressed in his lone navy blue suit and red polka-dot tie. He never went on a trip without forgetting something. This time it was his dress belt. That meant going through the day with his coat buttoned and hoping his pants didn't fall down. What the hell, he'd have to live with it.

He gently shook Carla. She mumbled something, pulled the sheet tightly around her, and snuggled deeper down in the bed. He went over to the bureau, located stationery, and left her a note. Looking at Carla reminded him of what she'd said about Judge Edgar Bryson, which further reminded him that he had a couple of bones to pick with Rusty. He left the hotel at a brisk walk, covering the six blocks to the courthouse in less than a quarter hour.

The Harris County Criminal Courts Building was pure county government, an uninteresting, plain structure of ten or twelve stories with a white stone exterior. He had some time, so he spent a few minutes watching the parade of rush-hour bus and auto traffic, and perspiring in the muggy Houston air. Jesus, but it was humid in the bayou. Bino had gone to law school in Houston, at South Texas College of Law, and once he'd received his sheepskin he'd vowed never to set foot in the town again. It was a vow that he hadn't been able to keep—there was just too much commerce between Texas's two largest cities for a Dallas lawyer to escape a trip to the bayou every once in a while—but that didn't stop him from hating the place. He'd seen all of downtown Houston that he wanted to see. He went over to the building entry, held the door while three women in business dresses brushed past without so much as a thank-you, and went inside.

The lobby guard, a chubby young guy wearing a pistol, gave him directions to the courtroom. He took the stairs up for the exercise and arrived in court fifteen minutes too early to visit the holding cell, so he sat down on a front-row spectators' bench to wait. Three other guys in suits with briefcases waited as well.

The man seated directly beside him said, "Hey, how's the hook shot?"

Bino turned his head and looked the guy over; long and lanky with thinning brown hair, green eyes with little laugh crinkles at the corners. "Jimmy Lankford," Bino said, extending his hand. "Long time." The great State of Texas was a very small world.

Lankford had a firm grip. "Damn near twenty years since the last time you-all beat us down here. You swished so many baseline jumpers that the scorekeep had to get a second sheet." He glanced at Bino's puffy eye. "What are you, a lawyer or a boxer?"

Bino winced as he touched his lip. "I still play a little basketball. Collision with the gym floor. Since you're asking, I didn't think Rice grads went to law school. I thought all you guys were engineers, sat around building bridges and whatnot."

"Sometimes it takes four years of college to find out what you *don't* want to do," Lankford said. "I went back to school after a couple of years, and now I spend most of my time arguing with the D.A. over how much time my clients are going to get."

"Along with the rest of us." Bino rested his ankle on his knee, leaning back. "I'm lucky to run into you. I'm a fish out of water in Harris County, so I wonder what I'm up against with this judge here."

Lankford glanced toward the other two lawyers, then leaned close and said guardedly to Bino, "You really want to know?"

"Please don't say it's that bad."

"For most cases, about what you get up in Dallas," Lankford said. "Stacked against the defense about 75–25, but all right. The client I've got today should be in misdemeanor court, but it's the fourth time he's walked off with a shirt or pair of underwear at Foley's, and they've bumped him to a felony. But he'll get an okay deal. You, though . . . if I took a wild guess, Bino, I'd say you're representing Rusty Benson."

Bino raised his eyebrows. "I got a sign on or something?"

"Seems you represent everybody that gets on television," Lankford said. "I watch the news, old buddy. Don't you have one of those Dallas cops under indictment in the fed?"

"Yeah," Bino said. "Tommy Clinger. Hey, I don't *try* to get in the newspapers. With Rusty Benson, we'd be better off if there wasn't any publicity. Today I got a plain vanilla bond hearing that ought to take about five minutes. With the coverage, I don't know. I might have to bring my lunch."

Lankford was suddenly serious. He glanced furtively toward the back of the courtroom, then said, "You'd better hold onto your ass with both hands on that Benson case, old friend."

Bino tilted his head. "How so?"

"I've got a client that's a diver. I'm talking out of school, but I've got some things you ought to know."

Bino cleared his throat, uncrossed and recrossed his legs.

"My client was one of the divers that helped haul Mrs. Benson out of that canal the other day," Lankford said. "The weird thing was, his deal was with the Channel Board and the HPD. Two days he spent, pulling up one wreck after another, and those cops weren't running makes on those old heaps. Harry thinks they knew what they were looking for all along. And he thinks the feds were involved."

"Fuck a duck," Bino said. "What made him think so?"

"According to Harry," Lankford said, "the entire time he's diving within a hundred yards of the spot where they finally located her car. They had the Caddy pinpointed. Then they told Harry and his partner to keep their mouths shut or else, and even paid them in cash as an incentive. This can't go any further, Bino, otherwise my client's liable to find himself locked up just for telling me about it. But the payoff, where they sent him for his money, was the Houston FBI office."

Bino cocked his head. "Just like that, huh?"

"Just like that," Lankford said. "If anybody finds out I—"

"You don't have to worry," Bino said. "And thanks for the information. I don't know what I'll do about it, the first order of business is to get my client free on bond. Tell you the truth, I probably won't be Rusty's lawyer after the bond hearing.

We've got a little conflict of interest problem, has to do with that cop I'm representing."

Lankford checked his surroundings once more. One of the other lawyers was watching; Lankford hitched himself around to face Bino, then said, "I don't want to nose into your case, so just tell me and I'll keep my mouth shut."

"You've already given me more help in five minutes than I've gotten from anybody," Bino said. "So please go on."

"Well, if I were you," Lankford said, "I wouldn't be expecting to get my boy out on bond. Not Rusty Benson."

"Oh, come on," Bino said. "Like him or not, Rusty's not any bond risk. Plus, you know the law, that hearing this morning is a probable cause. Before they can hold him they've got to put on evidence that he did it, and believe me, Rusty's got alibis up the yin-yang for the past two weeks." Almost as if he knew he was going to have to account for his whereabouts, Bino thought.

Lankford clicked his teeth together. "It doesn't work that way in Harris County, bucko. Dallas lawyers get their asses in a crack down here every day. Most local law enforcement has it in for the feds, but Harris County does whatever Uncle Sam says in these cases. I wish you luck, but if the feds want Rusty Benson in jail in Houston, Texas, then that's where he's going to stay."

The holding cell behind the 142nd District Court for Harris County had a barred door like a scene from a western movie. Behind the bars prisoners sat on a double row of iron benches, milled around aimlessly, or sat on the floor Indian style with their ankles crossed. There was a single stainless-steel toilet enclosed in chest-high partitions within the cell. As Bino and the deputy-in-charge approached, a black man who was built like a fireplug took a leak with the door open. The deputy said loudly, "Shut the fuckin' door, asshole." The prisoner sneered over his shoulder and kept on pissing.

Bino spotted Rusty seated on the far end of one of the benches, alongside a Mexican guy with a handlebar mustache. Rusty sat leaned forward with his forehead resting morosely on his lightly clenched fist, like *The Thinker*. He hadn't shaved and his watch and rings were missing; encircling his left wrist was a white plastic prisoner's ID band. He wore a khaki-colored jumpsuit with the words "County Jail" stenciled between his shoulder blades in large black letters. He wore no socks; his feet were in black plastic sandals and showed raw red marks where the sandals had pressed into his ankles and insteps. Even in this situation Rusty stood out; Bino couldn't help thinking of a matinee idol, Alec Baldwin perhaps, playing the part of a guy in jail.

The jailer rattled the door. "Benson. Your lawyer's here."

Rusty looked up slowly. His eyes were bloodshot beneath puffy lids. He showed a weak smile. "I'll bet I'm a lot gladder to see you than you are to see me," he said, getting up, approaching and wrapping big hands around the bars. A black guy and a Mexican guy had a race for the seat which Rusty had vacated. The black guy won.

The deputy said, "Rules are, you stand a foot apart. Don't pass anything between you other than pen and paper. I'll be sitting over there." He backed away and sat in a chair near the door leading to the courtroom.

"I've stood outside a lot of holding tanks, just like you have," Rusty said to Bino. "You get to think you know what it's like to be in here. Believe me, you don't."

Bino glanced behind him to where the deputy now read a newspaper, then said to Rusty, "We've only got a few minutes, so we've got to talk fast. First of all, you need to know, I got some pretty straight poop that the feds are involved in arresting you."

There was a slight shift in Rusty's gaze. Bino went on. "There's more. When did you and Judge Edgar Bryson get to be buddies?" He kept his expression calm and waited for some reaction.

And did he ever get one. Rusty sagged like a man punched in the solar plexus. He looked at his feet. "Who told you that?"

"What does it matter?"

Rusty looked up. "Well, it's nobody's business."

"Maybe it's not. But a judge palling around with a defense lawyer practicing in his court? Somebody will make it their business, if I don't."

Rusty pointed a finger. "I hired you to get me out on bail. That's all."

Bino's chin moved to one side. "That's right, you did. And I'll do my damnedest to. Tell you the truth, I don't think the state's got dick for evidence, and I think you'll get bail."

"That's all I want." Rusty backed away. "Are you through now?"

Bino looked at him.

"If you are, I've got some thinking to do," Rusty said.

Bino stepped back as well. "Yeah, Rusty, I'm through. You know, I just learned something good."

"Yeah? What's that?"

"That regardless of whether this murder beef is bullshit," Bino said, "things are looking up for my main client. You know, Tommy Clinger?"

"I thought we weren't discussing that case," Rusty said. "You and I."

"Oh, we're not," Bino said. "It's just that Tommy's going to be glad he's not the big fish in that federal investigation any more. If you want to see the whale, baby, go look in the mirror. See you in court, Rusty." He started to leave, then stopped and turned. "Oh, and Rusty. On the murder. Start thinking about a lawyer. Once you get released on bond, I'm outta here."

As he sat alongside Jimmy Lankford, waiting for the judge to arrive in court, Bino gave himself a pep talk. He had to get himself inspired. He'd taken Rusty's money and agreed to represent the guy, and like it or not, for the time being he was stuck.

Lankford pointed to the front. "Ready to meet the other side?"

Bino followed Lankford's direction. A man lounged at the state's table, talking to the bailiff. The guy was in his thirties

with coal black hair, sideburns chopped off even with the tops
of his ears. He wore a navy blue pinstripe, and his eyes had an
I'm-suspicious glaze about them.

"The prosecutor?" Bino said.

"Persecutor is more like it," Lankford said. "Roger Tiddle.
He handles special cases. Like yours."

"Nice guy?"

Lankford snickered. "Judge for yourself. Talk to me after
you meet the guy."

Bino went through the railing and touched the prosecutor's shoulder. "Bino Phillips," Bino said. "Here representing
Rusty Benson."

"Roger Tiddle," Roger Tiddle said, gripping Bino's hand
halfheartedly, without standing up. "Man, that's a nasty cut
over your eye. I don't think we've got anything to talk about."

This was another guy whom Bino wasn't going to like. The
list was growing. "Oh?" Bino said. "How come we don't?"

"If you want to discuss bail for your client, forget it. I'm
going to hold him."

Bino had now had it up to here. "*You* are? I must be in the
wrong country. I thought that was up to the judge."

One side of Tiddle's mouth turned up, like the smile of a
man partially paralyzed. "You know, you're right. It *is* up to
the judge. So that's who you should be talking to, not me." He
turned his back and continued his conversation with the
bailiff.

Bino very nearly grabbed Roger Tiddle by the collar and
hauled him to his feet. He controlled himself, however, smiling like a Baptist on his way back to the spectator section.
Whatever incentive he'd needed in giving Rusty a good effort
for his money, Bino now had in spades.

As Bino sat down, Lankford said, "Well?"

Bino crossed his legs, looked toward the prosecution
table, then grinned at Lankford. "Could stand some attitude
adjustment," Bino said, "couldn't he?"

• • •

If Bino's conversations with Jimmy Lankford and Roger Tiddle had begun to deflate his confidence in getting Rusty out on bond, his first glimpse of Judge Anson Griggs finished the job. To begin with, Griggs was a sawed-off little toad. Bino's own perspective, he thought, was likely distorted by gazing down at the world from his own six-six, but his experience with short guys hadn't been pleasant. The short men in his life seemed hell-bent-for-leather to make up for their lack of size by snarling and snorting at everyone within earshot, and the taller the person under the short guy's control, the more the short guy was likely to buck and rear.

The same deputy who'd taken Bino to the holding cell escorted Griggs into the courtroom, and the top of Griggs's head was on a level with the deputy's shoulder, the short-legged judge having to hustle to keep pace. Griggs's robe looked to be about three sizes too big for him, and the stack of files he carried in his left hand seemed bunched up in his sleeve. The jurist ascended to his throne and sat down, and since Griggs's chest and shoulders remained visible Bino assumed there were several cushions piled up on the judge's chair. Griggs swept the courtroom with a withering glare, then bellowed, "Beee seated," every bit as loudly as the bailiff had said, "Awwwl rise." As Bino sank into his own seat in the front row of the spectators' section, he decided that the hearing wasn't going to be much fun.

Roger Tiddle was doing a lot of prancing around on the prosecution side. Which wasn't all that unusual; a prosecutor arriving early in court was a dead giveaway that the case he was handling was high profile. In a situation which had received the TV and newspaper coverage that Rusty's had, the state's lawyer generally liked to see how much of the limelight he could hog. Bino turned around. The media section was jam-packed. As he started to face the front once more, the rear courtroom door opened with a swish of air. Marvin Goldman came in.

Jesus Christ, Bino thought.

Goldman wore a light tan summer-weight suit, and his goatee was disheveled as if he hadn't had time for his morning primping. A second man followed Goldman in—an FBI agent, of course, Bino thought, with sandy hair cut in a burr—and the two took seats in the very last row alongside a black teenager who was wearing a Simpsons T-shirt. Just as Goldman prepared to sit, he spotted Bino.

For just an instant, Goldman froze. He glanced at the exit as if considering making a run for it, then relaxed. Bino practically heard the wheels turning inside Goldman's head. He hadn't expected to run into his nemesis—in fact, Bino Phillips was probably the last person Goldman would expect to be representing Rusty Benson in a Houston courtroom—but now that Bino had spotted Goldman, the federal prosecutor was likely thinking, So what? As he sat, Goldman favored Bino with a shit-eating grin, lifted a hand to ear level, and waggled his fingers. He said something to the FBI agent, who looked at Bino and smirked. Warmth creeping up the side of his neck, Bino faced the front.

Judge Anson Griggs cleared his throat and said in a high pennywhistle voice, "The court calls Case No. 1190876, the State of Texas versus Russell Norman Benson." He peered around expectantly. Griggs had a thin face and sharp features, and Bino placed the jurist at forty-five, give or take a couple of years. Griggs displayed a thick shock of wavy red hair. "Are the parties present?" Griggs said.

Roger Tiddle shot to his feet like a jack-in-the-box and said loudly, "State's here and ready, Your Honor."

Bino climbed slowly up and folded his hands at the hem of his coat. "I'm Bino Phillips, Your Honor, down here from Dallas." He offered what he hoped was his most disarming grin.

Griggs favored Bino with a stoic blink. "So?"

Bino swallowed hard. "So . . . so, I'm here, Your Honor."

"I can see that," Griggs said. "Are you a lawyer? Or possibly a boxer?"

Tiny pimples of embarrassment stood out on Bino's neck as he touched his swollen lip. There was a muffled giggle behind him which Bino was certain came from either Goldman or the FBI agent. One of the bastards. "Sure, Your Honor, yessir," Bino said. "I'm a lawyer. Representing the defendant, Russell Benson." Bino wondered fleetingly whether Rusty could hear what was going on from his place back in the holding cell. If he could, Rusty was probably deciding about now that his attorney was a blithering moron.

"Well, I'm glad to get that much out of you," Griggs said. "Bailiff, bring the defendant in." Then, as the deputy exited out the door behind the bench, Griggs said, "Mr. . . . Phillips, you say?"

"Yessir, that's me," Bino said.

"Well, I don't know how they do it up in Dallas, Mr. Phillips," Griggs said with a glance at the prosecutor that was practically a broad wink, "but down here in the bayou, counsel generally sits with his client at the defense table. That okay with you?"

"Well, sure, Judge, that's . . . the way it's done where I come from." Bino went through the gate and stood behind the defense table. Boy, was this sawed-off pipsqueak of a judge having himself a good time. Bino poured himself a glass of water from a carafe which sat on the table, and gulped down the liquid in two big swallows. "I'll sure do my best to comply, Your Honor," Bino said. At that moment the deputy brought Rusty Benson in.

Bino just couldn't shake the feeling that Rusty was playing a role, that Rusty was in fact the star while the rest of those assembled—the deputy escorting Rusty in, the judge, the prosecutor, and, yes, Bino himself—were nothing but bit players. Even in his jail garb, Rusty seemed at ease. He strolled into the courtroom, hands swinging at his sides, and moved around behind the defense table while the deputy stood guard near the rail. Rusty whispered to Bino, "How's it looking?" His calm brown-eyed gaze rested on Tiddle, and then shifted from the prosecutor to the judge.

Bino hadn't forgotten the holding cell incident, and couldn't resist a little dig. He whispered to Rusty, "Marvin Goldman's sitting at the back. You got any idea why?"

Rusty's brow furrowed as he looked to the rear. His look was one of—anger? concern? Bino wasn't sure. Whatever emotion was flowing in Rusty at the moment, he sure as hell didn't seem *surprised* to see Goldman. Rusty said softly, "The sons of bitches." Bino didn't answer.

Papers rattled at the bench as Judge Griggs looked through his file. Griggs cleared his throat before saying, "The matter at hand, for the record"—the court reporter, a young black woman wearing a mini and displaying the loveliest pair of legs Bino had seen in a courtroom in a long, long time, rattled the keys on her shorthand machine—"is a probable cause hearing to determine whether the defendant is entitled to release on bail. Just a minute. Lucy, shut that thing off and come up here."

The court reporter walked primly around her table and approached the bench. Griggs leaned over and said something to her. She laughed prettily. The judge said something else and she nodded. Then she returned to her place, picked up a small stack of papers, and exited at the rear of the courtroom.

After she'd gone, Griggs folded his hands. "As I was saying, this hearing's to determine whether the defendant's entitled to bond. The state ready?"

Tiddle's heels clicked like a Nazi corporal's. "We've already announced ready, Your Honor."

"Yeah," Griggs said. "Yeah, you have. What about the defense?"

Bino thought he'd seen everything, but the exchange which had just gone on between the judge and the court reporter was a new one on him. He cleared his throat. "We are, Your Honor, but . . . Well, what about the court reporter? Aren't we making a record of this?" Jesus Christ, how was anybody going to appeal anything if there wasn't any record to send to the higher court? Come to think about it, an appeal without a record would be damn near impossible.

Griggs laughed and exchanged yet another knowing glance with Tiddle. Bino had been exposed to a lot of hometown referees in his time, both on the basketball court and in the courtroom, but the buddy-buddy looks between Tiddle and Griggs bordered on the ridiculous. Griggs said, "Oh,

Lucy? She's been needing some time off, and for a little hearing like this I thought I'd give it to her. We may not be as formal down here as you folks up in Dallas, but we get things done."

Yeah, thought Bino, I'll just bet you do. "If the court please," he said, "we'd just as soon have a record of these proceedings."

Grigg's eyes narrowed and his face reddened. "I'll tell you, Mr. Phillips. The court *doesn't* please, how about that? There are a lot of people waiting on us, so let's get this show on the road."

Bino straightened his posture. "Very well, Your Honor. Let the record reflect defense's objection, please."

Griggs smirked in the direction of the vacant court reporter's chair. "Uh? What record is that?"

Bino glanced at his client. Rusty looked detached, and even a little bit amused. What the hell could Rusty think was so funny about all this? "Just call it a slip of the tongue, Judge," Bino said.

"I'll tell you something else, Mr. Phillips," Griggs said. "Too many slips of the tongue in this court can buy you a contempt citation, and I wouldn't be forgetting that. Now let's quit fooling around. Mr. Tiddle, present your case."

As the prosecutor goose-stepped around his table and headed center stage, Bino mentally kicked himself. He'd been so caught up in the rigamarole with the court reporter that he hadn't even considered what evidence the state might present. Now he did. Probably there'd be testimony from Fuller, the Harris County cop, and maybe Jimmy Lankford's client, the diver who'd found Rhonda's body. Those witnesses' testimony wouldn't matter, Bino thought, because nothing they said could possibly place Rusty in Houston in the past week or so. So what could the state put on as evidence that Rusty should be denied bail? Goldman, maybe? Jesus, what could Goldman possibly have to say?

Tiddle stood in front of the bench and showed the judge a small stack of legal-size paper. "Our evidence is quite brief, Your Honor." He turned to the clerk, a mousy-looking woman

in a dark brown dress, and handed her one sheet from the top
of the stack. "Please mark this as Prosecution's Exhibit One,"
Tiddle said. While the clerk wrote something down in her log,
then affixed an evidence sticker to the paper, Tiddle walked
over and handed another sheet to Bino. "I didn't forget you,"
Tiddle said. "Copy for the defense." Then he went back and
stood with folded hands, waiting for the clerk to finish.

Bino looked the paper over. What the hell was this? He
was holding a copy of the indictment. The indictment was on
a printed form, showing the date of the grand jury return
along with some legal mumbo jumbo having to do with the
crime being "against the Peace and Dignity of the State of
Texas," whatever that peace and dignity happened to be. Inserted in the body of the form were two typed-in lines stating
that the grand jury charged that Rusty had intentionally
caused Rhonda's death, and that he'd done it during the commission of still another felony. Bino was dead certain that the
indictment wouldn't hold up because it failed to identify the
other felony, and that the capital murder charge against Rusty
was a lot of whistling in the wind. He showed Rusty the copy.
Rusty frowned.

Tiddle took the marked copy from the clerk and handed
it to the judge. "The state offers Exhibit One, Your Honor," he
said. Then he stepped back and waited expectantly.

Bino came around the defense table in a hurry. "Hold on.
Excuse me, I mean, objection. Your Honor, that's nothing but
a copy of the indictment. It's already a part of the written
record in this case, and it's only the state's allegation. By legal
definition, the indictment isn't evidence."

Griggs held the paper off to one side and squinted.
"Thanks for the lecture, Dallas counsel. We-all down here in
the bayou did go to law school, thanks. And you're out of order. The defense is going to get a chance to object. You mind
if I look this over first?"

Bino resisted the impulse to say, Well, fuck you, then, and
said instead, "Certainly, Your Honor."

Griggs made a big show of reading the indictment while
Bino nervously scratched the back of his hand. Griggs had al-

ready seen the frigging indictment, Bino knew, a copy of the
thing was right there in the judge's file. Finally Griggs looked
up and said, "Okay, I've read this. Does the defense have any
objection to the admission of this piece of paper into evidence?"

"As we stated, Your Honor, we do," Bino said. "That's a
copy of the indictment, and by legal definition it isn't evidence."

"Legal definitions from defense counsel aside," Griggs
said in a bored tone of voice, "objection overruled. I'm admit-
ting this."

"Jesus . . ." Bino said, then caught himself and said, "Your
Honor . . ."

"*Overruled,* counsel." Griggs pointed a finger. "And I'm
warning you for the last time."

Bino expelled air from his lungs and studied the carpet.
Seen from the corner of his eye, Roger Tiddle had the look of
a man about to ejaculate. Jesus, Bino thought, no wonder.
With judges like this one, prosecutors in Harris County didn't
have anything to do but jerk off, anyway.

To Tiddle, the judge said, "Anything else?"

Tiddle stood at attention. "The state rests, Your Honor."

Bino couldn't hold back any longer. "The state *rests?* Your
Honor, all this guy is going to do is put a copy of the indictment into evidence and then sit down?"

"That's what he said, Mr. Phillips," Griggs said. "Now since
you think so little of the state's evidence, let's see yours. What's
the defense got to say before I rule on the state's motion to
deny bond?"

Bino glanced at Rusty. The burden in a probable cause
hearing was on the state, and if the state couldn't put on any
evidence to show that Rusty was likely guilty, the court was required to grant bond. Any second-year law student knew that
much. Rusty quickly shook his head. Bino nodded and turned
back to the judge. "In view of the state's *evidence,*" he said,
"then I don't suppose we do have anything. The defense rests,
Your Honor."

Griggs smiled. "Hey, short and sweet, just the way I like

these hearings. Okay." He raised his gavel and brought it down with a pop. "The state's motion for denial of bond is granted. Bailiff, take this guy out of here and let's get on with the next matter."

The deputy left the rail, took Rusty by the arm and started to lead him back to the holding cell. All of the confidence Rusty had shown disappeared; his face had a disbelieving look and his complexion was ashen through his tan. His broad shoulders slumped.

Bino took a step toward the bench. "Wait a minute. Did I understand you to say you're holding this defendant without bail?"

Griggs shrugged, obviously enjoying himself. "Well, I said the motion was granted, didn't I? Or isn't that the way they do things up in Big D?"

Bino had had all he could take. "Well, then," he said, "I've got something to say. Yes, sir, that's the way they do it up in Big D, and that's the way they do it everyplace else, too. Only in Big D and everywhere else I ever heard of, the judge knows something about what's going on. This is the damnedest . . ."

Roger Tiddle showed a broad grin. Judge Griggs had an amused look as well, and his head was tilted slightly to one side. He raised his gavel once more.

"You may as well finish, Mr. Phillips," Griggs said. "Go on, buddy. You've already said a mouthful."

13

THE BARREL-CHESTED BLACK GUY, WHO CLAIMED TO HAVE THE best pussy for sale in Fifth Ward, and who insisted that he'd be back on the streets as soon as his girls could get together the money to pay the bondsman, offered his biscuit in exchange for a scoop of powdered scrambled eggs. "That biscuit *good*," he said, grinning.

The tall, skinny black guy put in his two cents worth, claiming, "Man, that ain't shit, one biscuit. Tell you what, you take my biscuit plus I gonna give you a pack of Nestlé's hot chocklit a kitchen dude gimme. That chocklit hard to come by." He claimed that he didn't know from nothing about the twenty-five-dollar paper of toot which had been in his pocket when the Houston PD had hassled him out on Montrose Boulevard. He looked satisfied, as if he thought he was offering a pretty good deal.

"Don't listen to this mothafuckah," the Fifth Ward pimp

said. "He get that chocklit from one of them homosectual dudes up in Tank 5C3 he's lettin' polish his knob. Man, that chocklit liable to have AIDS all over it."

Bino eyed the runny scoop of egg in his tray as he considered his options. "Fellas, I'm not that crazy about chocolate to begin with," he finally said. "But one of you guys got a cigarette?" It had been a month since he'd sworn off the three or four filtered Camels a day he'd smoked for years. A night in the county had weakened his resolve.

The Fifth Ward pimp grinned ear to ear, got up, and headed for his bunk. "Sho, man, I got some Bugler rollin' tobacco a dude left when he went to the streets. Don't have no gummed papers, though. Toilet paper work pretty good, you don't let it burn too fast." He lifted his mattress, dug underneath, and came up with a pouch of Bugler and a roll of toilet paper which had been mashed into the shape of a parabola.

The thin guy stroked his mustache as he sat across the table from Bino and continued to watch the powdered eggs. "Don't listen to that dude knockin' my chocklit, man. That Bugler? He got it from a crazy dude, dude used to stand over in the corner and piss on that tobacco so's nobody'd be hittin' on him for no cigarettes." He licked his lips. "Man, them eggs sho looks good."

Bino lifted his rump from the metal stool and adjusted his jumpsuit. The suit was a couple of sizes too small, and Bino's shoulders and arms felt as if they were bound by cable. "Hey, guys," he said, "I been trying to quit smoking anyhow. How 'bout if you two split the eggs?" He used a plastic spoon to divide the runny mess in half, shoveled one portion onto the pimp's tray, and gave the rest to the skinny guy. The pimp came over and polished his egg off in one swallow while the skinny guy picked up his portion with his hands and took small bites. Bino's stomach churned.

A uniformed deputy came down the corridor to stand outside the cell and peer in between the bars. He carried a clipboard. "Phillips," he yelled, and the sound echoed from bare concrete floors, ceilings, and walls. "Hey, Wendell A. Phillips. A.T.W."

"Hey, that's me," Bino said. He leaned over and said quietly, "What's this A.T.W.? What am I, in trouble?"

The two black guys exchanged astonished glances. Then the pimp said, "Man, you got to be kidding. A.T.W. stand for 'all the way.' You getting out, man, to the streets. Yo gulls must have come wid the bond money, huh?"

Bino showed a relieved grin as he climbed to his feet. "Yeah, they must have. You need to work the airport hotels more, pal. The pickings are better out there."

The pimp thoughtfully scratched his nose. "Ain't no bad idea," he said.

Carla wore baggy khaki shorts with suspender straps, along with a brown Esprit T-shirt and snow-white canvas Keds sneakers. The men who passed by on the sidewalk in front of the Harris County Jail did double takes as they glanced down at her legs. She said, "Dondi says you haven't really been in jail. He thinks you've been down here conferring with your contact man, giving him all these tapes where you've been recording everybody."

"Bully for Dondi," Bino said gruffly. He had the pants to his suit on, along with his white dress shirt minus the tie. His coat and tie were folded over his arm, and his other hand was shoved into his pocket. His clothes were rumpled and soiled from being stuffed into a bag in the jail basement. Bino now said to Jimmy Lankford, "Am I going to have to go to some kind of hearing, or what?"

Lankford was dressed in a robin's egg blue summer-weight suit and carried a thin brown attaché case. The sun had just risen above the skyscraper roofs, and the pavement and asphalt were quickly heating to egg-frying temperatures. "No, it's over," Lankford said. "We run down the street to the appellate court and they cut you loose. The district judge knows he can't hold you more than overnight, and once the appeal guys free you the lower court forgets the whole thing. It's just to remind the lawyer what can happen if you give the judge any lip. Half the lawyers in Houston have spent a night or two as a guest of the county." Lankford chuckled. "At least you got to confer with your client, close-up."

Bino rubbed his neck where it was stiff and sore from his sleeping on a rag-stuffed mattress without a pillow. "I didn't even get to do that," Bino said. "I didn't get to see anybody but Marv Goldman. He was standing by the door when that deputy took me off in handcuffs, and he said, 'Rough going, buddy.' Wait till I run into *that* son of a bitch again."

"Are you going back inside the jail to visit your client?" Lankford said. "Or have you had enough of Harris County for one day?"

"I've had enough of this place to last me a lifetime," Bino said. He flicked a mote of dust from one of Carla's suspender straps. "I'm not sure what I'm going to do. I've already told Rusty that I'm not his lawyer any more after the bail hearing. That was before that phony judge denied us, though, so now I guess the fee I collected has to cover appealing the no-bond order to the Texas Court of Criminal Appeals. That's going to take a couple of weeks, which means that Rusty's stuck until we can be heard. Jesus, I'm not even sure if I *can* appeal. They ran the court reporter out of the room before they pulled all that crap."

"I saw," Lankford said. "That happens so often in Harris County that I can answer your question. You appeal on the fact that there wasn't any record. The high court will remand, ordering another hearing with the court reporter present. Then they'll do it on the record, have the same identical evidence, and deny bail a second time. You'll have to appeal again, this time with a transcript, and the high court will reverse and order bail. But since you have to appeal twice, it means they can hold your boy twice as long."

"Sounds like a long road for the good guys," Bino said.

"It is," Lankford said.

Bino dug out his wallet, extracted a business card, and handed the card over to Lankford. "Send a bill to my office, Jimmy. Oh, and hang loose for me, huh? Before this is over I'm going to need a lawyer with some local knowledge. Right now I think I'll go over to the Houston Police Department and snoop around their evidence room. I want to look over the car they fished out of that canal and whatever stuff was with the body." There was a tiny slip of paper in his wallet along with the business cards. It was the receipt the jail people had given him last night when they'd taken his valuables. "I don't want any receipts from the Harris County Jail," Bino said. "They'll bring back crappy memories." He rolled the paper into a ball to throw it away.

Carla stepped quickly forward. "Give me that," she said. "I want Dondi to see it. You may not care what he thinks, but I have to perform with the guy."

Buck Fuller had done a lot of thinking about the promotion he'd taken, leaving his job as a detective to be an investigator for the Harris County D.A.'s office, and had come up with one plus: the pay. If it wasn't for the extra hundred bucks a month, he'd have gone to the sheriff and requested a demotion long ago.

Sitting in this fifteen-by-twenty office with a lovely view of the jail, and listening to two lawyers play one-up on each other, was a perfect example of what Fuller meant. As far as Detective Fuller was concerned, neither one of the lawyers was very smart. Not Assistant Harris County D.A. (for Dumbass) Roger Tiddle and not Assistant U.S.D.A. (for United States Dumbass) Marvin Goldman. The fact that Goldman was federal, though, made all the difference in the world. Federal guys, Fuller thought, had *everybody* by the balls.

Roger Tiddle was saying, "By the time Fuller here gets through with his investigation, we should have something solid to go on." Which about made Fuller swallow his bubblegum.

"Getting something solid isn't really that important. Not yet," Goldman said, which made Fuller think better of the situation.

"We can't just keep holding the guy," Tiddle said. "Eventually push is going to come to shove."

"You let us worry about that," Goldman said. "Sure, the appellate court will make you grant bond. Eventually. But I

figure we can delay that as much as a year. In the meantime
Mr. Benson's ass belongs to us." The A.U.S.D.A. sat across
from Tiddle. Tiddle tilted back with his feet up on the corner
of his desk. Goldman's legs were crossed. Detective Fuller was
on the small two-seater couch near the door.

"A year or whatever," Tiddle said. "Eventually it's going to
come down to it." He looked to Fuller. "Detective, exactly
what do we have on this guy?"

"In a word," Fuller said, "not shit. What we've got is a dead
lady submerged in an auto, and not a clue as to who put her
there. Our federal friends told us where to find the body, but
they won't tell us how they happened to direct us to one particular canal when nobody'd even reported the broad missing.
Good question, but I guess I'm out of line in bringing it up."
He lifted one thick leg and folded his hands over his knee.

"Well, you are out of line," Goldman said. "All I can tell
you is, national security."

"Or national bullshit," Fuller said, then wished he hadn't.

Tiddle pointed a finger. "Listen, Buck."

"I can let you in," Goldman said, "that what we're working
on . . . you remember Graylord?"

"The Chicago deal," Tiddle said, "where all the cops and
judges went to jail."

"That's all I can say," Goldman said. "If it's determined I
can give you more, that's a bridge we'll cross."

"We're sure busting our ass to help out the Dallas people,"
Fuller said. "How's that helping us in Harris County?"

Goldman yanked on his goatee. "Well, it would be nice
for you if the FBI doesn't start the same kind of investigation
down here. You get my drift?"

Tiddle folded his arms. Fuller stared at the floor.

"Look," Goldman said, "the guy popped his old lady. I
know it, you know it, he knows it. For now it's not necessary
for anybody to *prove* it. We're working on that, we got this cop
up in Dallas I think is about to tell us something.

"I don't want you to get the idea anybody's strong-arming
you into anything," Goldman said. "But you got to appreciate
the importance. Here we got a guy we know damn well has

been spreading money around to cops, judges, and whoever else will take it, for a year and a half we know about, but we got zero evidence. Then, boom, one day his old lady finds out she's had no exclusive license on the guy's dick, and what do you know? She's ready to talk to us, and man, does she have something to say. The guy had her popped, and there's no higher priority for us than getting this guy."

Roger Tiddle produced a handkerchief, blew his nose. "And your case up there against all those city cops . . ."

"For now that's on hold. Look, you guys work out?" Goldman sat up straighter, and Fuller's jaw dropped in astonishment as the federal prosecutor actually flexed his back muscles under his tailored black suit. "It's during the bench presses a lot of times that these things occur to me. One thing leads to another, you know? So we jumped the gun a bit on that cop indictment, but that's . . . okay. One of those cops is talking to us, and now we can work on Mr. Benson. We're moving along.

"And Bino Phillips," Goldman said, "Benson's lawyer? He's defending one cop, and now he's got Rusty Benson to worry about. If nothing else, we got the other side disorganized. Bino Phillips has now got problems."

"How did you like the problem the judge gave him?" Tiddle said.

"Hey, not bad," Goldman said.

Fuller leaned back and rubbed his eyes. The guys were boring the shit out of him. "You federal folks want to talk to Rusty Benson?" Fuller said.

Goldman seemed deep in thought for a moment, then nodded his head. "Yeah, we do. We're finding out things about him. Now it's time to see what he has to tell us, as long as we've got an incentive to give him."

"I got to tell you, Mr. Goldman," Fuller said. "I get the impression that Mr. Benson's a pretty tough cookie."

Goldman yanked on his goatee. "They all are at first. Where you warehousing the guy?"

"He's in lockdown on the eighth floor of the jail," Tiddle said. "That's where they keep all the capital murder guys."

"They've got an arrangement like that in Dallas County," Goldman said, "to separate what they call serious offenders. Private toilet, shower, all that shit?"

"Sure, yeah," Tiddle said. "We've got to let the guy take a shower every day. The Constitution . . ." He spread his hands, palms up.

"Fuck the Constitution," Goldman said. "We're trying to find out something from the guy. No, cancel that, I didn't say anything about anybody's constitutional rights. Everybody's got 'em. But you've got to improvise. You got a guy handing out disposable razors, right?"

"Right. Guy with a cart, once a day."

"Yeah, okay," Goldman said. "When he gets to Mr. Benson's cell he's fresh out, beginning today. Then the water, there'll be an individual cutoff for each cell if you're built to national standards."

"I suppose we are," Tiddle said. "They have inspections every so often."

"Sure," Goldman said. "So you just cut Mr. Benson's water off, and if he bitches about it, you know how tough it is to get a plumber. Let him go scraggly-faced and stinking, and late tonight we have a talk. And if that doesn't work . . ."

"I don't know how much we've got to deal," Fuller said. "I don't think we can do a thing with him on the murder, unless he decides to confess."

"He doesn't know that for sure," Goldman said. "If he doesn't say anything the first night, you just get the sheriff to decide he needs Mr. Benson's private cell for some really dangerous guys, and that Rusty Benson's such a lamb he needs to be in general population. Put him in one of the open tanks with the run-of-the-mill prisoners. He's a pretty guy, so maybe somebody cornholes him, right? And even if they don't, just let him live with those filthy motherfuckers awhile. You'll be amazed at what smelling a few assholes will do for a guy's attitude about whether he wants to talk to somebody. You telling me that down here in Harris County you don't know how to fuck with people?"

14

THE SUN-HEATED ASPHALT SURFACE COOKED BINO'S FEET through the soles of his shoes. The Houston PD Auto Pound was underneath the elevated inner-loop freeway. As Bino stood, hands in pockets, and looked Rhonda Benson's white Eldorado over stem to stern, a forty-foot trailer rig rumbled past overhead, vibrating the pavement. There were gray streaks on the Eldo's trunk and bumper where filthy water had dried. Rivulets of sweat ran down from Bino's hairline and dripped from the end of his nose.

"Looks pretty clean, considering where it's been," Bino said. "Must not have been under too long."

The uniformed policeman who stood nearby was around thirty, with blond hair already thinning and fat pouches sticking out over the back of his belt. "I've been told," he said, "to show you whatever you want to see. I don't have any instructions to make comments." He was sweating as well. As Bino watched, a trickle ran down the cop's forehead and soaked into his eyebrow.

The cooperation from the Houston PD was just what Bino expected. Exactly none. He looked for a moment at Rhonda's personalized license plate, and remembered the time at Crooked River CC when he'd seen her leaving the golf course in the white Caddy. RUSTY'S R. Rusty's redhead, tall, charming, just the thing for a guy to have around if he was moving up in certain circles. Which Rusty definitely had been. Bino was glad he didn't have to see what was left of her. The description on the medical examiner's report was enough to last for a lifetime.

"Well, do your instructions include," Bino said to the cop, "showing me what they found inside the car?"

The cop threw Bino a sidelong glance. "Mr. Phillips, you can look at whatever. I know what you're entitled to see, but I got no personal effects. Anything that was inside that car and wasn't fastened down, the property room's got." Visible beyond him through the glass door into the waiting room, Carla sat primly on a bench reading a paperback. Two cops hovered near the bench, scratching their rumps, chewing the fat, glancing at Carla and likely wondering the best approach to strike up a conversation. Bino hoped they didn't try the "What would you say to a little fuck?" routine. Carla flipped over a page and pointedly ignored the guys.

Bino returned his attention to the cop. "Funny, but I don't see any dents in this car. Couple of whiskey-bumps, maybe, but nothing major. Almost like somebody lowered it into that canal on a winch instead of driving it over the edge."

The cop shrugged. "I just work here."

Bino expelled air in a sigh of exasperation. "Can you tell me how to get to the lab?" he said. "Or am I supposed to look it up in the phone book?"

The cop showed a deadpan blink. "That's easy enough. Over in the main city building, fourth floor."

Bino squatted down on his haunches and peered at the Eldo's underbody. "Anybody over there in particular I should ask for?"

"Miss Sims. She's the most helpful on things like what you're after."

Bino nearly lost his balance and steadied himself with a hand on the Eldo's bumper. "Yeah," he said. "I'll just bet she is."

Miss Sims walked as if she could have carried a razor blade sideways between the cheeks of her ass without cutting herself. Her HPD uniform was tailored like a man's and there didn't seem to be any curves in her body. She compared the three-by-five card in her hand with the metal tag on the evidence drawer, then unlocked the drawer and slid it weightily open. She stood stiffly aside. "Everything's in storage bags. You can't be here alone, and you're not to open the bags and touch what's inside."

"They told me you'd be helpful," Bino said.

Eyes with short brown lashes widened beneath unplucked brows. "I beg your pardon?"

Bino was glad he didn't have to do a stand-up comedy routine with the HPD as an audience. "How much time have I got?" he said.

Miss Sims checked her watch—plain digital face, black acrylic band—and showed an irritated frown. "It's not how much time *you've* got. It's how much time I've got to stand here. Ten minutes." Bino halfway expected her to unholster and raise her service revolver like a starter's gun.

"Okay," Bino said. "Thanks." He picked up the first clear plastic Ziploc bag and held it at eye level. Inside were a round compact with a flower design, a shiny gold tube of lip gloss, and a couple of mascara brushes. He tossed the bag back into the drawer and went on to the next one. This bag contained matchbook covers from Vincent's Seafood Restaurant and Casa Rosa Mexican Cuisine, both located in Dallas. Ordinarily the Houston PD would have zeroed in on these, and by now should have had investigators in both eating places asking if anyone had seen Rhonda there in the past few days, and who had been with her. Since the Mounties thought they already had their man—Rusty—Bino doubted that the cops had followed up on the matchbook covers. Okay, Bino thought, we can get a leg up on the prosecution just by having Half-a-Point Harrison collect his bets the following week at Vincent's, then pay off the next day over at Casa Rosa, asking a few questions in the process. He dropped the bag containing the matchbooks back inside the drawer.

The next Ziploc held two box seat tickets for the game at Arlington Stadium between the Rangers and White Sox on April 26. The date was nearly three months ago, just a few games into the season. The tickets were torn in half and had been used. Bino tossed the bag and picked up the next. This time Bino squinted at a quarter-size two-pronged digging tool of dull gray metal, a gadget used by golfers for repairing ball marks on greens. DIG 'EM UP FOR THE SHOOT 'EM UP was printed on the tool in tiny black letters, Bino chuckled under his breath. Barney Dalton was one helluva poet. He tossed the digging tool. The next bag contained a pair of big, round, I'm-a-starlet sunglasses. Toss the . . .

Wait a minute.

DIG 'EM UP FOR THE SHOOT 'EM UP.

Conscious of Miss Sims watching from a hip-cocked stance with folded arms, Bino softly dropped the bag containing the sunglasses and reached out for the Ziploc holding the digging tool. He held one corner of the bag between a thumb and forefinger.

Well, whaddya know.

"Find something?" Miss Sims said.

Bino tossed the Ziploc into the drawer and stood back. "Nope, nothing. Just reminded me that I ought to take up golf, get my mind off of some things. I'll be going now, ma'am. Thanks for your time."

Bino watched Carla's thigh muscle flex and then elongate as she crossed one leg over the other, her feet propped up on the edge of the sitting area table, adjusting her position so that the light from the hotel window fell across the book in her lap. Her mouth was drawn in concentration. Bino leaned back against the king-size headboard, picked up the bedside receiver, and punched the long-distance 8 on the Hyatt Regency phone. He waited for the dial tone, then entered the area code and direct line number for the pro shop at Crooked River Country Club, up in Dallas. He wore boxer shorts and was freshly showered and shaved.

After three rings there was a click over the line, after which a youthful male voice said, "Golf course, Danny."

Bino folded his arms and braced the receiver between his neck and shoulder. "Yeah, this is Bino Phillips. Barney around?"

"Hold on." There was another click, followed by an easy-listening orchestral version of "New York, New York," an arrangement which a couple of Bino's clients would call "shoplifting music." In about fifteen seconds a third click sounded, followed by Barney Dalton's Texas-twang tenor saying, "Bino. We're full up on tee times, if that's what you're—"

"That's good," Bino said. "I won't be having the time to play. Listen, Barn, when's the club tournament? You know, the Shoot 'Em Up."

"That's a partnership tournament," Barney said. "I don't know anybody hard up enough to play with you." There was a raspy metallic sound in the background. Bino pictured Barney standing beside the workbench at the rear of the pro shop, talking on his speakerphone while using the vise to change the loft on his four wood or pitching wedge. Barney adjusted his clubs around like a maniac. Bino wondered briefly if more loft on his own driver would lower his handicap.

"I wouldn't have time to practice anyhow," Bino said.

"I don't think practice would save you," Barney said.

"Ha, ha. When's the tournament, Barn?"

"August 6. You know, there is one guy in the Eighth Flight—"

"I don't want to *play* in the damn thing, Barney."

"That's a relief," Barney said.

"And I really don't want to know when the tournament starts."

"Well, what'd you ask me for?"

"You remember when we played with Rusty Benson?" Bino said.

"I'll never forget it. Look, if you're calling to borrow poker money . . ."

"Just before we teed off, you gave us all one of those little two-pronged gadgets for fixing ball marks, said DIG 'EM UP FOR THE SHOOT 'EM UP."

"Sure, poyanna," Barney said. "Fucking weed grows flat to the ground like a spiderweb, a month ago our greens were ate up with the stuff. The digging tools were the greenskeeper's idea. Way we figured, if every member pulled up one clump of poyanna on every green while they were playing their round, by the time we had the tournament the greens ought to be in pretty good shape."

"I remember that," Bino said. Carla flipped over a page, raised her head to smile fleetingly at him, then returned to her reading. Bino said, "What I need to know, exactly when did those digging tools come in? One week they weren't available, the next week you had a whole basketful sitting up by the register."

"I could look it up," Barney said. "We bought 'em from some outfit out in Arlington."

"It had to be," Bino said, "sometime between the fourth and the tenth. The tenth, Monday, that's the day we played with Rusty. Time I was out there before that, seven a.m. tee time on the Fourth of July, so early I couldn't hit myself in the ass with a paddle."

"What's unusual about that?" Barney said.

"The point is," Bino said, "that I'm pretty sure you weren't handing out those things on the fourth. It's important for me to know exactly when you first put those digging tools out by the cash register. I found one of 'em in . . . it was left in a car has to do with this case I'm handling."

"Well, I could look it up, like I said, but I remember. I was unpacking those cartons the afternoon of Wednesday the fifth."

"I need to be sure, Barn. Jesus, that's—"

"I know it was Wednesday, because there's this lady comes

in for a lesson Wednesday afternoons. She showed up just as I was setting the basket out, interrupted me to go to the tee. She's got this godawful banana-ball slice that—"

"So if one of those digging tools was inside a car in Houston, and that car was found in a bayou canal on Monday the tenth . . ."

"You crazy? What's a car doing sunk in a canal?" Barney said.

"I need to know a couple of things, Barn. One, check your records to make sure you're right on the date you set out the digging tools. Second, and this is going to mean looking at restaurant tickets, swimming pool sign-ins, tennis court reservations—"

"Now hold on," Barney said. "Me and the tennis pro don't get along too good, he wouldn't like me fucking around in his business."

Bino rolled his eyes. "Make peace with the guy, Barn. You never know when you'll need somebody, you know? I got to know the last time Rusty's wife was out at the club."

"That's easy," Barney said.

"What's easy?"

"You're talking about Rhonda Benson, right?"

"Sure, Mrs. Rusty Benson," Bino said.

"She's the broad. That's who I gave the lesson to, on Wednesday afternoon."

Bino's jaw slacked. He couldn't say anything for a couple of seconds, then said, "Your memory's failing you. Rhonda Benson was out of town all that week, Rusty told me—" He closed his mouth with a near-audible snap of his jaws.

"Well, she may have been out of town that week," Barney said. "But on Wednesday the fifth, she was right here on the practice range. And now that you mention it, something funny. She told me not to tell anybody, especially Rusty, that she was here that day. You learn around one of these country clubs, you don't know what's going on between anybody and their old ladies. When somebody tells you to keep your mouth shut, you do it."

Bino sat up straighter on the bed and Carla shot him an

inquisitive glance. He showed her a just-a-second wink, then said into the phone, "Are you sure it was her, Barney?"

"She had on white shorts looked like she painted 'em on," Barney said. "Some of these women I might forget. Rhonda Benson, never. It was her, Bino. Take it from old Barney here."

Running Half-a-Point Harrison down, Bino knew, would take some doing. Half had four or five favorite Vegas hangouts and might be in any one of the places. Lunchtime narrowed the choices a bit—Half was too tight with the dollar to dine on the Strip; he'd likely take in either the $3.49 buffet at the Four Queens, which included a free fifty-cent keno ticket, or the all-you-can-eat deal in the Sombrero Room at Binion's Horse-shoe—but locating Half, Bino knew, was at the very least an hour-long chore.

Carla was getting antsy. Her periods of concentration on her book had shortened as Bino talked to Barney on the phone, her irritated glances more frequent. Bino paused with the phone book open on the bed, his index finger beneath Las Vegas on the area code map. "Listen, this is going to take awhile," Bino said.

Carla stood, raised up on her tiptoes, and stretched. "It's already taken awhile. Police auto pounds and sitting around hotel rooms I can do without. *Laying* around hotel rooms, now, that's a different story." She looked the king-size over foot to head and arched an eyebrow.

"It's business," Bino said.

"Who's that you were calling about Rusty Benson's wife?"

"A golf pro. Friend of mine."

"That's business?"

"It's what I do. Representing the guys I do, I talk to all kinds of places. Bookie joints, whorehouses . . ."

"How enlightening," Carla said, hands on hips. "What does a golf pro have to do with Rusty Benson being in jail?"

"Nothing, personally. He knows some things I need to work on Rusty's next bond hearing, if the appeal works, plus some of this stuff can help another client of mine. Tommy Clinger."

"Who?" Carla said.

"He's a . . . that's not important. The point is, I'm going to be tied up and don't want you to get bored."

Carla looked at the ceiling. "Great fun. I bring this guy to Houston, barely get a good humping from the guy before he's in jail and I get to spend the night keeping my own feet warm."

"How could your feet be cold? It's hot as—"

"It's a figure of speech, sweet thing. In addition to that I've had a tour of the jail and the police auto pound. I was hoping this afternoon we could see something at least a little cheerier. Like skid row or someplace."

"Look, Carla, I didn't plan this. I just wanted you to know this would take awhile, so if you wanted you could do something else."

She pooched out her lower lip and blew upward. Her bangs lifted in the draft, then settled back down on her forehead. "You bet I can find something better to do. You have yourself a good time, sport." She headed for the door, her bottom twitching.

"Carla," he said.

She went out into the hall with a swish and a click.

Bino stood and took two steps in pursuit, then paused, picturing the scene in the hallway that was likely to follow, him charging after Carla, Carla standing in the elevator doing a toetap while the doors slid shut in his face. And the other hotel guests peering out of their rooms to see the cause of all the furor, while Bino stood in the corridor in his underwear. He thought, To hell with it, and retreated to the bed. Carla was cute and fun and all that, but her feistiness could be a massive pain. Bino gingerly touched the swelling above his eye.

Half-a-Point Harrison wasn't at Binion's Horseshoe, nor at the Four Queens, nor inside Lily Langtry's at the Golden Nugget, where Half occasionally liked to chow down on the noon Chinese buffet. Bino then tried the Sports Book at the Fremont Hotel, catty-cornered across the street from the Golden Nugget, only to learn that Half had been there two days previously, had bought three winning tickets on the

Dodgers playing at home against the New York Mets, but hadn't even returned to cash in.

Forty-five minutes later Bino was totally disgusted. After no telling how much in long-distance charges—he'd even systematically called up and down the Strip, from the Stardust all the way to the MGM—he wasn't any closer to locating Half than he'd been when he'd started. He decided to try his own office in Dallas, to see if Half had called and left a message. He should have checked with Dodie to begin with, but after her icy tone during the call the night before last, he cringed at the thought of talking to her. He sucked in his pride, punched in his number in the Davis Building, and listened to the series of rings on the line.

After the third ring Half-a-Point Harrison picked up and said, "Yeah, lawyer's office."

Bino gritted his teeth. "What the hell are you doing there?"

"What you think I'm doing? I'm doing what you ought to be doing, giving this little girl a break so she can use the bathroom. Which I wouldn't have to be doing, except that you're off running around with some broad."

Bino pictured Half, thin with a pencil mustache, wearing a vest and tab collar which made his tie stick out from his chest, sitting on the edge of Dodie's desk with a skeptical tilt to his mouth. The tab collars had been out of style for twenty years, which bothered Half not one iota, and Bino wondered where Half still bought the damned things. Half had never married and had no kids, and hovered over Dodie like a mother hen. Sometimes Dodie spent weekends out at Half's farm in Mesquite, subbing for him on the phone taking baseball and football bets, and Bino had feared for some time that if the law were to bust Half's bookmaking operation on the wrong day Bino's entire office staff would be in jail.

"I don't mean, what are you doing at the office," Bino said. "How come you're in town at all? I've been calling all over Vegas."

"I got tired of it," Half said, "after three days. Always do, Vegas gets old in a hurry. Plus, when I called last night the little girl said you were out screwing around as usual. So I thought I'd better—"

"Screwing around?" Bino said. "Dodie told you I was screwing around?"

"She's too sweet to say that," Half said. "What she said was, you went to Houston. I had to dig the part about the broad out of her."

"Well, I'm down here, mainly, representing a guy. Rusty Benson."

"They got newspapers up here, Bino. There was a nice photo of you on your way to jail. Nice going."

"The courts down here are crazy as hell," Bino said.

"Sounds to me like *you're* crazy as hell," Half said.

"Look, I need you to get on something. And I need a copy of your notes on this to go in Tommy Clinger's file."

"I thought you were down there representing Rusty Benson."

"It's a long story. As soon as I wrap up a couple of things my deal with Rusty is over. But in trying to get Rusty out of jail I've found some things out that I think we need to know to help Tommy Clinger. That clear?"

"As mud," Half said. "But I don't guess it's any different than any of the other shit you get yourself into."

Bino ignored the remark. "I want court dockets for the last year, countywide. Make a list of every case where Rusty Benson's shown to be the lawyer for the defendant."

"That's one helluva big pain in the ass, Bino."

"It'll take a lot of work," Bino said. "Then you'll have to go do a records search at the county clerk."

"I don't like going to county records," Half said. "Too many guys over there know me."

"So tell Dodie to go," Bino said. "I want the disposition of every one of Rusty's cases, how much time the defendant got, whether charges were dropped . . ."

Half said nothing. Faint static crackled over the line. Bino shifted the phone from one ear to the other.

"Half?" Bino said.

"I'm writing. How much time have we got to do all this?"

"ASAP. I want the same search done on federal criminal cases in Dallas. There's probably fifty state cases on file for every federal, so the fed stuff shouldn't take all that long. And

Half. I want particular attention paid to cases that turned up in Edgar Bryson's court."

"Bryson?" Half said. "Ain't he the religious nut?"

"He professes to be. Right now he's presiding over Big Preacher Daniel's trial."

"I know a couple of guys," Half said, "that he made believers of. You ever checked the sentences Bryson hands out?"

"I only tried a couple in front of him," Bino said, "and had to appeal both. He won't stay inside the federal sentencing guidelines if he decides he personally doesn't like the guy."

"So how come Bryson?"

"Just a hunch. Look, the feds are behind what's happening to Rusty down here in Houston. Goldman was in court yesterday. They can only have one motive, wanting Rusty to inform on somebody. I'm hoping the somebody's not Tommy Clinger, but I think it's to Tommy's best interest to check out what old Rusty's been up to. Oh, and Half, one more thing."

"I already got plenty of things," Half said.

"We're probably going to know some of Rusty's clients. Or my clients will know them. If we've got contacts, we want to talk to them."

There was a pause, after which Half said, "It bothers me, and you're the lawyer. But it bothers me that you're supposed to be Rusty Benson's lawyer and you're checking out all this other shit."

"I told Rusty up front," Bino said, "that if I discovered anything representing him that'd help Tommy, I'd use it. I'm not going to screw the guy around, though. Tomorrow morning I'm going to see Rusty at the jail and tell him exactly what I'm up to. He can like it or lump it. And if what I'm doing makes him not want me to appeal his bail denial, then he can hire himself another lawyer."

"The papers up here," Half said, "are full of hints that the feds think Rusty may have offed his old lady because she was about to inform on him and some other people. 'Unnamed sources,' you know how they write it up. They're saying Rhonda was hiding out under federal protection."

"Jesus Christ," Bino said. "That was in the paper?"

"Today's edition. You figure there's anything to it?"

"Until I'm sure," Bino said, "I've got no comment one way or the other. But I'll tell you one thing. People afraid for their lives don't run around taking golf lessons."

"*Golf lessons?*" Half said.

Bino rubbed his eyes and switched the phone from one ear to the other. "Forget I said that, Half. Just thinking out loud, okay?"

As soon as Carla exited the elevator on the ground floor of the Hyatt Regency, her demeanor changed. All of the hip-slinging anger gone from her walk, she crossed the lobby rapidly in an all-business posture, checking her watch three different times on her way to the front exit. A uniformed doorman held the entryway open for her, standing aside and saying briskly, "Have a good day, miss." Carla didn't act as if she noticed the guy.

She made her way down two city blocks, hustling through one intersection as the yellow warning light changed to red, shooting furtive glances over her shoulder every hundred yards or so. When she was out of sight of the Hyatt Regency, her walk slowed and her breathing returned to normal. She dug in her handbag, withdrew a Kleenex, and wiped perspiration from her forehead and upper lip, an attractive young lady in tasteful walking shorts with suspender straps, drawing appreciative glances from men passing by, ignoring the glances without so much as a smile of acknowledgment.

She paused near the center of the block and flagged down a cab, climbing quickly inside and looking both ways before closing the door, giving the driver her destination in precise, measured tones. The driver, a thin black man with a clipped Jamaican accent, said, "Yes'm," moved the arm downward to start the meter running, then wheeled out into thickening midafternoon traffic.

Twenty-five minutes later the cab—a blue and white Plymouth with a Budweiser ad suspended over its trunk—exited Southwest Freeway and pulled underneath the awning at the

Red Carpet Inn, a motel built in two three-story sections. There was a marquee over the entry, ballyhooing Crystal Malone on the cocktail hour piano in the Scarlet Room. Carla handed a twenty up front to the driver, then got out and crossed the drive to enter the cool motel lobby. She passed two rows of couches on which businessmen sat reading newspapers, went by the check-in counter without so much as a glance, and entered the cocktail lounge. She paused, listening to tinkling piano music as her eyes grew accustomed to the dimness. There were only two tables occupied, both near the pianist, and three lone men sat at the bar. Carla approached the bar and slid onto a stool beside a man in a coal black suit. She ordered Cutty neat, water back.

As the bartender freepoured Scotch into a rock glass, Carla turned to the man seated next to her. His head was down, and he was drinking orange juice. He wore a goatee. Carla said, "He knows she was in Dallas last week. He's checking around."

The man yanked on his goatee. "I'd expected you to be in touch long before now," Marvin Goldman said. "Jesus Christ, if we're going to work this out, you need to tell me what the hell's going on. How does he know?"

"It's the first time I've had a chance to get away, without acting gitsy," Carla said. "Without tipping everybody and their dog off." She took a filtered Virginia Slim from her handbag, lit, and blew a plume of smoke across the bar. "He called some golf pro where she took a lesson."

"That club they all hang around. She was supposed to stay home. That should be an example to you, it's what can happen when you—"

"I told you, Mr. Goldman. As soon as I could, here I am."

"Well, we aren't just screwing around here," Goldman said, grimacing. "We've got too much at stake. Look, blow that smoke in some other direction, will you?" He took a clear glass ashtray, extended his arm in front of her, and placed the ashtray on the counter as far on the other side of her as he could reach. "I'm lying to cops, FBI agents, and everybody else to keep you a secret," Goldman said, "and I can't even find out what you're doing. If I didn't know better, I'd say you and Bino Phillips were having too good of a time."

Carla checked her makeup in the back bar mirror. She ran her little finger across her upper lip. "What gave you that idea?" Carla said.

15

"**T**HING THAT GETS ME," MANCIL ADRIANI SAID, "IS HOW THEY put that fucker up without modern equipment. For two centuries you couldn't build anything taller than William Penn's hat in this whole fucking town. There's a story about that." He was seated on a park bench, dressed in perfectly ironed khaki chino pants along with an oversize red knit polo. His thinning hair was washed and fluffed out. He reached into a small paper sack and tossed a couple of peanuts across the sidewalk. Three pigeons bumped over on ungainly feet and pecked around after the peanuts.

The man beside Adriani was in his sixties, wearing bifocals in dark plastic frames. He wore a lightweight cotton Jesse James overcoat and his gray hair was windblown. He reached in his pocket and produced a palm-size clear glass vial, half full of amber liquid. "It's something new I'm recommending," he said in a distinct Northern accent. "Abericinine. Disappears from the system in less than twenty seconds, absorbed right into the bloodstream. It contains some arsenic compounds, laced with—"

"I give a shit what it is?" Adriani grinned and nudged the man with his elbow. "You always treat me right, Charles, I got no problem with you. You say the stuff's okay, I buy that. First time you don't treat me right, then we got something to talk about." He tossed more peanuts, made a clucking sound, looked satisfied as additional pigeons joined in the hunt. He looked up, then up further still, his head reclining on his neck as he gazed at massive stone blocks, at William Penn directly overhead, the brim of the hat shadowing the face and hiding the hat's crown from view. "Story is," Adriani said, "that some contractors up here got in bed with a few politicos, made it worth their while to change the city ordinance so they finally could build a few skyscrapers. I think they fucked up the town. This country needs some historical values, you know? I can't stand crooked political fuckers."

The older man replaced the vial in his pocket and leaned back on the bench. "These additional ingredients are expensive, but worth the difference."

"I met some of those assholes," Adriani said, "doing time. Most guys in the joint I keep my mouth shut, I figure what somebody did to get in there is their own business. But these bastards were fucking up American history, you know? I give 'em all hell. Got other guys to give 'em hell, too, and they deserved every bit of it. I mean, what would Benjamin fucking Franklin say?"

"I've had to double the price," the older man said.

Adriani sat up straighter, swiveled his head to look at the gray-haired man, the eyes distorted by thick bifocals. "Say," Adriani said, "you wouldn't fuck old Mancil around, would you? I think you know better. If you say twice the price, I just make the difference up from my guy. But if I catch you fucking me around . . ."

"My costs are much higher," the man said.

"So I'll buy it." Adriani tossed peanuts. There were now twenty or thirty of the clumsy birds, a couple of the pigeons venturing halfway across the sidewalk in Adriani's direction, then scuttling for safety as two young women in jogging suits went by. "Pisses me off, too," Adriani said, "what they done to the Liberty Bell. When I was a kid they had it real nice out in the open. Now they got it down the street in a building looks like Buck Rogers constructed the fucking thing. People don't know nothing about historical preservation." He dug in his pocket, produced a thick roll of hundred-dollar bills, and counted the money out on the bench. "I don't understand your outfit, Charles. Damn near as hot up here as it is in Texas this time of year, you're wearing a fucking overcoat. Looks like you'd burn up in that thing."

The older man leaned forward, intently watching Adriani stack the money, brought the vial back out, and set it on the bench. "Ozone layer's dissipating," he said. "Protecting my skin."

"I'm damn sure glad," Adriani said, "the women in that *Sports Illustrated* don't think like you. Would really fuck up the swimsuit issue, you know? Two thousand, Charles? I got a plane to catch." He looked up once more at William Penn. "Pisses me off I got no more time. I come in at eleven, got to leave at four. I had time I'd go in that city hall and give some people a piece of my mind, fucking up these historical landmarks around here."

Adriani walked a couple of blocks south from City Hall Square and hailed a cab at the corner of Sansom and Broad. He had two hours before takeoff, so he told the cabbie to take the scenic route, tooling at a leisurely pace east on Chestnut through Independence National Historic Park. They passed Congress Hall. Adriani curled his upper lip at the glass enclosure surrounding the Liberty Bell. He thought they could at least have built the structure with rustic logs, make the fucking thing look historical.

Then they dallied through South Philly, a detour from the direct route to International Airport. Adriani watched remorsefully through the backseat window, looking at unswept

streets the width of bowling lanes, cars parked bumper to
bumper all along the curbs, old brick buildings housing dry
cleaners and small Italian restaurants.

One of the restaurants, Timpanic's, Adriani recalled,
served the best fucking mussels this side of Boston Bay in an
open-air courtyard. Once when he was twenty-three Adriani
and Jimmy Ditulio, Jimmy Dit they called the guy, had entered
Timpanic's around eight in the evening. Shoulder to shoulder
they'd strolled in, smiling hidy-do to the waitress, pretty young
thing in an apron with a faint mustache on her upper lip,
Jimmy Dit and Mancil Adriani saying, One of these days, darlin', one of these days when you're getting off, we'll go have us
some fun, huh? And she'd grinned back at them, liking the attention, smiling at the two young Italian men as they'd saun-
tered into the courtyard where an older man named Angelo
Bedell was eating his dinner. Angelo Bedell, surrounded by
his wife and seven kids, had paused with one mussel half
pried from the shell. He'd dropped shell and all onto his
plate, his eyes knowing, understanding full well what was coming, glancing frantically about for an escape route for a second or two. Then he'd showed a sort of resigned acceptance
as Jimmy Dit and Mancil Adriani had leveled identical WWII
German Lugers and pumped four 9mm slugs apiece into Angelo Bedell. Adriani had gotten satisfaction from seeing the
waitress, smiling moments ago, put both hands over her
mouth and scream at the top of her lungs. He'd paused on the
way out to bend and kiss her on the cheek, that's how much of
a stupid jackoff he'd been in those days, had kissed the broad
with her looking right at him for identification purposes. He
and Jimmy Dit had strolled leisurely down the block, dropping the Lugers and gloves into a garbage can. The kissing incident had worried them enough so that Adriani and Jimmy
Dit had had a talk with the waitress's sister, after which the
waitress had lost her memory.

Adriani ducked back in the cab as he spotted two guys familiar to him, Ralph Demoin and Arthur Caterine, two guys
in jeans and T-shirts ascending to street level from the stand-
up crap game below Arnold's Sandwich Shop. He would have

liked to stop and speak to Ralph Demoin and Arthur Caterine, two all right guys Adriani had never had words with, and
maybe drop in below Arnold's to renew some old acquaintances. But if he were to acknowledge the guys, his life ex-
pectancy would shrink a few years.

Adriani directed the cabbie to halt in front of a clapboard
building with a counter displaying newspapers from around
the globe. Handing a twenty to the driver, he told the man to
fetch him a *Houston Chronicle* and to keep the change. Five
minutes later, the *Chronicle* folded under his arm, Adriani told
the driver he'd seen enough, he was ready for Philly International.

At 3:25, fifteen minutes from boarding his L.A. flight,
Adriani settled down at the gate and looked through the
Chronicle. He tossed aside the front page and sports, and went
straight to the metropolitan section, zeroing in on an article
headlined "JAILED ATTORNEY WELL KNOWN IN DALLAS CRIMINAL
COURTS." He digested the story word for word, learning that
Russell Benson had a strong record of getting guys acquitted
or their sentences reduced. By the time he'd finished the
story, the gate attendant was calling his flight. Adriani folded
the paper tightly and dropped it on a chair as he moved up,
boarding pass ready, to stand in line.

It was a fuckup, Adriani thought. I'm going to regret doing that broad.

16

WHEN CARLA RETURNED AROUND FIVE-THIRTY, CARRYING A shopping bag, Bino was sitting up in a chair watching senior golf on ESPN. She dropped the bag onto the king-size as she said, "I picked up a few things. I see you're through on the phone."

"Watching this Trevino proves to me," Bino said, "that technique has nothing to do with it. Guy swings the club like he's driving nails."

"First the telephone, now the golf. God."

He picked up the remote and clicked off the set. "I thought we'd have a nice dinner. Your show's at eight, right?"

"On the dot," Carla said, shrugging out of her suspenders, undoing and stepping out of her shorts, bending to fold the shorts, wearing tan bikini panties. "And it's going to cost you, buster." Her features relaxed. "What are you finding out?"

Bino stood and walked over to the closet, opened the

door, and withdrew navy Dockers on a hanger. "Finding out about what?"

Carla pulled her cotton sweater up over her head, her breasts compressing with the movement, her hair tousled, slightly messed by the sweater. "Rusty. So, did he kill Rhonda?" She blinked.

Bino buttoned and zipped the trousers, took a tan woven belt from the closet, and threaded the belt through the loops. "I'm not sure," he said, "and I don't want to know. For now I'm only worried about Rusty's bail, and I'm treating him just like any other client. Whether he did it or not isn't my problem. I imagine it's something Goldman would give his eyeteeth to find out."

Carla froze for an instant, her head down, then resumed her rummaging through hangers holding her performing costumes. "*Who'd* give his eyeteeth?"

"Marvin Goldman," Bino said. "He's the U.S. Attorney down here hawking me."

Carla selected snug white pants with Indian princess braid down both legs. "I thought maybe he'd confessed to his lawyer," she said.

Bino reached in past her and grabbed a white Izod knit. "Not me, babe. If I find anything out, though, I'll let you know."

At one o'clock in the morning a guard clanked a private cell open on the eighth floor of the Harris County Jail and shone a flashlight inside. "Get up, Benson," he said.

In a few seconds Rusty Benson stepped into the corridor, blinking. He had a stubble of beard. "Can I get a drink?"

The guard cuffed the prisoner's hands. "Come on."

"I'm dying of thirst."

"I said, come on." The guard led Benson to the elevator, then took him down to the third level and through the cat-walk over Main Street into the District Attorney's offices. The prisoner's feet shuffled in jailhouse slippers. The office was dark, the way lighted by occasional desk lamps illuminating

covered typewriters and computer terminals. Midway through
the open-bay work area was a row of four cubicles enclosed by
six-foot partitions. Inside one of the cubicles a light burned.
The guard led Benson in and sat him down in a chair with a
slatted back. As the deputy cuffed Benson to a chair arm, the
prisoner blinked dully around at Roger Tiddle seated behind
a desk, at Marvin Goldman and Buck Fuller seated in chairs
identical to the one in which Benson sat. All three lawmen
wore slacks and sport shirts. The desk was bare except for a
pocket-size tape recorder. Tiddle said to the guard, "Give us a
half hour." The deputy nodded and left.

"How you holding up, Rusty?" Goldman said.

Benson nodded. "Marv. Things could be better."

"You can make them better."

Benson rubbed his handcuffed wrist, not saying anything.

"You can come on over," Detective Fuller said, "and we'll
help you."

Roger Tiddle watched with his fingers pyramided, touching his lips.

"I could use a drink of water," Benson said.

Goldman massaged his bicep. "I suspect you could."

"We've got your hit man, Rusty," Fuller said. "He's talking
to us."

Benson dropped his wrist. The handcuff clinked. "You
do? What's his name?"

Fuller and Tiddle looked at each other.

Goldman bent his wrist and looked at his flexed forearm
muscle. "Come on, you're not going to bullshit this guy." He
relaxed his arm. "We do have somebody talking to us up in
Dallas, though. Terry Nolby."

Benson scratched his stubbled cheek. "Oh? How's Terry
doing?"

Goldman chuckled and murmured, "Shit." He placed a
lightly clenched fist on the desk. "How long do you think
these guys can hold you, Rusty?"

"I hadn't thought about it."

"Well, you should. Six months without bond, then maybe
with bail you can't post. Three or four million. You can be

here a couple of years while they're fucking with you."

Tiddle remained unmoving, his fingers before his lips as he said, "I think that's conservative."

"You shouldn't be talking to me without my lawyer," Benson said.

Fuller's eyes grew big and round. "Do tell."

Benson sighed and rubbed his forehead. "What do you want? I'm not copping to any kind of murder, you can forget that."

"Suppose we were talking," Goldman said, "just Dallas things. More cops, maybe a judge or two."

"I'd want to keep my law license," Benson said.

Goldman and Tiddle exchanged a look. Goldman said, "That's not possible, Rusty, you know that. Likely you're going to do a piece of time. Year or two, but you can do it federal. Tennis courts and shit."

"You'd move me, right?"

"Tonight, if you give the word," Goldman said.

"And we're forgetting about any state charge? Period, I'd have to have that."

Goldman indicated Tiddle. "This man would help me on that."

"I'd want a bath first," Benson said. "Christ, I smell like a horse."

"I'm not believing this," Detective Fuller said. "I thought this guy would be a helluva lot tougher."

Goldman winked at Benson. "Tough's one thing," Goldman said. "Smart's another." He looked at Tiddle. "Call your guard, Roger. Rusty cleans up nice, believe me."

17

BINO GOT UP THE NEXT MORNING, CREEPING AROUND ON TIPTOES so as not to disturb Carla, slipped into his blue suit, and prepared to leave the room. He paused for a moment in the doorway, watching the milk-skinned girl slumbering peacefully on her side, one bare rounded hip showing with the folds of the sheet tucked around her thighs. He winced as he touched the scratch on his shoulder, then did the same as he gingerly touched his eye.

He covered the seven long blocks to 1301 Franklin Street, rehearsing in his mind what he wanted to go over with Rusty Benson. He had to be careful, doing what he could to help Rusty get out of jail and at the same time protecting Tommy Clinger's interests. Keeping the two cases apart wasn't going to be easy.

The deputy behind the desk, a lantern-jawed black guy whose head was shaved, was the same wiseass who'd been working the property room when Bino had retrieved his clothes after his own stint in jail. The deputy smirked in recognition. Bino ignored the guy, lowered his head, and filled in the blanks on the sign-in register. The deputy spun the register around to read, glanced at Bino, then returned his attention to the page.

Finally the deputy looked up and said, "I've got to make a call."

To which Bino replied, "Why? The record shows I'm Mr. Benson's lawyer, and I'm supposed to be able to see him anytime I want."

"I know who you are," the deputy said, "and I know the rules. And I've got to make a call." He left Bino drumming his fingers, retreated from the counter and picked up a phone. He was on the line a couple of minutes, then returned to the counter to say, "You're out of luck."

Bino frowned. "If I don't get to see my client in a hurry," he said, "*you* may be out of luck."

One corner of the deputy's mouth tugged sarcastically to one side. "I'm here to serve you, Mr. Phillips," he said, meaning, Fuck you. "Really I am. But I've got a real problem with letting you visit Mr. Russell Benson."

"Sounds to me," Bino said, "like you're wanting more problems than you've already got."

The deputy grinned. "Maybe I am. But I can't let you visit anybody which isn't in this jail."

Bino's chest deflated like a ruptured tire. "Huh?"

"As of this morning, we've got no Russell Benson as a prisoner. Couple of other Bensons. One hot-check guy, another in for rape. You want to see one of them?"

Bino looked down, then back up. "What's happened to my client, then?"

The deputy folded burly arms. "You know better than that, Mr. Phillips. The only thing we're authorized to say about Mr. Benson is that he's not currently a prisoner." He looked toward the lobby exit. "I'll give you more than I'm supposed to, though. If I wanted some answers, I'd talk to those guys." He gestured with his head.

Bino turned. Standing near the lobby entrance in ani-
mated conversation were Roger Tiddle, Marvin Goldman,
and the same FBI agent who'd been Goldman's shadow in
court at Rusty's bond hearing. The Harris County prosecutor
was wearing a charcoal gray suit while Goldman was in slacks
and a formfitting green knit shirt. Bino said over his shoulder
to the deputy, "Thanks," then crossed the thirty steps over to
the three men with his hands balled into fists.

Goldman was in the process of handing a business card
over to Tiddle. As Bino approached, the Assistant U.S.D.A.
was saying, "Any questions you get, you just refer 'em to me."

Bino stepped in between Goldman and the FBI agent and
looked down on Goldman. "Okay," Bino said, "I'll be the first
questioner. Where in hell is my client?"

"You're looking better this morning, buddy. Your eye's not
as swollen, and you're moving around better." Goldman
scratched his head through his too-black hair.

Bino's gaze hardened. "Looks like you're moving around
pretty good yourself, Marv. Where's my client?"

Goldman now exchanged looks with Roger Tiddle. "You
mean Rusty Benson?" Goldman said.

"No, Marv," Bino said. "I mean Jeffrey fucking Dahmer.
Who the hell do you think I mean? I'm talking about the guy
jailed in the phony bond hearing, which hearing I'm about to
appeal the shit out of."

Roger Tiddle now cleared his throat. "I'll help you on that
one. We've withdrawn our request to hold Mr. Benson without
bond. He's no longer in our custody."

Bino got it. He alternated his gaze between Tiddle and
Goldman. "What about the murder beef?" Bino finally said.
"You dropping that one, too?"

Tiddle studied the floor.

Bino held a stiffened finger underneath Goldman's nose.
"Well, I got a message for you to deliver, Marv old buddy."

Goldman shrugged. "A message to who?"

"To Rusty Benson," Bino said, "at whatever fucking safe
house you're hiding him in. You tell old Rusty that I just resigned as his lawyer, and that he owes me another thousand

bucks. That's the charge for the hassle I've been through. Plus, there's a policy of mine. Anytime my client decides to become a federal snitch, my fee doubles. You tell old Rusty that for me, will you, Marv?"

During the pell-mell taxi ride to Hobby Airport, Bino was too busy with his own thoughts to have much to say to Carla. He wasn't sure, in fact, exactly why she was coming along. When he'd charged into the room and begun tossing his luggage together, she'd been sitting up in bed naked as a jaybird, but by the time he was ready to go she was dressed in loose-fitting jeans, a pullover cotton jumper, and brown Cole-Haan loafers. She'd hustled along with him to the elevator and through the lobby, and had hopped into the cab in front of him before he could raise an objection.

At Hobby he left the taxi at a dead run, used his credit card in the machine for a one-way ticket, and, with Carla dogging his tracks, arrived at the gate five minutes before the Southwest Airlines flight was ready for boarding. He checked in at the counter, received a boarding pass, then stepped with Carla out into the corridor with his carry-on suitbag slung over his shoulder.

She leaned against a pillar, crossed her ankles, and looked up at him. "Now would you mind telling me what's the big emergency?" she said. "Or is it just that you're tired of me?"

"I tried to explain at the hotel," Bino said, "that things were blowing up right and left. I've got some huge fires back at the office. My deal with Rusty Benson is over with, so there's nothing to keep me here."

She compressed her mouth into a pout. "There isn't?"

He suddenly felt two inches tall. "That's not . . ." he said, and gently touched her hair. "Hey, I didn't mean you. It's business, okay? You've only got, what, one more night to perform in this town?"

"That's not the point," she said.

"Hey, I know that," he said. "Believe me, I do. You'll be

coming home tomorrow. Look, I've got these two guys, Barney and Half, doing some things for me. What I found out this morning over at the jail tells me I've got to get a move on."

"Which is what?" Carla said, interested.

"Which is that your friend and mine Rusty Benson has suddenly decided he'd rather have Goldman for his lawyer than me. He's decided that Goldman has a better chance of keeping him out of jail, and he's probably right." Bino checked his watch. "Look, I don't have time to explain all of this. Just trust me that it's not you I'm running from. I'm running *to* someplace."

"What is it that you've got them doing?" Carla said.

A little warning bell tingled inside Bino's head. "Got who doing?"

"Those guys you said. Barney and . . . Half?"

"Half, yeah. Half-a-Point," Bino said thoughtfully. Then, as gently as possible, "Tell me something. Why is it you're suddenly so interested in all that?"

Her gaze shifted so that she wasn't looking directly at him. She took on the same expression that Bino had seen on one of his burglar clients, Wimpy Madrick, whenever anyone asked Wimpy if he was the guy who'd stolen the stereo and TV.

"I mean, hey, Carla," he said. "Don't take this wrong, but good times are good times and business is business. So, why the sudden curiosity?"

"Curiosity?" she said, licking her lips, then firming her mouth to say, "I was just making small talk."

The gate attendant was now calling the flight for boarding.

"Look, Carla, we can talk later," Bino said. The warning tingle had grown to a full-fledged anvil chorus, another *not-quite* feeling that he couldn't put his finger on. "I'll see you back in Dallas, okay?" He kissed her on the forehead. "I've got to get on this airplane, babe."

"Sure," she said. She took three or four small steps in the direction of the airport lobby, then turned and raised her voice. "Bino."

He had started toward the boarding line, but now turned. "Yes?"

She looked at him for a full fifteen seconds, then dropped her gaze. "Nothing," she said. "Nothing that can't wait." She smiled. "We've had fun together, hoss. Let's don't forget that, okay?"

18

BINO LANDED AT DALLAS'S LOVE FIELD, RETRIEVED THE LINC, and drove directly downtown to his office. Dodie did a double take as he came in, then closed the file she'd been studying and laid it aside. "You still owe me the seven-fifty," she said. She wore a plain cotton tan minidress, and her hair was tied back into a ponytail.

Bino sat in her visitor's chair. "That's all you've got to say? Not, Gee, we've missed you, or anything?"

"Well I could say something tacky like, 'Where's your girl-friend?' " Dodie said. "But I won't." She held out her hand, palm up.

He reached in his pocket and went through his bankroll, located a five and two singles, and dropped them on her desk. "You'll have to trust me for the fifty cents," he said.

"I'll keep that in mind."

"Look, Dode," he said.

"You've had several calls," Dodie said, thumbing through a stack of pink slips in businesslike fashion.

He scratched his chin. If that was the way she wanted it . . . "For now," he said, "hold all calls that don't have anything to do with Tommy Clinger. And get in touch with Tommy and tell him I need to see him, pronto. Tomorrow morning, if he can get down here. Most of the other calls, you know how to handle. The ones that require a personal touch from me, well, they'll just have to wait."

Her nose wrinkled. "A personal touch from you?" She looked once again through the call slips. "I don't think any hookers have been calling. If they do I'll tell them you'll personally touch them." She smiled daggers.

He pointed a finger. "Pretty good, Dode. Hey, that's a good one."

"You think so?"

He stood, doing his damnedest not to show his irritation but failing miserably in the attempt, and gestured toward Half-a-Point Harrison's door. "He in?" Bino said.

"Last time I checked," Dodie said, not looking up.

"Well, don't forget to call Tommy," he said huffily.

"I'm not the one around here who forgets things."

He opened his mouth to make a crack, then thought the better of it. He nodded at the top of Dodie's head, then went into Half-a-Point Harrison's cubbyhole.

There were two phones in Half's office, a red one and a black one. He was on the red, saying, "The number on Texas can move. We got no word on Juan Gonzalez's sore back. If Gonzalez plays the odds'll change. Home run power." He glanced up, held a hand out toward his visitor's chair, and listened to the party on the line.

Bino sat, scooted his rump forward, and crossed his legs.

"What do you mean, call you?" Half said. "You want the changes, you call me. This ain't no Sports Central here." He hung up. "Bino. I been trying to call you at the Houston Hyatt."

"It's good I wasn't there," Bino said. "Talking to me might've interfered with the bookmaking calls."

Half wore a tight-fitting vest with his tie yanked down and his collar undone. His coat hung on a hall tree in the corner.

He inserted a toothpick between his lips and grinned. "I take care of all business," he said. He reached inside his middle desk drawer and tossed two stacks of paper over in front of Bino. One pile was handwritten yellow legal sheets, the other computer printouts in alternating shades of green.

"What're those?" said Bino.

Half propped a knee against his desk and moved the toothpick to the corner of his mouth, there to dangle. "What you asked for. The yellow pages are lists of Rusty Benson's cases in state court, the printout's from the federal district clerk. I got Rusty's federal cases underlined. The ones in Edgar Bryson's court have the case number circled. What else?"

Bino picked up the yellow legal pages. "You got dispositions on these state cases?"

"Third column," Half said. "On the federal printout the case status is on the far right, whether it's still pending or if the guy's already pled or gone to trial."

Bino relaxed. Half-a-Point Harrison's income as an investigator was about ten percent of what he made brokering bets—from lawyers, county employees, and even a few prosecutors—and he looked on his investigative chores as part of helping out a buddy. Half and Bino went all the way back to small-town Mesquite, when Pop Harrison used to haul the two kids around in the back of his pickup, and buy them Grapette soda in a bottle and licorice sticks from a jar inside a drive-in grocery that smelled of fresh cold cuts and cheese. Bino's parents were both dead and gone—his mom in a pileup with an eighteen-wheeler, his dad from a heart attack a few years after that—and most of his Christmases and Thanksgivings were spent at the Harrisons' Mesquite home, munching on drumsticks and watching the pro ball games on television. Bino said, "Looks like you've done a pretty good job."

"What'd you expect?" Half said.

Bino picked up both stacks and rattled the pages. "You see any pattern here?"

"Depends on what you're looking for," Half said. "His murder and rape clients get hammered just like anybody else's. I got to say, though, that if some of your guys find out what Rusty's people are getting on the bullshit charges, the drunk driving and shoplifting, you're going to be minus a few clients."

"He's making good deals for them," Bino said.

"Yeah, you might say that. He's got a guy, I know this guy. Runs a poker game and football store out in East Dallas by the golf course. Murphy Litton."

Bino nodded. "Fat Murphy."

"Sure," Half said. "You know him, too. Not a particularly brilliant guy. The numbers are going to make a bookmaker rich in the long run, and that poker game is the real berries. He's knocking down the pot, fifty cents, a buck or two when the pot gets bigger. In a ten and twenty game he's going to cut five or six hundred a night, depending on how long the game lasts.

"But Fat Murphy's not satisfied with waiting," Half said. "He knows his football customers, so he shades the numbers. Say the guy's a Texas fan. Murphy knows that, knows the guy's going to bet Texas, so he knocks points off the spread. Doesn't realize the guy's probably betting two or three other bookmakers, and is a cinch to find out the real number and that Murphy's screwing him."

"I've heard," Bino said, "that his poker game's not the straightest spot in the world, either."

"You've heard right," Half said. "He runs professionals in and charges them a fee to sit in with the square johns. Murph gets it coming and going. Not only is he cutting the game, the sharpies are buying a seat from the guy. Trouble with that is, once the mooches take a few baths, they tend to get pissed off, you know?"

"Which translates," Bino said, "into complaints."

"Not a football season goes by," Half said, "that two or three of Murphy's customers don't make anonymous phone calls, not to mention the poker players' old ladies that are already bitching downtown because their old man doesn't bring enough home to feed the babies. Keeps Fat Murphy's tit in a wringer."

"Six times"—Half held up all five fingers on one hand,

the index finger on the other—"old Murph's been busted. The first three, they're misdemeanors where he pays a fine. Numbers four and five, Rusty Benson gets dismissed. Number six, that was this spring the case come up, that's enhanced into a felony because of the three prior misdemeanors, right? The standard D.A.'s deal on the felony is reduction to a misdemeanor and sixty days in jail, right?"

"Plain vanilla," Bino said. "That's the standard proposition."

"Yeah, only not with Fat Murphy Litton. He gets probation on the beef, can you believe it?" Half reached across the desk to rattle the stack of yellow paper. "There's a bunch of 'em in there. Hookers run in eight and ten times, winding up with maybe a loitering ticket referred back to city court. Nothing that's going to get the newspapers on anybody's ass, like early parole for rapos and whatnot. But they're deals no other lawyer in town could swing."

"They're all vice squad busts, right?" Bino said.

"Every one I found." Half leaned back and folded his arms.

"Which would require," Bino said, "some prosecutor's cooperation in addition to the vice squad's. It takes an Assistant D.A. to reduce the charges, but if the vice squad cops aren't cut in they're going to bitch to somebody over the A.D.A.'s head."

"Way it looks to me," Half said.

"Jesus Christ," Bino said. "Goldman is going to make one earth-shattering street sweep out of this one. I can see his list now, it'll make the cop indictments on Tommy Clinger and those guys look like a Little League batting lineup. Judges, D.A.'s, you name it. With Rusty to name names, old Marv's probably already got calls in to *60 Minutes* and *The New York Times*." He squeezed the bridge of his nose between his thumb and forefinger. "I wonder how Rusty's been handling the payoffs on all this crap."

"I thought you might wonder," Half said. "So I went out and had a talk last night with Fat Murphy Litton."

"Oh? I didn't know you and Murphy were tight."

"We ain't," Half said. "But you have to know how to talk to the guy. I just dropped in on Murphy's poker game and mentioned to him on the sly that I'd seen a couple of his players before, playing in the professional tournaments at Binion's Horseshoe. First thing you know, Murphy takes me out in the kitchen to visit."

"Wants to make sure you won't blow his cover," Bino said.

"You got it. Now, Murphy don't know exactly how Rusty Benson makes these deals. All he knows is, if you want the right consideration it's going to cost you extra. He gives the money to Rusty, and where it goes from there Murphy's got no idea. Murph had one pretty hot item for me, though."

"Yeah?" Bino said. "What?"

"Rusty's wife, Rhonda Benson, now deceased. She's been in bed with Goldman."

"Jesus Christ," Bino said. "She had more class than that."

"Tune in, Bino. I didn't mean she was screwing the guy. She was so hot at Rusty when they split the blankets, she went straight to the feds. Apparently Rusty put the word out that he wanted to know what safe spot Goldman was keeping her in. All of Rusty's clients were supposed to be keeping their ears to the ground."

"So all that stuff he told me at the golf course," Bino said, "about how he thought she was visiting her sister . . ."

"Was a lot of bullshit," Half said. "He had no idea where Rhonda was, at least as of last week. Last week Fat Murphy talked to Rusty, and he was still looking for her."

"I should have figured this out. Would have, eventually. All of which puts Rhonda's killing in a different light." He slapped his forehead. "Jesus, a hit. I need to come to the party. That's why Rusty wanted witnesses as to his whereabouts. He spent five hours on the golf course with Barney and me, then met me and that Kinder guy out at Arthur's. He wanted to know where Goldman was keeping her so he could notify his contract man."

"And Rusty and Goldman," Bino said, "have been bullshitting each other. Man, would I like to've seen that, Goldman telling Rusty about the deal he was rigging for Terry Nolby, and Rusty acting like he was lapping it up, all the time wanting to know where Goldman was keeping Rhonda. And now that he doesn't have Rhonda any more, old Marv's just made a deal with Rusty." He reached out and picked up the computer printout. "How 'bout these federal cases, Half?"

"I ain't had time to do anything about them," Half said. "Want me to start?"

Bino stood and snatched up both piles of paper. "Let me think on that. I'll go over this printout. It might be there's enough here that I won't need you to do anything else."

Half reached in his drawer and pulled out his betting slips. "I hope not. My business is suffering, you know?"

Bino stopped in the reception area long enough to say to Dodie, "You find Tommy Clinger?"

She stood before the file cabinet with one drawer open. She reached in and pulled out a file. "Did do."

"You tell him to come in tomorrow morning?"

She slid the drawer closed. "*Didn't* do."

He cocked his head. "Huh?"

"Where I located him was in the shower. His wife says he's going to call me back." She carried the file around behind her desk and sat down.

Bino looked at his watch. "That's good. I need him earlier. Tell him, six-thirty. I want him to meet me at Joe Miller's Bar."

She rolled her eyes. "How original."

He ignored the crack. "It'll give me time. I've got to go check on a contract killer."

Now she looked interested. "One of your clients? Or just another drinking buddy?"

"Neither. I know somebody that can probably tell me where to find one."

"You're not *that* mad at Mr. Goldman, are you?" Dodie said.

"Almost," Bino said. "But, naw. I'm trying to find out who might have done a contract on somebody."

Dodie blinked. "Well, if you find out, let me know. I might have a job for him."

19

BINO THOUGHT THAT THE LINC MIGHT BE TRYING TO TELL HIM something. As he exited Highway 114 to turn south on O'Connor Road, just a mile or so west of Texas Stadium, the engine hesitated and nearly stalled. The white Lincoln Town Car wasn't behaving, and it was the first indication of any trouble in a hundred and nine thousand miles. He'd been a maintenance freak with the car—oil changes every three thousand miles, annual checkups—and he'd made up his mind that the Linc was his until the fenders fell off. But suddenly, just as he was about to cruise into Las Colinas subdivision, the Linc acted as if it was going to quit on him. As he drifted powerless to one side of the road, however, the engine smoothed out and the car picked up speed, and by the time he'd made the sweeping turn onto O'Connor the motor was hitting on all cylinders. He wondered briefly if the Linc knew where he was headed, and if the hesitation had been some kind of protest. Can't be, he thought, it's only a car.

He went south through new-money Las Colinas, home of the here-today-gone-tomorrow fast-buck crowd, and marveled as he always did over the size of and contrast between the different houses. There were modern architecture monstrosities sitting alongside Spanish-style homes complete with adobe brick fronts and red-tile roofs, and next door to the Spanish home might be an English Gothic with rounded towers at its corners. If Bino was running Las Colinas, he thought, he'd pass a residential building code. Anybody building an ugly house had to pay a fine.

He passed the residential district and slowed, bending to peer out the right-hand window to search for addresses. He cruised in front of a strip shopping center holding a Toys "R" Us, a Tom Thumb Supermarket, and a Bally's President Spa, and then made a sharp right-hand turn into the far end of the parking lot. He moseyed in front of the Tom Thumb, braking every fifty feet or so to bounce roughly over a speed bump, and parked nose-on to the curb in front of the Bally's. Visible through the picture window fronting the building, two men and three women trudged away on stair climbers. Bino turned off the key; the Linc's engine died with a final ominous post-ignition shudder. Bino got out, made a face at the Linc as he locked the driver's-side door, then strolled across the sizzling concrete to enter the health spa.

He was conscious of sounds, the rubbery *clop clop* of feet on stair climbers, the faraway *clunk* of someone lowering a freeweight onto its stand. On his left was a natural fruit juice dispenser; behind the counter on his right was a petite bottle blond in a thigh-length pink leotard. She wore no makeup and didn't need it. She smiled at him like someone on a commission, and said brightly, "Welcome to President's." The chart on the counter told him that if he'd sign up before August 1 he'd get a discount on the initiation fee. The young lady's leotard was cut away in front to reveal taut stomach muscle; Bino's own midsection felt suddenly softer than it had just moments ago.

"Hi," Bino said. "I'm looking for someone in here."

"Oh?" She frowned and looked down at her sign-in roster. "Who?"

"Annabelle Tirelli. Or Mrs. Dante, could be either one."

She ran a finger down the column. "Mrs. Annabelle, it says. You want to go back? She's doing pecs, I think."

Bino wanted to say, Doing what? But he kept his mouth shut and circled the counter toward the rear of the weight room. The girl bent over to lift a box from a lower shelf, showing buttocks like pumped-up basketballs.

He went down the aisle between two rows of Nautilus equipment, and passed a guy who was examining his flexed triceps in a full-length mirror. Bino's own muscles tightened involuntarily.

Annabelle was on a sixty-degree padded incline bench attached to a Nautilus, her upper arms extended out, elbows bent, hands up in the locked position as she forced the tension bars up beside her ears. The cords in her neck stood out with the effort. Her leotards were lavender, her honey-blond hair tied behind her head, terrycloth bands on both wrists and around her forehead. Her tensed thigh muscles rippled under spandex. Bino thought her figure even better than twenty years earlier, when she'd bounced up and down and led cheers in Moody Coliseum while he was playing basketball.

He went and stood before her with his hands in his pockets. She was at maximum extension when she spotted him. Her arms relaxed; the tension bars rolled outward. Air escaped her lips in a sigh. There was a fine sheen of perspiration on her cheeks and upper lip. She smiled, showing one slightly crooked front tooth.

"Did you just happen in?" she said, slightly breathlessly. "They have a membership drive."

He adjusted his tan knit polo around his waist. "I came to see you."

"Well, aren't I the lucky one," she said. Her biceps were bunched, a crease in the flesh where her upper arm joined her shoulder. "How did you know where I'd be?"

"You know the answer to that."

The laugh crinkles around her eyes tightened. "I do?"

"Those two musclebutts you referred to me last month."

"Yes, aren't they beautiful?" she said. "Keep them out of jail, love. It would be a shame to waste all that on prison punks."

"A steroid selling beef isn't that serious," Bino said. "I'm working on it. Probation, likely, they've got no records."

"Hip, hip, hooray," Annabelle said.

Bino backed up to straddle a padded bench, and sat down. "Anyway, they delivered your message."

One plucked eyebrow arched. "Oh? Did I give them a message?"

"I guess it was a message," Bino said. "It was a handwritten itinerary of your workout schedule, on the letterhead of this place."

"Maybe I just wanted you to know I was getting back in shape."

"You've never looked *out* of shape to me, babe," he said. "I've always said, told everybody, you look like you could still cartwheel from the fifty to the goal line."

"Looks are deceiving," she said. "At least they were. My legs were getting like dough." She reached down to stroke her inner thigh.

Bino had to admit that her workouts were . . . well, working out. She'd always been a fanatic about the way she looked. Which, Bino thought, was part of the problem with her. "I need to ask a favor," he said.

"Excuse me? I thought you came as a result of my message."

He firmed his expression. "We need to talk, Annabelle."

She laid her head back against the inclined bench. "Up front, down the corridor, there's a juice and salad bar. Give me a few minutes to finish toning." Her eyes showed a wanton twinkle. "Then I'll be ready for you, okay?"

The juice and salad bar was behind a glass cafeteria-style counter, in a long room with full-length mirrors covering three of the walls. Bino felt out of place as he pushed his tray along, dropping a fork and spoon on top of a folded paper napkin, looking over an array of sandwiches on saucer-size paper plates, an olive and a miniature pickle impaled on a toothpick stuck through each individual sandwich. All he saw was wheat bread, which Bino supposed contained no additives and crap. He wondered briefly how far it was to the nearest 7-Eleven, where he could get a loaf of good old Mrs. Baird's.

He pointed at one of the sandwiches, and leaned over to say to the girl behind the counter, "It's chicken, huh?"

She wrinkled her nose. "It's soya. Tastes like chicken."

I'll just bet it does, Bino thought. He said hopefully, "How 'bout the beef?"

"It's soya, too," she said. "We don't have any meat here."

"Oh."

"You want the beef?" she said.

"No. No, just checking." He continued on down the line, finally ordering a drink called a strawberry/banana smoothie. The girl tossed fresh strawberries and banana chunks into a blender, added crushed ice and water, and whipped up something resembling a daiquiri which she served him in a plastic cup. He fished out two singles and approached the register. The girl trotted down behind the counter to punch computer keys, then grinned at him. "That'll be three-eighteen, sir," she said. Bino mumbled to himself as he poked the dollar bills back into his pocket and came up with a five. She gave him his change. He stumped over to a waist-high table and sat on a stool.

The only other customers were two guys at a nearby table, men in their twenties wearing muscle shirts, their triceps like thick twisted rope. Bino sat up straighter and glanced in the full-length mirror, then took a deep breath and stuck out his chest. One of the two guys smirked at him. His ears reddening, he had a sip of strawberry/banana. It wasn't bad.

In about five minutes Annabelle appeared, striding confidently in from the corridor, patting her forehead with a towel draped around her shoulders. She nodded and smiled, and he lifted his cup in a toast. She went through the serving line, then approached with one of the godawful phony chicken sandwiches and a cup of water. She sat on the stool beside him and crossed her legs as the two burly guys threw appreciative glances in her direction. Then the two looked at Bino as if to say, Who's the out-of-shape asshole sitting with the fox? Involuntarily, Bino squared his shoulders.

"Do you have a sore back or something?" she said.

He relaxed. "No, I'm okay. How've you been?"

"Bored."

Annabelle spent her life in a state of boredom, which Bino supposed was one of the reasons he'd come home from law school class one day to find her gone. "Sorry to hear that," he said.

"Are you planning to excite me?" She took a tiny bite from one corner of her sandwich.

" 'Fraid not. I'm just not a very exciting guy."

"That's not what I remember," she said, chewing, "from the last time we were together."

During the time he'd been defending a federal judge, Bino had weakened and taken her to bed for the first time since their divorce eighteen years ago. He swallowed hard. Her current husband was into a lot of different things, one of which was making guys dead. "I need your help with something," he said.

"Translating into, Dante's help," she said. "The last time you pumped me for mob information, at least I got a good screwing out of the deal."

He picked up his cup and swirled pink liquid around. "I'm coming to you because I know that nobody else can assert the influence on Dante Tirelli that you can. You're in a real strong position, Annabelle."

She smirked. "Does that mean I'm not going to get the screwing?"

"What I need is," Bino said quickly, "I've got a case where I think somebody's paid somebody else to do a contract killing."

She huddled closer to him and looked around the room. "*Shh.* Information's one thing, but being a stool pigeon

against my husband won't make for real spiffy marital rela-
tions."

"Not him," Bino said. "He's got nothing to do with this.
But the chances are ninety-nine percent on the Bino Phillips
scale that a pro did this job. What we've got is a woman looking like a victim of a nut. Later, though, it turns out to be very
convenient for certain people, people with a lot of stroke, that
she's dead. Making a killing look like something different
than what it was, that's a signature of only one group of folks."

She relaxed. Bino felt a little bit sorry for Annabelle, being in a marriage where she had no way out other than feet
first, but Annabelle had known exactly what she was getting
into. She'd been a poor little rich girl all her life, and her marriage to Dante Tirelli had the same motive as her earlier marriage to Bino Phillips—something that would be fun for a
while, and when things quit being fun she could simply walk
away. Only with Dante Tirelli it hadn't worked out the way
she'd planned, and never would.

"What would be my incentive other than sex?" Annabelle
said, taking a bite of her sandwich.

"This time," Bino said, "it would be Dante's incentive. The
dead lady had nothing to do with the Outfit, and neither do
any of the other players. Mob contracts are all family affairs.
The guy that did this, because of the method, he's either an
Outfit guy or had some training from one. That means that
somebody's taking in work on the side, and if that's true he's
doing it on the sly. His *capo di tutti,* or whatever they call them
these days, isn't going to like one of his people acting as an independent, and is going to want to know about it. Brighten
up, babe, you'll be doing something that old Dante will like."

"Dante doesn't like dealing with the New York guys. He's
been forced into it lately on the gambling, he thinks because
of you."

Bino felt a slight chill. "Why because of me?"

"The New York people being in on the gambling in Dallas
is a trade-off. Something they did for him a while back. I'd be
raising my neck and saying, Here, honey, go ahead and cut
my throat, if I elaborated on that, but you should be able to

add two and two." Annabelle folded her arms on the table. Her breasts bunched under taut spandex.

He got her drift. He'd agreed once to represent a lovely person named Buster Longley, who was in the process of trying to make a plea bargain deal in return for tattling on a guy named Winnie Anspacher, who in turn had held information not so favorable to Dante Tirelli. Longley had died in jail under less than pristine circumstances, and though Bino had figured the murder to be mob related, he'd never had any confirmation up to now. "Sure," Bino said. "Buster Longley."

"You said that," Annabelle said. "I didn't."

"Hey, Annabelle, I didn't have anything to do with who Longley was or wasn't going to roll over on. That deal was in the hopper before I ever talked to the guy." The story was almost the truth, and Bino put on his best Honest Abe expression.

"You should tell Dante that, not me," Annabelle said.

"Whether I'm popular with Dante or not," Bino said, "it'll be a feather in his cap to transfer information about somebody in the Outfit doing hits on their own. And it'll score points for you to be the bearer of the tidings."

"I've got better ways than that of scoring points," Annabelle said. She winked.

"Be that as it may," Bino said, "here's what I need. The lady was found in Houston. Three days before that, she was in Dallas taking a golf lesson."

Annabelle rolled her eyes. "I hope you weren't teaching her. God."

"Hey, I've really improved since we were . . . you know, married. But no, I wouldn't have the time to give lessons. The point is, the guy's likely in either place, Houston or Dallas. There are only a few people that do things like this, and it shouldn't take much for Dante to figure out who he is. I want his name in return for furnishing the information that it's going on."

"You're talking about Rusty Benson's wife," Annabelle said. She assumed her phony Brooklyn accent, which under some circumstances Bino thought was cute as hell. "Even da mob reads da paper," she said, then in her normal Texas voice, "I have to tell you, Dante nearly rolled off the couch laughing when he read you were in jail."

"I'm glad somebody thought it was funny," Bino said. He took on a serious look. "Look, babe, I'll be indebted to you."

She took the toothpick from her sandwich and popped the olive into her mouth. "I'll have to think on how to bring it up," she said. "And you will owe me, buster. Don't think I won't collect, either."

Bino studied her, the ageless face, the eyes that twinkled with a strange sadness and even some desperation. He was going to owe her. So far he'd owed Dodie and Carla as well. If he didn't get some answers soon, he'd be in debt to everybody in the whole fucking state. He stood and stepped back from the table. "Sure," he said. "How about if I join the health spa and put you down as the one that referred me? That'll give you a break on your dues, won't it?"

20

BINO WAS TEN MINUTES LATE IN GETTING TO JOE MILLER'S BAR. He left the Linc in between a Range Rover and a Buick Century, then jogged up to and opened the padded door and stood just inside the entry looking around. He spotted Tommy Clinger all alone in a back booth, quickly skirted the bar—nodding in return to a brief hello from Melinda the bartender—and slid in across from Clinger. "Been here long?" Bino said, and then regretted the question as he noted the half-full drink in front of Tommy, the full one waiting near Tommy's elbow, Tommy's vacant look as he lifted the half-full glass to his lips. Guys in Tommy Clinger's predicament had plenty of time.

"Just awhile," Clinger said. "Molly dropped me off on the way to the grocery store. I told her I'd call when I was ready."

"Shouldn't take too long," Bino said. He sensed a presence near the booth, Melinda waiting expectantly with one hip thrust slightly out. Bino ordered a Budweiser draft. Clinger held his glass out and nodded. Bino's gaze dropped as Melinda sashayed off to fill the order, her outline dim in the muted light from behind the bar.

"Operating with one car's a problem sometimes," Clinger said. "We have to work it out. When Molly has to go someplace, pick up the kids or whatever, I just stay home. She's been job-hunting."

Bino experienced a pang of sympathy. A lot of criminal lawyers told him they'd passed the point, years ago, of feeling sorry for clients, but Bino never had. "You're still on leave with pay, huh?" Bino said.

"For what it's worth," Clinger said, finishing off one drink with a gulp, setting the glass aside, moving the full glass over in front of him. "Never has been worth much. With the additional expenses we've got . . . Molly needs to get used to working. I don't know how long I'm going to be away." His chin sagged and the flesh under his eyes was puffy.

"Cool it, Tommy," Bino said. "Nobody knows for sure that you're going to be away at all." Melinda delivered a frosty mug with a thump near Bino's elbow, set a fresh highball in front of Clinger, and toted Clinger's empty away.

"I've been on the other side of this a long time," Clinger said, "and I've seen these guys. They get out on bond and run around town like nothing's going to happen to them. Then, boom, one day they're gone and the wife's left with nothing on the table. I know the odds. We're getting ready for it, best we can."

"I'm working on some things," Bino said. He took a sip of beer, the liquid cold and bubbly, tickling his throat.

"I see that you are," Clinger said. "Rusty Benson. Asshole lawyer for an asshole snitch."

"I was afraid that would bother you."

One of Clinger's shaggy eyebrows lifted. "Bother me? Why would it bother me? My wife and I are giving the last nickel we've got in this world to this guy, I look in the paper one day and there he is, traveling all the way to Houston fucking Texas to help out Terry Nolby's lawyer. Why would that bother me?"

"Look, you got a right," Bino said. "But I was looking after you, too."

Clinger snorted.

"Hear me out, Tommy," Bino said. "And it's none of my business, but all that booze won't do anything but keep you in a resentful state of mind."

"Is it the booze?" Clinger said, knocking off a slug. "Or am I finally learning what the assholes I've been chasing knew all along, that once you're gotten, you're gotten, and all these fucking lawyers are good for is to take your money?"

Bino's jaw protruded. "Yeah? Well, maybe you're right, but I'll tell you one thing. You got more than most, my friend. You got a wife and a couple of fine kids, if you don't go off the deep end and lose them. If you do, Tommy, it'll be your fault. Not any lawyer's. Not any feds. Just yours."

Suddenly, Clinger broke down. He sobbed aloud, tears streaming down his cheeks. He pulled a handkerchief from his pocket, wiped his face and blew his nose.

Bino's tone gentled. "It's tough, but I've got to get through to you. You're taking a screwing, Tommy, but let's don't pretend you're lily white. You told me yourself, you knew all this was going on, all these cops with their hands out. Now, if you'll listen to me, and if you haven't gotten too drunk sitting here feeling sorry for yourself, I'll tell you exactly what I'm pretty sure is going on, and what it's going to take to get your balls off the chopping block."

Clinger stared vacantly off. "If I just hadn't taken the job to begin with . . ."

"Well, you did," Bino said, "and that's that. Okay, first of all, your trial's put off sixty days, but believe me that it'll never come to pass. Any day now, you can look for Goldman to dismiss the charges against you, Nolby, and the rest of the cops."

Clinger looked hopeful.

"But when that happens," Bino said, "it's just a lull before the next indictment that's coming. Now that indictment, that's the one Goldman's really going to get his cookies on. It's going to include you and the same police guys, plus some judges, plus whoever Goldman can think of that'll give him more press coverage. Rusty Benson is one dirty lawyer, in case you don't already know."

"I mind my own business," Clinger said. "I've heard he did a good job for some people."

"He damn sure did," Bino said. "He did the best job that a little money spread around in the right places can buy. Rhonda Benson was talking to the feds, which is why Rhonda's not with us."

"Now wait a minute," Clinger said, pointing. "I never had Rusty Benson, never had any business with the guy. And I damn sure know nothing about any judges getting fixed."

"That won't matter," Bino said. "You'll have to take my word on this, Tommy, but what I'm going to tell you is based on many years of fucking with Goldman. It'll be a conspiracy beef, likely with a couple of RICO counts thrown in. It's called tarring everybody with the same brush, and it won't make any difference if you never even heard of most of the people involved, you're going to get convicted just by association. The law is crazy as hell, but here's how it works. Say you're in on taking the heat off of a whorehouse or two, for street information like you said. Now, say that same whorehouse is doing business with Rusty Benson, who in turn is buying off a couple of vice squad cops and a judge or two. The law says that makes you a part of a conspiracy with the judge, even if you've never met the guy."

Clinger seemed to shrink in size. "I know those laws are broad."

"Broad as hell, and it gets worse as we go along," Bino said. "Now, not only does Goldman have Terry Nolby on his team, he's got Rusty Benson."

Clinger's jaw dropped in shock. "I thought Benson was charged with killing his wife."

"He was, but that didn't keep Goldman from manufacturing a deal. The state guys in Houston will do whatever Goldman tells them with regard to the murder beef, and Goldman would make a deal with Charles Manson if he thought Charlie could finger a few jurists."

"That's tough for some people if Rusty's going over,"

Clinger said. "But he doesn't know anything about me to tell about."

"No, but he's got enough on other people Goldman's going to indict to make it rub off on you. Unless my plan works."

"Unless your *plan* works? Jesus Christ, my house is pledged to secure your legal fee, you'd by God better have a plan."

Bino looked down, then back up. "Call me when you sober up, Tommy." He started to rise.

Clinger reached across and put a hand on Bino's arm. "Don't go yet," Clinger said. "I'm listening."

Bino sat back down. "Not for you am I telling this. For just you, the way you're acting, you could have your legal fee back and go fuck yourself. I happen to think a lot of your family, which translates that I think you'll be all right yourself one of these days. But I don't need the kind of pressure you're trying to put on. Understand?"

Clinger took a drink. Slowly, he nodded.

"Here's what I think may work," Bino said. "The only thing a guy like Goldman will listen to, and don't get me wrong, the guy's got power that'd scare God to death. But all we can try to do is know something, and I don't mean you being an informant. I've told you before how I feel about snitches, I won't represent one. We need to know something that, if it comes out, is going to screw up Goldman's case. Then let him understand what we know, and understand that if he doesn't keep the heat off of you, we'll use it."

"What the hell could we possibly know," Clinger said, "that's going to scare the United States Attorney?"

"That he's doing business with a guy," Bino said, "that's had his own wife killed, and is making the state let this guy off the hook on a murder charge if he'll testify. Bad publicity is the only thing that'll scare Goldman."

"I thought Harris County already knew that."

"I'm not sure. Know it, maybe, but I don't think they've got evidence. I won't go into it all, Tommy, but that business down there in Harris County was nothing but a sham to get Rusty into jail where they could play with the guy. I don't think they've got piece of evidence one."

"Well, if they don't, what makes you think you do?"

"I've got connections even the U.S. Attorney doesn't," Bino said. "And I've already got feelers out. Pretty soon I think I may have something."

"You'll excuse me," Clinger said, "if that doesn't completely take the load off my mind."

"Excuse you? Sure I will," Bino said. "And there's a lot I can't answer. Such as, How did Harris County know where to look for Rhonda's body? Like I said, Tommy, I'm working on it." He reached across the table and took Clinger's drink. "In the meantime, you lay off the hooch," Bino said. He swallowed the liquor in two big gulps. The drink was bourbon, not Bino's favorite, sour mash to boot. "You go home and tell Molly you love her," Bino said, exhaling liquor fumes. "Before this is over, I might be doing enough drinking for the both of us."

21

AFTER CLINGER HAD GONE, DINO WENT BACK INSIDE JOE Miller's for one beer, just to be sociable. He ran into a couple of friends and made a night of it, half staggering into the parking lot at fifteen minutes till one and listing over to where the Linc was parked. He jabbed at the door lock with his key a couple of times, then finally got the hang of it, unlocked the door, fell inside behind the wheel, fished around in the glove compartment for an Elvis tape, and squealed rubber onto Lemmon Avenue with "Suspicious Minds" vibrating his eardrums. He was feeling no pain.

He drove out to Vapors North, weaving from one side of the road to the other and praying he didn't run across any squad cars, and crawled through the residents' lot at five miles an hour. Finally he inched the Linc into his numbered slot, proud that he didn't scrape the blue Mazda which was his next-door neighbor's pride and joy. He alighted and took two

steps toward the building, then halted. The suitbag he'd
hauled to Houston was still in the Linc's trunk. He went back,
opened the trunk, and hefted the suitbag. Then he staggered
across the parking lot, through the breezeway, and alongside
the pool. He listed sideways and nearly fell in the water twice
as he made his way to his apartment.

He'd already unlocked and opened his door before it
dawned on him that the lights inside his apartment were on.
Jesus, had they been on all week? No wonder his fucking electric bill was so high. Visible through the entryway were his giant Mitsubishi television screen and his fireplace of uneven
white brick. The TV was on; Whoopi Goldberg was interviewing Burt Reynolds. Bino paused, scratching his head. Had the
TV been on when he'd left on Tuesday? Jesus, he couldn't remember. He stepped inside and dropped his suitbag.

He sensed movement on his left. Hands the size of Christmas turkeys gripped his upper arms from behind. A huge
dark-haired young guy, wearing a dark suit and tie, rose from
the sofa and faced him. Bino was just drunk enough to grin.

"Dirk," Bino said. "How you doing?"

The last time Bino had seen him, Dirk had been a floor-
man/bouncer at one of Dante Tirelli's gambling joints, a con-
verted tennis club out in far North Dallas. He had a habit of
rolling his head around as he flexed his neck muscles, and regarded Bino as though he didn't think that the white-haired
lawyer was very funny. As his partner kept Bino's arms pinned
from behind, Dirk stepped forward and conducted a pat
search. He shook down both trouser legs from ankle to
crotch, ran his hands underneath Bino's belt, then moved his
open palms up both sides of Bino's rib cage. Bino giggled and
said, "That tickles." Dirk stepped back and wound up to throw
a punch.

From within the kitchen Dante Tirelli said loudly, "I want
you to hammer the fucking guy, I'll say so. I got a carload of
punks to choose from, I got to pick the one thinks he's
Sylvester Hambone. You two let our friend Mr. Phillips be." He
bent down and peered through the opening above the bar.

Dirk showed a disappointed leer and retreated to sit once

again on the sofa. The hands released their hold on Bino's arms, and he turned. He'd expected as much. His other old buddy from the gambling joint, about twice Dirk's age and bald as a billiard ball, with a thick neck and broad shoulders, nodded. Dirk did a lot of prancing around, Bino thought, but the older man was all business and a lot more dangerous. "What's new, Ralph?" Bino said.

"Ain't nothing new," Ralph said. He was chewing a toothpick, which he now shifted from one corner of his mouth to the other. "Good seeing you," he said, then sat down beside Dirk.

Tirelli had the refrigerator open, rummaging around inside. He wore an orange oversize knit golf shirt and tan form-fitting slacks. His hair was iron gray, his forearms sturdy muscle.

Tirelli said as he poked around, "All you got in here is cold pizza and a bunch of beer. Don't you keep no orange juice?"

Bino moved nearer the bar. He was sobering up in a hurry. "You look in the freezer?" he said.

Tirelli jammed his hands in his pockets. "Yeah."

"Then I got no juice."

Tirelli's square jaw tilted as he studied the floor. "You don't live too healthy, Phillips. You got beer and whiskey and pizza. Don't you ever take no vitamins?"

"My secretary, that's . . . Dodie, you don't know her," Bino said. "She's got all these catalogues, says I ought to be taking some beta-carotene. Last week I bought a bunch of carrots."

"You ought to listen to her." Tirelli bared his teeth like the wolfman, and Bino thought the burly gangster might charge around the counter and bite him. "You see these?" Tirelli said.

"Yeah, I guess so," Bino said. "See what?"

Tirelli ran his index finger across even upper teeth. "These. Sixty-two years old, all I got is a coupla fillings." He clicked his teeth together. "I go to the dentist maybe twice a year is all. Vitamin E, I take a thousand units twice a day. Got the gums of a fifteen-year-old."

Jesus, Bino thought, his teeth do look pretty good. Bino himself had one tooth, lower right, which was sensitive to cold, and Bino had wondered if he should have the thing pulled.

Tirelli found a large glass in the dishwasher, dropped in ice from the freezer, and filled the glass with tap water. "You want some? One of those fucking beers or something?"

In fact Bino had been thinking of a beer just before he'd entered his apartment. The mood had left him. "Nothing for me," he said.

Tirelli turned from the sink and raised his glass to his lips. "Oh, hey. I fed your fish. You oughtn't to go off and leave the fish without any food." He sipped.

Bino glanced at Cecil's tank. The Oscar looked contented, floating between waving fins, his eyes at half-mast. "Thanks," Bino said.

Tirelli reached beneath the counter. "Where you come up with this relic?" He stood holding Bino's Mauser pistol, the German make that Bino had taken as a fee from a burglar. The burglar was now doing ten years and likely wishing he had the gun back.

"A guy gave it to me. I thought it was in my bedroom."

"It was," Tirelli said. He indicated Dirk and Ralph, still seated on the sofa like the Rowdy Twins. "Those guys look around. It's what I pay 'em for." Tirelli laid the gun on the counter and came out of the kitchen. He waved come-on, said, "Let's talk in here," then led the way back to the living room. He then said, "I can't stand that fucking phony Burt Reynolds guy," switched off the television, and sat on the end of the sofa beside Dirk. Bino flopped in an easy chair. He was angry over having his bedroom searched, but realized that it wouldn't be smart to read the riot act to this trio.

"You look like you do some working out," Tirelli said.

"Push-ups," Bino said. "Sit-ups sometimes." It was a lie; the last time he'd tried push-ups he'd collapsed beside Cecil's tank and hadn't been able to get up for a quarter hour or so.

Tirelli slapped his own flat midsection. "You need to keep it up," he said. "Your age, what, forty-two?"

"Three," Bino corrected.

"Your age you can get by with a lot of shit. You wait ten more years it'll show. You don't watch yourself, time you're sixty you'll be running around looking like Big Bird, tall as you are."

Bino squared his shoulders the same way he had at the salad and juice bar, when the two young musclemen had smirked at him.

"Just a little advice," Tirelli said, "seeing as how we're sort of brother-in-laws. That what you call it, Dirk? Guys married to the same woman, huh?"

Dirk showed a broad grin, and Bino wondered briefly what Tirelli's trick might be, getting a smile out of the guy. Bino thought, Maybe I should ask to borrow Tirelli's joke book.

Tirelli propped an arm on the back of the sofa and sipped more water. "While we're talking workouts, I thought that might be what you had in mind, going out to the President's this afternoon. Las Colinas, that's awfully fucking far for you. They got no workout places closer in your neighborhood?"

Bino crossed his legs and thought, Uh-oh. He kept smiling and hoped his grin didn't look as terrified as he felt.

"You know, Annabelle," Tirelli said, then shook his head and grinned. "What a woman, huh? Annabelle, she really thinks she's independent, don't she?"

Icy prickles began at the base of Bino's scalp. "Yeah, I guess, at least she used to be. It's been a long time."

"Yeah," Tirelli said, "but you'll remember, right? Sure you will, brother-in-law. You tell Annabelle she can't do something, she's gonna do it come whatever.

"That's why," Tirelli said, sipping, "I don't press her. She thought I was watching her she'd really get uptight, might not give old Dante no pussy a coupla weeks or something, you know?"

"I can't imagine her not giving you any . . . cutting you off," Bino said.

"You'd know about that, brother-in-law." Tirelli bent forward and placed his glass on the coffee table. "So I don't keep

no official watch on her, but she's got to have protection. Even
a man like me, a man in the restaurant business, you never
know when some enemy's going to come fucking with a guy's
old lady. What's happened is, since Annabelle's been working
out, a couple of my guys getting really built up themselves.
Getting some legs on 'em, working those stair climbers. Good
for the guys."

"Really healthy," Bino said. He had a sudden flashback,
the noise of the electric stair climbers as he'd stood at the
President's counter talking to the cute little blond. He was
conscious of Ralph, chewing on a toothpick two spaces to
Tirelli's right.

"Now old Dirk here," Tirelli said, pointing sideways,
"when we got the call you'd been talking to her, Dirk wanted
to go find you and break your fucking neck."

Bino swallowed hard. "Old Dirk did, huh?"

"But I tell him, Naw," Tirelli said. "Annabelle, I trust the
woman, otherwise I wouldn't be married to her, right? Tell you
what, Dirk, I told him, I bet no sooner than Annabelle gets
home she tells us all about it, right? I tell you that, Dirk, or
not?"

Dirk grunted. Bino shifted nervously in his chair.

"And sure 'nuff," Tirelli said, "first thing when she comes
in . . . Hey, brother-in-law, all that working out's sure making
her look good in them leotards. You think?"

Bino smiled. "I didn't really notice."

Tirelli scowled. "You didn't? How come?"

"Well, yeah, she looks," Bino said, then cleared his throat
and said, "she's always had a cute figure, even back in college."

Tirelli shook his head, grinning. "Man, you college guys.
Got all the answers, right? I tell you, though, it's good for her
she brought the subject right up, that you'd been to see her.
Told me all about it. Now I'm an easygoing guy, but Dirk's a
young buck and gets real mad, he thinks somebody's hiding
something."

Tirelli leaned back and crossed his legs. "So she tells me
right up you're looking for some guy. I got to ask you, how
come you think I'd know something about somebody croaks

people? I got a place with the best crab claws in town, people lining up outside, what I want somebody croaked for?"

"I knew you used to live in New York," Bino said. "I just thought you might have some acquaintances."

"That I do," Tirelli said. "That I do, my friend, and I'll tell you something. Nineteen sixty-seven I come to Dallas, a little burg back then with what, four hundred thousand? You think I like the weather or something? Roast your ass in the summer, got no real good winter with Christmas snow and shit. Ain't no place in this world I like better than the City, so why you think I move down here?"

"Less competition in Italian restaurants?" Bino said hopefully.

"I know some people up there," Tirelli said. "You grow up Bronxside you get to know a few. I never was into a lot of heavy, you know, leg-breaking or whatever, but I knew some guys. Guy, maybe, had a sports book out on Long Island, another guy sold a few numbers up on Fifty-seventh between Broadway and Sixth. Those guys all had ten-block territories, you walk up around, say, just south of the Park you're doing business with another guy.

"But I moved to Texas," Tirelli said. "You know why? Because I wanted away from all that *Godfather* shit. All those guys into illegal stuff I don't need. What I am is a restaurant man."

"I like your spaghetti carbonara," Bino said. "With some broccoli on the side."

"Ain't bad, is it?" Tirelli said, looking thoughtful, crossing his legs. "But if I was into all this gambling and shit like people think, I'd have a couple of problems right now. The main problem I'd have, these New York guys have started doing business down here, and now I'd have a bunch of partners I don't want, guys from up north that run sports books and shit. Which makes me glad I'm in the restaurant business and not fucking in nothing illegal. But even if I got nothing to do with these New York people around here, I hear a few things. This guy you're looking for, Annabelle says he's in Dallas or Houston."

"One or the other," Bino said. "The people letting the contract wouldn't bring in anybody from way off."

"New York people got no such friends around here," Tirelli said. "And even if they did, nobody's going to do no hits without the right kind of direction. Not no New York guy that has any connection to these people I know. But I asked around. And there is a guy. Only there's a problem. This is a Philadelphia guy. This Liberty Bell motherfucker, he might be your boy."

Bino continued to grin, showing his attention, wishing that he hadn't had so much to drink. Dirk sulked while Ralph put a soggy toothpick in his pocket, fished out another packaged in cellophane, tore the wrapper away, and put the fresh toothpick in the corner of his mouth.

"This guy," Tirelli said, "is part of a Philadelphia unit that these New York guys don't know too good. This guy ain't too popular around because he's in that federal witness program. Funny thing is, the guy's got nobody to hide from, but hey, the feds going to support a guy, give him a new address, what's he care? The guy thinks some family's after him, but the people he snitched off to get in the program weren't connected to anybody made. They were some stupid fucking bankers up east, had this guy croaked was gonna testify against 'em, so who cares? And incidentally, my friend, that particular arrangement was outside this guy's family, so they'd cut him off before he got to be a snitch. But the guy wants to think he's hiding out, let him. Only time he's got a problem is if he wants to talk to the feds about any made guys. Then he's dead."

Bino said, "He's whacking people while he's in the protected witness program?"

"You seen that movie, too, huh?" Tirelli said. "Anybody talking about whacking people got it straight from the screen and don't know what the fuck they're talking about."

"That's me, okay," Bino said.

"But what's to prevent him?" Tirelli said. "He's got a pad, the government's paying the rent, all kinds of phony ID, who better to do a contract? Now, I'm going to do you a favor, brother-in-law. I got this guy's real name, address, and phony witness protection monicker wrote down on a card in my pocket." He patted the front of his shirt.

Bino straightened in surprise. "You've got the name and address of a federal witness? That's supposed to be Top Secret Number One."

Tirelli snorted. "You shitting me? We know, not *we*, these New York guys, yeah and Philadelphia guys, too. They can give you the address for every federal witness there is, tell you what time of day the guy takes a shit if you want to know. If the occasion comes up that he's a danger to somebody made, then we just off the guy. *They* off the guy, I'm getting to know these people so good sometimes I think I'm one of 'em."

"Easy mistake to come by," Bino said.

"Federal witnesses getting croaked," Tirelli said, "never makes no newspapers. The feds keep that quiet on account of it makes them look not so bright." He reached in his pocket and brought out a business card. "Now I told you there's a problem here."

"I knew it couldn't be this simple," Bino said.

"Chances are still this is your guy. He's been croaking guys for money all over ever since he's been in the program. Everybody knows it that needs to. But the thing is, he lives in Houston."

"That's sure the right location." Bino reached for the card.

Tirelli held the card to his chest. "Ain't finished yet. Guy lives in Houston but the word is, he don't do nobody *in* Houston. He's got to travel to take a job."

"Maybe he made an exception," Bino said.

"Not likely," Tirelli said. "This thing you're doing, the woman found in Houston? I was you, and this Philadelphia guy did her, I'd start thinking he done her someplace else. How the broad winds up in a Houston ship channel, that's a sixty-four-dollar question."

"If everything else fits," Bino said, "I'd still have to say it's probably him. I'm shooting from the hip anyway, and this is the best I've come up with. I owe you one."

Tirelli held the card gingerly between a thumb and forefinger. "Not for long do you owe me. We're fixing to get square."

Bino frowned. "How'm I going to do that?"

Tirelli looked to his right. "Ralph, the man's got a question."

Ralph regarded Bino deadpan, the toothpick dangling. "I heard."

"Okay," Tirelli said. "You got an answer?"

Ralph reached inside his coat. "That I do."

Bino tensed, ready to dive for cover.

Ralph pulled out an envelope-size folder, like the ones which usually held car rental contracts. "Won't cost you a thing, Mr. Bino. Beano, however you say it. We paid you up for a year."

Jesus, Bino thought, they've bought a life insurance policy. He gulped. "How much is the principal?" he said.

"Ain't much," Ralph said. "Thirty bucks a month or something."

"No, I mean, how much do you get if I die? Croak."

Ralph leaned forward to exchange glances with Tirelli around Dirk, who continued to look glum. Ralph said, "Die? You ain't going to die." He waved the folder. "This here's a membership at President's. The one close to you, just north of here on Belt Line Road."

"Just our little gift," Tirelli said. "Now you can get in shape all you want, only it ain't going to be necessary for you to drive all the way to Las Colinas. That membership ain't transferable, if you understand what I'm telling you."

22

MANCIL ADRIANI THOUGHT THAT LOS FUCKING ANGELES WAS one of the only places in the world where he'd less like to live than Houston fucking Texas. He wasn't sure, though, it might be a dead heat between the two. He moved nearer the window to peer down at bumper-to-bumper traffic on Wilshire Boulevard, eighteen floors below, then raised his gaze to look out across the Pacific Ocean toward Catalina Island. He squinted. Might be he was seeing some whitecapped breakers rolling toward shore, but could be an illusion due to his imagination and his wanting to see. A lady had told him during the elevator ride up that on a clear day one could see from the penthouse suite all the way to Catalina Island, but this wasn't any clear day. The smog was so thick that the autos on the Santa Monica Freeway, only a few blocks to the south, were barely visible, and no way was anything out at sea that resembled any fucking island. Catalina Island, Adriani thought.

Twenty-six miles across the sea, and all that shit. Man be lucky to see twenty-six *feet* in that pea soup out there. Wasn't as hot as Houston, that was a plus, but Jesus, what a choice between the two burgs. Give Mancil Adriani a Philly steak sandwich dripping with provolone any old time, a walk up to city hall and a seat in the park beneath William Penn's hat, share his sandwich with the pigeons and let the world go by.

He turned from the window, approached the man in the swivel chair from the rear, ran his finger underneath the cloth behind the man's head to be certain the gag was secure, walked around and sat on the desk facing the man. Adriani rested his palm-size Llama .380 on his thigh. The man's wrists were strapped to the arms of his chair and there was a wide spandex band around his chest, holding him upright. Socks were stuffed in his mouth, secured by spandex wound around his head. His salt-and-pepper hair was center parted and his eyes bugged out. The eyes were watery blue. He breathed rapidly through his nose. Got to slow his breathing, Adriani thought, the timing has to be perfect.

"I don't want you to worry anybody's going to shoot you," Adriani said. "Robbery, that's all that's going on here. You understand me? Nod your head." He snugged up his right gray work glove.

The chin moved up and down, the flesh slightly red below the spandex. The tightness around the eyes seemed to loosen some, the guy telling himself that at least he was going to live.

Adriani wore mustard-colored coveralls with Riverside Air Conditioning Service written in script on a white oblong patch above the pocket. He'd done time at El Reno with an old honky-tonk owner, a guy taking a fall for peddling speed to truckers stopping by. The guy used to say to Adriani, "You show me a sumbitch with a sign on his pocket, I'll show you a man that's fixing to get drunk and start some shit." The memory made Adriani smile. He reached out for the wrist nearest him and felt the man's pulse. Still fast, but not racing as much as it had been just a minute ago.

"So you can't get hurt," Adriani said, "unless you do something dumb like yelling for those secretaries outside. Far as they know I'm just screwing around with your thermostat, right?"

Another nod, the expression more calm. The chin lowered slightly, folds of the neck drooping over the pale blue collar and nearly obscuring the knot on the dark red tie.

"Now that we have this understanding," Adriani said, "I'm going to cut you loose. Then you're going to get up and hand me whatever's in that wall safe. Remember I'm holding this gun."

The man nodded rapidly as Adriani loosened the strap on the right wrist, paused to watch the red mark fade as circulation took hold. Just about right, Adriani thought. He undid the other arm, watching in satisfaction as the skin quickly regained its normal color. We walkin' and talkin' now, Adriani thought.

"Don't move," Adriani said, waving the pistol, going around behind the chair, glancing out the window at the ribbon that was Wilshire Boulevard, bumper-to-bumper traffic like toys. "We're taking it slow and easy, all right? I don't want you having a stroke on me." Adriani took the spandex from around the man's chest, stood back and rolled the stretchy stuff up like an Ace bandage as the man rubbed his wrists, then massaged the back of his neck. "I'm taking the gag off now," Adriani said, sticking the spandex bonds into his pocket. "Only, no talking. No quick movement, you don't start up out of that seat till I tell you. Hey, that's good, you're learning to nod without being told. Before I'm outta here we'll have it down pat, huh?"

Adriani removed the headband, reached around to yank the white athletic socks from the mouth, getting to the tricky part, cramming the spittle-dampened socks into his back pocket. He dug into his side pocket for the ring, slipping the ring onto his middle finger, being careful to avoid the quarter-inch pin protruding from the metal surface. He took a step back. "Now, don't look at me, I don't think you want to remember my face too good."

The man seemed collected now, breathing normally, sitting relaxed in the chair awaiting instruction. Adriani in-

clined his head for a side view, watching the red indentations
fade from around the man's mouth and under his nose. Working like a charm, Adriani thought. He clapped the man lightly
on the shoulder, saying, "Okay, time to move," and caught the
slight intake of breath, the quick sideways jerking motion of
the head as the pin pricked the skin. "On up now, over to the
safe," Adriani coaxed gently, liking now the man's expression
changing from one of surprise to a puzzled look, the man's
hand coming up to rub his shoulder where the pin had pene-
trated just enough so that it was too late for anything to save
this guy.

"The safe. Yes," the man said softly, then rose and took
one step as Adriani counted to himself, thousand seventeen,
thousand eighteen, the man stopping, turning to Adriani with
a look of pain, a remembering look, recalling with sudden
hopelessness the sticking of the pin. The sight of Mancil Adriani's pug-nosed face was the last thing the man would carry
with him to wherever people went when they weren't no more.
The man clutched his chest, his face relaxing once and for all
as he crumpled. His forehead bumped the edge of his desk as
he went to his knees, then pitched headlong to the floor.

Adriani bent over the corpse, satisfied himself that the
bonds and gag had left no telltale marks, and that this over-
worked fifty-one-year-old hotshot fucking business executive
was going down in history as a heart attack victim. Adriani
took his time, putting the tools carefully away in the box, sliding the ring and pin into a protective padded envelope, adjusting the thermostat to seventy-one degrees, and backing
out into the reception area while saying to the silent office
and dead man inside, "Sorry to bother ya, but the super says I
got to fix that thing today." The slim receptionist typing away,
not even aware that Adriani was standing there. She turned
and smiled impersonally as Adriani said, "That'll take care of
him, now I got to check the other one," then hurried into
Whitley Morris's office before it could dawn on her that
maybe this blue-collar air-conditioning asshole shouldn't be
barging in unannounced.

Morris was seated behind his desk, signing checks, and

looked up with a startled gasp. "I didn't know you were going to—"

"Won't take a minute," Adriani said, going in his toolbox for a screwdriver, moving to the thermostat, leaning over a mahogany credenza stacked with computer printouts to make an adjustment. "Now if it gets too hot in here, Whitley, you just turn this screw back to the left," Adriani said. He turned, grinning. "You gimme five minutes' head start, then you go in and find the guy. He's got a bad heart, what can you say? Job's finished." He went to the door. "Oh, and Whitley, send me one of them pictures of your new old lady. The one of her on the wing with her skirt blowing up around her ass, okay? Hey, I like the looks of that broad."

The overalls wound up tight and stuffed inside a big leather business satchel, the balance of the abericinine, vial and all, flushed into the City of Los Angeles sewer system, Mancil Adriani stepped out of the water closet in the men's room and washed his hands. He wore a blue-black Armani suit, thirteen hundred bucks off the rack at Houston's Galleria Mall and an extra three bills for the tailor, Mr. Rich-but-Conservative washing his hands in the eighteenth-floor men's room.

He left the building at the Wilshire Boulevard exit and carried his satchel a leisurely two blocks oceanward to Rodeo Drive. There he watched the women in knock-'em-dead dresses going in and out of the shops, banging hell out of the credit cards. It was an hour before Adriani hailed a cab, and he left then only because the smog was burning his eyes. Stinkhole that it was, L.A. sure did have the broads, that was one thing he'd have to say for the town.

One hour and fifteen minutes later Adriani stepped into a phone booth at LAX inside the Delta terminal. He punched in the zero before the area code and number, needing operator assistance in order to call collect, gazing out the plate-glass window at the airport traffic, yellow Hertz and red Avis buses. The elevated revolving restaurant stood on four legs like an attack bug from *Star Wars*. Adriani liked his own reflection in the glass, thinking he should dress in a suit more of-ten, go to some nice places with a classy piece of ass on his arm.

After the party had accepted the call, Adriani said, "I got your message off my machine. Why am I not surprised?"

He listened, a smile on his face for the benefit of passersby, nothing in his expression to indicate how ticked off he was. Then he said, "Why *should* I be surprised? I already found out you didn't tell me the fucking guy was a lawyer. Al-ways problems when you get one of those guys mixed up in . . ."

The voice droned in his ear as Adriani directed his smile to a uniformed Delta flight attendant, who stopped nearby waiting for the phone. Behind her she pulled luggage on wheels, tugging the suitcase along by a leather strap. Adriani said, "Just a minute," then smiled at the flight attendant once more and indicated a man down the way who'd just hung up and who was moving quickly toward the security gate. She nodded and hauled her luggage to the now-vacant booth.

Adriani bent his head and said into the mouthpiece, "If I got to I got to. Funny thing you got two broads to do, you only told me about one." He listened some more, rolling his eyes, then said, "Look. Tomorrow, same place." His expression changed to a scowl, replaced immediately by the public-image grin. "Hey, I give a fuck tomorrow's Saturday. Same place, I said. Up to you how you get there, but I'll tell you something. You forget me, somebody's liable to wind up hunting you. See you tomorrow." He bent his free hand and shoved his wrist against his side. "That's what I said. We get in shit over this, pal, you better hope they don't put us in the same cell to-gether. You're in a world of hurt if they do."

Within five minutes Adriani stood at the ticket counter, trading his one-way to Houston for an open-ended L.A.-to-Dallas-to-Houston, nodding his thanks as the agent explained about savings if he'd make a twenty-one-day advance purchase and stay over Saturday night. Then he poked his new ticket into his inside breast pocket, hefted his satchel, and walked quickly toward the metal detectors. The security gate re-minded him that he'd dropped one helluva good Llama .380

into a dimpster dumpster just outside the terminal. He hated to lose the pretty little piece but had no way to transport the gun to Texas with him. It nettled him as well that, in addition to the extra expense of the Dallas stopover, he was faced with the prospect of doing one more murder without compensation. When you're fucking with lawyers, Adriani thought, there's always loose ends.

23

FROM SEEMINGLY MILES AWAY HALF-A-POINT HARRISON SAID, "Gin."

Bino rolled over and sat up. Foul body oder assaulted his nostrils.

Seated on top of the covers, Half showed Bino a crooked grin. A deck of cards was split in two piles, one facedown, the discards up. Half's hand of cards was fanned out showing gin. Wimpy Madrick sat across from Half and was scowling. He turned his cards around so that Half could see them. "Thirty-nine," he said, his wizened head cocking to one side. "Thirty-fucking-nine." Bino closed his nostrils against the smell, which, strong as it was, was lighter than usual. When he was doing time in county jail, Wimpy really tended to ripen.

Wimpy started to drop the spent cards on top of the deck. Half reached out to stop him. "*Hoh-old* it," Half said. "I count forty-three."

Wimpy looked puzzled. "Lessee, then." He began to peel the cards out of his hand one at a time. "Three. Thirteen. Twenty-three . . ." Flop. Flop. Flop. Flop. He neared the end of the stack. "Thirty-nine. And four makes forty-three. Like I said, forty-three."

"You said thirty-nine," Half said. He picked up a pad and pencil. "That's out in the first two games." He marked the scores down, then tossed the pad aside. "Funny you made that error. Thirty-nine only puts me out in Game One." He squinted suspiciously.

Bino leaned bare shoulders back against the headboard. "You guys know there's a table out in the kitchen? Also maybe a table or two over at your own homes?" The air-conditioning whispered and blew a cool draft. Bino sneezed.

Half paused with the deck split in two parts, ready to shuffle up. "They got tables a lot of places. Those other places don't got you."

"Jesus, I need to sleep," Bino said.

Half shuffled the two stacks and pushed them together. "Jesus, you need to listen."

"Listen to what?"

"To Wimpy."

Bino opened his nasal passages. The odor was sickening. He closed his nostrils and breathed through his mouth. "I listen to Wimpy all the time." He sounded like a man with a cold.

Both men turned to look at him. Finally Half said, "Usually you listen to Wimpy telling how he's going to pay your fee soon as he makes a score, or how he can't pay you 'cause his last try for a score landed his ass in jail. Now he's got something to say."

"Yeah," Wimpy said. "I'm saying if these cards don't turn around I'll have to go to stealing to pay off."

"You'd be stealing anyhow," Half said. "This gives you another excuse." He threw a sidelong glance at Bino, then split the deck to shuffle again. "Wimpy's got something about Rusty Benson."

Bino pushed the covers aside and swung long legs over

the edge of the bed, and stood. "Why didn't you say so?"

"I just did," Half said.

Wimpy looked up. "Going to cost you."

"So what else is new?" Bino said.

"I don't mean deducting from my legal bill," Wimpy said. "I got to have cash."

Bino picked up his pants from a chair and fished in his pocket. "I'm a little short there." He snapped his fingers. "Half, you got a little cash you can let me have?"

Half's mouth tugged to one side. "Wimpy owes me already, from this gin."

"You'll be loaning it to me, not him. I'm guaranteeing your money." Bino grinned.

"Trouble is," Half said, "you owe me, too. From the last time you and I played."

"I'm good for it," Bino said. "You know that."

"I guess I can stand it," Half grumped. "But carrying every burglar and lawyer in town can get heavy."

Bino went over and entered the bathroom. In seconds he returned carrying a big fluffy towel, which he tossed in Wimpy's lap. Wimpy looked up, regarding Bino with one eye skeptically closed. "Take a shower, Wimp," Bino said. "If we're going to be visiting awhile, we need to be in the same room."

Bino couldn't say that Wimpy Madrick cleaned up pretty well, but at least the odor was gone. Wimpy came into the kitchen wearing overalls with suspenders, and no shirt. Dark patches sprouted from his underarms and naked chest. The hair on his head was soaked, combed straight back on the top and both sides, and Bino made a mental note to dispose of his comb and buy another the first time he passed a drugstore. Wimpy had a thin wrinkled face and a long skinny nose, and his bare arms looked like thin sticks. Bino's towel was draped around his neck. He flopped morosely down in a kitchen chair. "Your soap stinks," Wimpy said.

Bino was tilted back with his ankles crossed on the table. He wore running shorts and a T-shirt with COUNTRY 96.3 emblazoned across the chest, and blue Nikes with no socks. The printout from federal court was spread out across his lap, and he'd been going over Rusty Benson's cases. He'd earlier trekked out to the parking lot to retrieve his briefcase from the Linc, and had dumped his traveling clothes from his suitbag into one corner of the hall closet. He'd taken two Nuprin, but his sinuses still throbbed from his night on the town. "It's scented Irish Spring," Bino said. "Smells real nice."

"It stinks," Wimpy said.

Bino raised his voice. "Half, Wimpy thinks my soap stinks."

Half-a-Point Harrison was on the living room sofa, visible through the opening over the counter. He hunkered over the phone with his betting sheets spread out on the coffee table. It was a quarter to twelve; major-league baseball action would begin in fifteen minutes on the East Coast. The phone rang insistently. Half peered over his shoulder. "Hell, *Wimpy* stinks," Half said. "How's he going to know if the soap stinks?"

Bino said to Wimpy, "What kind you usually use? When you bathe."

Wimpy shrugged. "Some stuff I picked up down at the county. Last thirty days I done, I made off with five bars. Last week."

"The county furnishes Lava," Bino said. "Peel your skin off."

"At least it don't stink," Wimpy said.

Bino glanced at the printout. He'd already made check marks beside two cases, both handled by Rusty in Edgar Bryson's court, and he was less than halfway through the list. One was a cocaine possession charge, third offense. The guy had pled out and Bryson had sentenced him to ninety days in the federal section of Mansfield Jail. The federal guidelines for a third-time coke beef were anywhere from thirty to fifty months, depending on the amount of coke involved. A federal judge was required to state the reasons on the record anytime the sentence was less than federal guidelines, and Bino had made a note to look up the file jacket and see what Bryson had had to say. Bino dropped the printout on the table, lowered his feet to the floor, sat forward, and leaned on his elbows. "You look in pain, Wimpy," Bino said. Wimpy always looked as though he was in agony, and liked for people to inquire.

"Rotten tooth," Wimpy said, pointing at his jaw. "Need to see the dentist."

Bino pictured Dante Tirelli. "You ever take vitamin E?"

Wimpy gingerly laid his palm on his cheek. "Huh?"

"Vitamin . . . never mind. Let's hear your story."

"Oh, that. I done time with a guy."

"There's more guys you've done time with than that you haven't," Bino said. "What guy?" In the other room, the phone jangled once before Half picked up the receiver.

"Time before last," Wimpy said. "Maybe the time before that, I ain't sure. Three, four months ago. This was a boiler room guy."

"Oil?"

"Some oil, yeah. Stocks, anything where you can hustle the mooch over the phone, this guy did. Twenty, thirty salesmen on those 800 lines. Guy used to brag he done a half million a month sometimes, but most of those guys are fulla shit. Young guy, fast talker. I think it was the state securities people busted him."

Bino knew the type. The man would have been college educated, more than likely, with the salesman's easy manner about him. Bino pictured such a character bunking down in the same cell with Wimpy Madrick. County jail made for strange bedfellows. Bino interlocked his fingers behind his head. "High-rolling Harry," he said.

"You're getting the picture."

Bino glanced toward the kitchen counter. "You want coffee?"

"Black."

Bino stood, dug a clean cup from the dishwasher, picked up the glass pot from the Mr. Coffee burner, and poured steaming liquid. "So you were doing time with the guy," he said.

"Ninety days, you remember the beef. Burglary you got

reduced to misdemeanor trespass. This guy was in jail waiting for somebody to post bond. Which none of his buddies on the outside were in any hurry to do, it looked like to me. Every day the guy was saying he'd be out tomorrow. Two, three weeks this went on."

Bino set the coffee in front of Wimpy, picked up his own cup and poured a refill, adding powdered cream. "Let me guess. He borrowed commissary money from you."

Wimpy straightened. "How'd you know?"

Bino carried his coffee around and sat. "I know you. You're always a soft touch for these guys."

"So I am," Wimpy said, sipping, making a face. "These guys're laying around, got no smokes, ice cream. Kind of pitiful, you know?" He patted the front of his overalls, which had no pockets. "Speaking of which, you got a smoke?"

Bino thought for a second, then reached in a drawer for his lone remaining pack of Camel filters. He tossed the cigarettes to Wimpy, then furnished a disposable lighter and an ashtray swiped from Joe Miller's Bar. Wimpy lit, inhaled, and blew smoke toward the ceiling. "Hundred bucks he got," Wimpy said.

"That's a lot of ice cream."

"He smoked, too."

"Rusty Benson his lawyer?"

"Right on."

"So what have you got," Bino said, "that I'm interested in hearing?"

"Well, you damn near lost me as a client," Wimpy said, "when I seen how much good Rusty Benson does for this guy."

"Jesus, would *that* be a blow," Bino said. "You'd be in trouble having Rusty. I hear he makes his clients pay up."

Wimpy held his coffee in both hands, like a man accustomed to guarding his belongings. "This guy had a lot of heat. The D.A. was hollering for his scalp. It's tough when one of these pisswilly prosecutors gets a hard-on for a guy."

"You're telling me," Bino said.

"But first thing you know, the guy's over in federal court. Don't ask me, the state drops the charges and all of a sudden, boom, he's being indicted on a federal beef. Same thing, same case, only now the feds are charging the guy with mail fraud."

"That's done every day," Bino said. "His lawyer makes a deal with the feds to take the guy, the state always agrees to drop the charges once the feds step in. They got enough folks in their penitentiaries as it is. Federal jails got boo-coo room."

"I'm hip to that," Wimpy said. "So the next day he's shipped out to federal custody over to Mansfield. Last we see of him down at the county."

"Jesus, that's all you know?" Bino grabbed the federal case printout and ran a pencil down the list. "What's this guy's name?"

"Never forget it," Wimpy said. "Stanfield T. Morton. Always used the 'T,' like he's some kind of fucking big shot."

The name was on the list, all right, with the notation that the case had been transferred from state to federal court. To Judge Edgar Bryson, of course. According to the printout, the case hadn't been disposed of as yet. There was a notation, however, that Morton was currently free on his own personal recognizance. With a judge's cooperation the case could be set off practically forever. Bino looked up. "You know anything about this guy you haven't told me?"

Wimpy set his coffee down and sucked on his cigarette. The air was getting hazy. "Plenty," Wimpy said.

"Such as?"

"You forgot about the hundred simoleons this guy owes me. Softhearted I might be, but I don't forget these things. About a month after I'm back on the street, I'm out in North Dallas, close to Preston and Royal Lane. Minding my own business."

"Or casing one of those big homes out there," Bino said. "Or let me guess, you were looking for directions to Texas Stadium."

"Yeah, whatever," Wimpy said. "Anyway, I'm standing there with my hands in my pockets and, boom, there's the guy. Stanfield T. Morton in the flesh, cruising along in, get this, a fucking Jaguar. Hundred bucks he stiffed me for not two months earlier, now he's tooling around in a sixty-thousand-dollar auto."

"Those swindler guys," Bino said, "they get back on the street and in action . . ."

"They can come up with some bread," Wimpy said. "Now my friend Stanfield T., at this particular time he has the misfortune to stop not fifty feet from where I'm standing. I hotfoot it over to the curb, open the door, and slide into the seat right next to the guy. He looked like he seen a ghost. I hold out my palm and I say, 'Old buddy, How 'bout my hundred bucks?' He goes through the bullshit, you know? Plays like he's looking in his pocket, and guess what?"

"He doesn't have it," Bino said. "That kind of guy never does. He's forgotten to go to the bank or something."

"Yeah, it's always something. But it don't work this time with me," Wimpy said. "I lean back and I say, 'Well, until I get my hundred, you got you a companion. Where you go I go, *pardner.*' "

"That threat should have gotten you paid in a hurry," Bino said.

"He says, Well, I'm on my way to a meeting, where I'm going to, lessee, *close a deal*, I think this fucker called it. Says he'll meet me back at that same street corner in a couple of hours. I had a big picture of that so, 'Yeah, okay,' I tell him, 'you can close this deal with me along to make sure you ain't getting screwed.'

"I expected more bullshit, tell you the truth," Wimpy said. "But he throws the Jag in gear and away we go. First thing I know we're headed east on Northwest Highway, and guess where he was going?"

Bino pictured the area, Northwest Highway near Preston Road, and rolled his eyes. "Arthur's."

Wimpy's forehead tightened. "How the fuck you know that?"

"Lucky guess," Bino said. "It's the spot where a lot of heavyweights go."

"We roll into the parking lot," Wimpy said, "and one of these twerps in a uniform runs up and stands right in our path."

"Valet parking attendant," Bino says.

"Been me," Wimpy said, "I wouldda run over the little

shit, but not Stanfield T. He gets out like he's Donald Trump, gives the kid a bunch of shit about not scraping his fenders. Then Stanfield T. borrows a dollar to tip this punk. What an asshole, huh?"

"Well, maybe not," Bino said. "You don't tip something you're liable to find some dents."

"Not if the bastard wanted to keep all his teeth would he dent *my* car," Wimpy said. "Anyhow, in we go. It's about, five, five-thirty and it's happy hour."

"There a combo playing? Cute little singer, looks Oriental?"

Wimpy started. "How the fuck you know that?"

"I go there, to Arthur's sometimes."

"You're a big fucking sucker, then," Wimpy said. "Hey, you know it's two bucks for a beer in that joint?"

"It's expensive," Bino said. "Tell me something, Wimp. What were you wearing?"

"Slacks and a sport shirt. Why?"

Slacks and a sport shirt were Wimpy's idea of duding out. Likely the same outfit he'd worn to a sentencing once. The slacks were orange, the sport shirt bright green. "Just wondering," Bino said.

"We met these guys," Wimpy said. "Rusty Benson was one, and I don't mind telling you I was glad to see somebody that probably had a little scratch in his pocket. I was beginning to think my buddy Stanfield T. Morton was going to drink on me, at two bucks a beer. There were three of these guys at a big round table. One of 'em, this soft-looking guy in a fancy suit, kept telling about his own scam, some kind of deal selling Vegas tour packages."

"Jesus Christ," Bino said. "Pete Kinder."

Wimpy tugged at his ear. "How the fuck you know that?"

"I . . . just a minute, Wimp." Bino studied the printout in earnest, squinting, reading each name, finally pausing over the very last entry on the list. Kinder, Peter S. Mail and wire fraud, represented by Rusty Benson in Judge Hazel Burke Sanderson's court.

Case dismissed Thursday, three days after Bino had talked to Kinder at Arthur's; two days after Rusty's arrest in

Houston. Bino mentally kicked himself; he'd only been studying cases in Edgar Bryson's court. Jesus, if Rusty had been in
jail at the time, what lawyer had represented Kinder in the dis-
missal motion? Bino knew the answer to that one. Kinder's
charges had been set aside on the motion of the United States
Attorney. Goldman. Had to be in chambers, Bino thought,
back there in the judge's office with no one around to witness
what was going on. Goldman had dug up another stool pigeon. Bino said to Wimpy, "I met the guy once, with Rusty."

"The whole bunch of 'em," Wimpy said, "was buyin'
rounds and tippin' waitresses like it was going out of style. Except for Stanfield T., of course, the guy owes me the hundred
bucks which ain't got two cents in his pocket. Not for long,
though. The Pete Kinder guy comes up with a bankroll you
wouldn't believe, starts doling out money, one for you, one for
you, that kind of shit. Only time in my life when some high
roller tells me he's going to close a deal and it's not a lot of
bullshit. Kinder gives Stanfield, must have been five thousand
dollars, a hundred-dollar bill at a time."

"You get your hundred bucks?" Bino said.

"You shitting me? I snatched two of 'em before Stanfield
can get the money in his pocket and then give me some song
and dance. I been knowing this kind of guy for years."

"*Two* of them?"

"Yeah. A hundred he owes me plus a hundred for the irritation of getting fucked around for so long."

"You swiped an extra hundred," Bino said.

"Hey, guys like Stanfield, he never missed it. He was going
to tip it off to some waitress if I don't get it. These guys get a
big wad in their pocket . . . I got to make a living, you know?"

"Ever think of getting a job?" Bino said.

Wimpy's eyes widened. "What for?"

"Never mind." Bino glanced into the living room. Half
now had the fifty-one-inch Mitsubishi tuned in, a life-size Jose
Guzman on the mound, stretching, checking the base run-
ners, going into an abbreviated windup with ducks on the
pond. Half had taken off his shoes and had his stockinged
feet up on the coffee table. The phone sat ready near Half's

right big toe. Bino said to Wimpy, "You get any idea why this
Kinder was being so generous?"

"I figured it was none of my business," Wimpy said. "But,
yeah, I found out." Wimpy tugged on his earlobe. His hair was
drying, split ends frizzing out around the sides of his head.
"Stanfield tells me, in between drinking one highball after another, *four* bucks apiece for those fucking things and this is
happy hour. Stanfield tells me, he says, 'When things are going good I spread a little cash around. Give it to old Rusty for
investment purposes.' That way he gets busted, he's got credit
with the lawyer."

"Maybe you ought to try that yourself," Bino said. "Build
up an account."

"What Stanfield tells me, Rusty gives some of the money
to this Kinder guy, who salts it away with this stockbroker.
Then when any of Rusty's clients run out of cash, the broker
sells some off this account and feeds it through Kinder back
to the guy."

"You hear any of them tell the broker's name?" Bino said.

"He's the other guy sitting there at the table. These guys
all start getting boozy, they start toasting him. Larry some-
thing-the-fuck."

"You didn't hear his last name?"

"Might have, I don't remember. I ain't looking to make no
investments. I need a stash, I leave a little with this hooker I
know."

"Someone you trust," Bino said.

"Not necessarily," Wimpy said, "but if the hooker goes and
pisses my money off at least I can take it in trade. Some stockbroker loses your cash, what you going to do about it?"

"What did the guy look like, this Larry?"

"About your age," Wimpy said. "Only this guy's in better
shape, looks like he does something besides sit around on his
ass. Maybe lifts a few weights."

"I'm thinking about doing some of that."

"Well, you ought to. All you pretty boys, you don't realize
you get older you start to sag."

Bino patted his own midsection, picturing the health spa

membership which Tirelli had bought him. "Say, I know a guy that's a stockbroker, runs in some fast company," Bino said. "His name's Larry, come to think about it, I went to college with the guy. Guy with a thick head of hair, dresses nice . . ."

"I don't know about that," Wimpy said. "Could use some more color in his outfit."

"Maybe a little conservative for your tastes," Bino said. "He looks in shape, maybe like a defensive back."

"I don't know from shit about football players," Wimpy said. "What this guy looked like to me, maybe one of these nekkid dancers, only too old to wave his dong for the ladies no more."

"Yeah, but you get the idea," Bino said. "Larry Murphy, that ring a bell?"

"I told you, I don't remember. But that sounds like the guy. When the broads come over to the table, I thought he was gonna strip right there, the way he was flexin' his muscles. I can't stand assholes like that."

"They had women with them?" Bino said.

"I was about to tell you," Wimpy said. "All these guys, when they got money the first thing they think is getting some pussy. One of these broads was the dead lady. Rusty Benson's old lady, only I didn't know who she was till I seen her picture on television. She sat across from him, acted like she wasn't attached to nobody."

"This was a few months back?" Bino said.

"April, I think. Now, don't ask me, but this Kinder gives her a few hundred which she packs away in her purse. She and Benson don't hardly speak. Looking back on it, I think the only reason them broads dropped by the table was for her to pick up some money. I figured, none of my business, maybe she left something with this stockbroker to invest for her. Her and the other broad was talking about going home to change, like they were living together."

"Could have been," Bino said, "while Rusty and Rhonda were separated. They weren't getting along for a while, which would explain why they weren't on such friendly terms. Jesus, a roommate?"

"Roommate, housemate, how I know what the fuck they were sharing?" Wimpy said. "I thought I was giving you something new, till you said you already knew the broad."

"Not real well," Bino said. "I just saw her around. How could you miss her, the way she used to gallery golf tournaments in those bare midriff numbers. Had the flaming red hair."

Wimpy looked puzzled, then his features relaxed. "Oh. I ain't talking about the Rhonda Benson broad you said you knew. I mean the roommate."

Bino tilted his head. "I didn't say I knew any roommate."

"Yeah, you did. Right when I told you about Stanfield T. taking me to this joint. The singer with the band."

Bino had his mouth open to speak, but now paused. He frowned. "Jesus, you mean Carla?"

"I don't know her name, but yeah, the cute little Oriental-looking broad. Man, what I wouldn't give."

"Wimpy, you sure you're remembering right, that these two women were living together?"

"I got no problem with my memory," Wimpy said.

Bino leaned back and expelled air through his lips. Jesus, this was . . . He grabbed the printout, began with the first line, and went all the way through the list. No way could this be, not Carla. Nope, no Carla Carnes, nowhere. Bino felt somewhat better. Wimpy must have heard them wrong, Carla must have just stopped by the table during her break, maybe for a drink. There was a *guy* named Carnes on the federal printout, but no Carla. That's a relief, Bino thought, for a second there I thought . . .

Wait a minute.

He moved the pencil back up the list and stopped with the point beside the name Carnes, Christopher C. The other columns across read: 3, HAB Writ, Pending. Court 3 was Judge Hazel Burke Sanderson. The code in the second column meant that the old heifer had approved a writ of habeas corpus, which normally meant an order transferring a prisoner from the federal joint to a local jail so the prisoner could testify for the government in some poor schnook's trial. The writ for Carnes, Christopher C., was still pending, which meant that the guy was probably in federal custody out at Mansfield, where he would remain until the U.S. Attorney was finished with whatever he'd wanted the prisoner for to begin with.

Carnes, Christopher C.

Two C.C.'s, Carla had said.

Bino rocked back and looked at the ceiling. "Jesus fucking *Christ . . .*"

"Listen," Wimpy said, "you ain't fixing to have a seizure or something."

Bino sighed. "Naw, I'm all right. I'm just thinking, maybe I've been getting screwed in more ways than one."

"Everybody's getting screwed, one way or the other," Wimpy said. "You're just finding that out, huh?"

24

BINO WATCHED NIGHT FALL THROUGH HIS KITCHEN WINDOW. HE stared morosely out as the sun set, making way for twilight to crawl across the courtyard in dismal, ever-deepening shades of purplish blue. An occasional star twinkled bravely through the light Dallas smog. He continued to sit, his chin thrust out, his arms folded in disgust, his long legs stretched out to their fullest, his ankles crossed on the corner of the table. He'd fixed a Scotch on the rocks a couple of hours earlier but hadn't touched the drink. The dark amber liquid faded in color as the ice cubes shrank, then melted completely away. The Natalie/Nat King Cole duet tape he'd put on the stereo had long since run its course, and pops from the stand-up speakers occasionally punctured the silence.

Finally he swiveled his head. The kitchen was in darkness, the single courtyard gaslight throwing weak rays on the table and making shadows on the floor. The digital wall clock to the

right of Cecil's tank showed seven minutes after nine. Cecil's
eyes were closed, the Oscar floating motionless near the white
gravel on the bottom. Bino rose, flipped on the fluorescent
light over the sink, and poured the diluted Scotch down the
drain. Then he slouched disconsolately into the den, flipped
the tape over, and pressed the PLAY button. Natalie and Nat
crooned in unison into "A Blossom Fell," father and daughter
blending their voices across the gap of time. Bino flopped
down on the sofa and stared at the phone.

Finally he picked up the receiver and punched a number
in. After four rings a click sounded in his ear, then a soft and
friendly female voice said, "Hello?"

He got up and trailed the cord behind him as he walked
over to reduce the volume on the stereo. "Hi, Dode," he said.

There were four solid beats of silence, after which Dodie
said, "Hello." The word now followed by a period, the tone
less friendly.

Bino sank back down on the sofa. "I was just wondering
what was going on," he said.

"There were a few calls after you left the office yesterday. I
didn't bring the messages home with me. Maybe I should've."

"No, I mean," Bino said, moving his rump forward on the
cushion, "what's going on with you?"

"I'm pretty well caught up on the pending files. I should
have the next six months' docket on your desk Monday
morning."

"That's not what I was calling about."

"It isn't?"

"Nope. I was wondering, just, how you're doing. Maybe if
you've got a few minutes to talk."

More silence, followed by, "Let me guess. Your girlfriend
dumped on you."

He sat up straighter. "Why would you say something like
that?"

"Because nobody's shot at you that I'm aware of."

"Huh?"

"In the past nine years you call me at home for two reasons. Either somebody's dumped on you or somebody's shot

at you. If I think it over I might remember another reason, but it's always something that's got you all mopey."

"I'm not all mopey, Dode," he said, then under his breath murmured, "not exactly."

Her voice took on a cheerier tone. "You're not? Well, then, it was nice talking to you."

"*Dodie.*"

Ten more seconds of silence, then, "Yes?"

He leaned back and reclined his head. "You ever have anybody you thought you could trust, anybody like that lie to you?"

"Not anybody really important lately. The really important people don't care enough about what I think to lie to me. They just blurt out the truth and think it's—"

"Now wait a minute. You mean me?"

"—funny if I get upset. Why, no. Why would I be talking about you?"

"Well, *I* certainly care enough about what you think to . . . oh, hell, Dode, you know what I mean. It's why I confide in you."

"She *did* dump on you, eh?" Dodie said.

Bino looked at the ceiling. "Not entirely."

"Yes, she did. I can tell. Ha, ha."

"What I was wondering," he said, "if you're not doing anything, maybe I could come by."

"I have a date."

He looked at the clock. "Kind of late to be going out. With this Robert?"

"With this, that's my business. It's Saturday night, in case you don't know it. Things don't start jumping until ten, ten-thirty."

"I could be there in fifteen minutes. We could chat for a half hour or so."

There was a rustling noise on the line, likely Dodie switching the phone from one ear to the other. She'd be sitting on the edge of her bed, or possibly in her kitchen talking on the wall phone. "So I can sit at your feet and bow?"

"Come on, Dode, give me a break."

"Okay, I'll give you a break. I'll tell you what I think."

"That's what I want to hear," Bino said.

"I think that as a boss you're a jewel. As a guy, well, you've got fifteen years on me, and you've got the maturity of a teenager."

"I try to think young," Bino said.

"I think you go around chasing everything with a skirt on, and that whenever your moral deficiency gets the best of you, you call up anybody that'll let you cry on their shoulder. I just resigned from those ranks."

"You're not being fair."

"So the lesson is," Dodie said, "if you're going to make your bed, you have to pay the fiddler."

"That's if you're going to dance," Bino said. "If you make your bed you have to lie in it."

"You ought to know," Dodie said. "You've sure laid in a few."

"*Moral deficiency?*"

"So the thing is," Dodie said, "that if you're going through life as a continuation of adolescence, that's your business. I just work there. You and your friend Barney can get conked every single night of the world, and you can sidle up next to every female you see at the bar and show her a pantomime of your old hook shot. But whenever you feel these pangs of remorse, don't come crying to me. My shoulder's wet enough as it is." In the background Dodie's doorbell ding-donged. "That'll be him," Dodie said. "So, see you on Monday, boss. Enjoy your mopery, okay?"

After Dodie snubbed him, Bino spent nearly three hours going over the state and federal court lists around five times each. He was glad he hadn't drunk any Scotch, and during his three hours of study he sipped ice water. For what he had in mind, he needed a clear head.

The legal shenanigans in which Rusty had been involved for the past three years or so didn't seem to be as far-reaching as Bino had first thought, and of that he was glad. To Bino's

way of thinking, the justice system as a whole stunk to high
heaven to begin with and could do without additional black
eyes. He'd located five more federal cases—all in Edgar
Bryson's court, all clients whom Rusty had represented—that
reeked of under-the-table carrying-on. All of Bryson's Bible-
banging and public display of being tough on crime now
turned Bino's stomach. Judge Hazel Burke Sanderson had
been a thorn in Bino's side ever since he'd been practicing
law, but at least the old heifer was honest. Bino wondered
what goods Rusty must have on Bryson to turn a judge whose
salary was a hundred and forty thousand a year. Must be
something heavy, Bino thought.

State court was a horse of a different color because, as op-
posed to the federal system, state district judges had little or
nothing to do with sentencing under a plea bargain agreement. In a state beef, the judge accepted whatever sentence
was agreed on between the defense lawyer and the prosecutor. Bino had located what he was sure was a connection in
Rusty's wheeling and dealing on state cases, a third-chair
felony prosecutor in the 476th District Court named Arnold
Bright. In seven different cases—one a habitual felon rap
plea-bargained down to ninety days' county time—where
Bright was the prosecutor, Rusty had made deals that Houdini
couldn't have negotiated. Bino knew Arnold Bright, a guy who
played a lot of golf (and gambled high as a kite on the course,
Bino had heard), drove a BMW, and lived in a twenty-five-hun-
dred-dollar-a-month town house behind the wall at Northwest
Highway and Preston Road. The exclusive address was far outside Bino's own income bracket, and completely out of the
question on an Assistant D.A.'s salary unless the guy had something going on the side. The lure of big bucks was a tough
thing to cope with, Bino knew. But in his own early days in
practice he'd rented a garage apartment in East Dallas and
had nursed a 1960 Chevrolet Impala through two transmis-
sions and a blown head gasket, and as far as Bino was concerned, whatever happened to Arnold Bright was just tough
shit. He had no sympathy for the guy.

One judge, one prosecutor. And a guy like Rusty Benson

to bring the whole mess together. Bino tilted his glass, glugged cold water, and crunched vigorously on an ice cube.

At fifteen minutes to one in the morning he trudged into his bedroom, stripped, and put on old faded jeans and a short-sleeve Levi's shirt, letting the shirttail hang out around his hips. Then he stuffed his bare feet into scuffed and dirty Nike sneakers, snatched his car keys from the dresser, poked twenty dollars into his pocket—which was all that was left of the hundred he'd bummed from Half-a-Point Harrison in order to meet Wimpy Madrick's demands for giving information—turned off all the lights except for the lone bulb above Cecil's tank and the fluorescent over the kitchen sink, and left the apartment. He skirted the pool, underwater lights casting wavering blue-green shadows on the concrete, went through the breezeway, and crossed the parking lot. He climbed in the Linc, and within ten minutes was just another pair of headlights headed west on LBJ Freeway. Office buildings were outlined in the darkness like squared-off mountain ranges.

He arrived in Duncanville at a few minutes before two. When he'd been in high school, his hometown of Mesquite had had quite a basketball rivalry with the Duncanville Farmers, and back then he'd known his way around the small South Dallas County town of Duncanville pretty well. No longer. Instead of the dusty town square, lone main street, and drive-in movie Bino remembered, Duncanville had grown into a mini-metropolis complete with freeways and shopping malls. He'd been to Carla's duplex only once before, when he'd driven her home on the morning after he'd met her, but thought he wouldn't have much trouble finding the place. Was he ever wrong. After four or five incorrect turns and doubling back, which found him at the same intersection where he'd begun his search, he stopped in an all-night drive-in grocery and bought a map. Then, stopping every block or so to turn on the interior lights and check his directions, he finally parked in front of the duplex at a quarter to three. He got out and looked around. Up and down the street, random porchlights glowed.

Though he'd followed the map carefully, he still wasn't

certain he had the right place. So, looking right and left, and fearing any second he'd hear either a warning yell or the blast of a shotgun, he crept up and opened the mailbox. He thumbed a Bic disposable lighter to read the top envelope on the stack, and indeed it was a water bill addressed to Carla. After shutting the mailbox, he walked across the lawn to the porch. The house was a squatty one-story with a shingled roof, identical on either side of the wall separating the two living quarters. He took one step up onto the concrete porch and paused to look around.

He seemed to be the only person stirring, and given the hour, wasn't surprised. Cars, pickups, and minivans sat in driveways up and down the block, and parallel along the curbs. Across the street from the Linc sat a dark four-door sedan, either a Ford or a Chevy, and Bino thought that someone was behind the wheel. He squinted. He must have been imagining things.

He tried the doorbell, and a high-pitched *ding-dong* sounded from within. He waited. No one came. He rang the bell a second time. Still nothing.

There wasn't any car standing in Carla's drive. When he'd brought her home the morning after he'd met her, he seemed to recall a little red auto. Well, she'd have to show up eventually. He sat down on the porch, leaned back against the lone wooden pillar, and stretched out his legs. In seconds his eyelids drooped. His head sank down on his chest, and a series of deafening snores split the silence of the neighborhood.

As the white Lincoln Town Car pulled up to the curb and the tall guy got out, Mancil Adriani thought, Who the fuck is *that* long drink of water? Guy must be six-six or so, kind of a shifty-looking character in jeans and a denim shirt, looking all around as he approached the broad's mailbox. The jeans were ankle length and the newcomer wore no socks, which Adriani personally thought was disgusting. Guy going around without socks must be some kind of fucking hillbilly.

The man approached the mailbox, paused to look up and

down the street, then opened the box and reached inside. Can you believe this shit? Adriani thought. Guy driving a Lincoln running around dressed like some street asshole, now he's robbing the mail. Adriani had met some of these types in the joint, guys who swiped old ladies' welfare checks, and personally had no respect for the fuckers. If he hadn't had business, Adriani might've called the police and turned the guy in. He reached down on the seat beside him, felt the grip on the Beretta .380 automatic which had set him back fourteen hundred bucks from a guy in North Dallas who'd guaranteed the gun to be untraceable, then touched the handles on the wire cutters with which, a half hour earlier, he'd disconnected the telephone. What luck, huh? Not only was the broad not at home, she was about to get her mailbox burglarized.

A beam from a streetlamp illuminated the stranger, and what Adriani had thought was a goofy hat of some kind turned out to be a mop of snow white hair. He's going to steal mail, Adriani thought, he needs to cover his head. Somebody'll pick that hair out of a lineup in a minute. The guy stuffed the mail back inside the box and headed across the lawn to the house. She's got no welfare check, Adriani thought, now he's breaking in.

The stranger paused, turned, and squinted directly at Adriani's rented Fairlane. Adriani cursed under his breath and sank down out of sight, grabbing up the Beretta and easing back the hammer as he did. He waited, holding his breath, then slowly raised up and peeked out. Jesus, Adriani thought, now he's ringing the doorbell. Real smart asshole, waking up the whole fucking neighborhood. What he needs to do is go on inside. If somebody's home, either blow them away or run like hell.

What the fuck is this? Adriani thought, now the guy's sitting down on the porch. Sitting down, leaning back against the pillar and . . . Adriani heard a noise, sat up straighter, and turned his ear toward the porch. Jesus Christ, he thought, the fucking guy's snoring his ass off. Doesn't even have enough sense to go around the side of the house where nobody's going to see him.

Adriani brushed lint from his perfectly ironed chinos and tugged on the sleeve of his perfectly ironed knit polo. He clicked the .380's trigger and eased the hammer softly into the slot. Doing the woman was just part of business. Killing the dumb white-haired bozo was going to be a bonus.

A sweeping beam of light shone in Bino's face for an instant, then moved on. He opened his eyes as a red Mustang pulled up in the drive and stopped. He checked the time; three-thirty now. Jesus, he'd been asleep for a half hour; anyone seeing him had likely wondered what the big dumb white-haired bozo was up to. He yawned, then used the wooden pillar as a crutch to haul himself up into a standing position.

The Mustang's lights extinguished and Carla got out, dark hair bouncing in the light of the moon. She was dressed for a rock performance, in skin-tight dark pants and a bolero top with puffed sleeves. She looked toward the Linc, then centered her gaze on the porch. She took a frightened step backward, and for just an instant Bino thought she was going to dive behind the wheel and make a run for it. Then she came forward, the fleeting hesitation having told the story, the welcoming smile nothing but window dressing. Bino folded his arms, leaned against the pillar, and waited for her.

She came up on the porch with the smile painted in place, her glasses dangling from a chain around her neck. She lifted the glasses and put them on, then stood on tiptoes and nuzzled his jaw. "Whee, my knight-errant awaits," she said. "We came in from Houston this morning. Where have you been? I've been trying to call you."

He searched his memory. His visit with Wimpy had lasted a couple of hours, and before that he'd been asleep. He hadn't left his apartment all day, and his answering machine had been turned on the entire time. He recalled glancing at the red light on the machine as he left for Duncanville. The light hadn't been blinking. "I must have been out," he said. Somewhere on his left, a cricket *chirupped*.

"We've got a new gig, down in Deep Ellum," she said. "I wanted you to come by."

He played along. "Just as well, I was beat. Don't know if I could have survived another night in a club."

"It's what you're used to," Carla said. "I never get sleepy before four in the morning."

Bino recalled the frenzied nights they'd spent together in Houston. "I noticed that," he said.

She giggled. "Well, come on in, hoss." She unlocked the door and entered the duplex, reaching around the jamb and turning on a light as she did. Bino followed her in.

She'd done a neat interior decorating job. On all four walls were photos of Carla in performance; some showed her in cocktail dresses while in others she wore black skimpy come-on outfits, something like Madonna. In each photo she held a microphone; in two of the pictures strumming guitars were in the background. Another featured Dondi, drums and all, visible over her right shoulder. There was a mock fireplace in the living room, and the centerpiece of the mantel was a shiny gold trophy. The statuette affixed to the trophy was a girl in a milkmaid costume, hoisting something over her head which resembled a lumpy football. Bino strolled over and read the inscription. Sweet Potato Queen, 1984. Carla Pease. Many moons and many dreams ago. Bino turned to face her and leaned a shoulder against the mantel.

She closed and locked the door and secured the chain. "Hot set tonight, even had Dondi do a gangsta rap number. Funny crowd down in Deep Ellum, some pretty nice people, but, God, a lot of weird-looking freaks. I practically ran to my car when the show was over." She spoke rapidly and avoided looking directly at him.

Her furniture was light tan imitation leather. Bino sat in an armchair, crossed his legs, and didn't say anything. The thermostat kicked in the air-conditioning. A vent blew soft cool wind.

There was a stand-up bar near the entry to the kitchen, dark stained wood with ornate carvings. Carla bounced over and stood behind the counter, then cocked her head. "Scotch, right?"

"That's what I drink," he said.

She brought up two rock glasses, a padded bucket, and a

pair of tongs. As she dropped half-moon shards of ice into the glasses, one shard at a time, she said, "I think I'll join you."

Bino swept his gaze around the walls. "I like your pictures."

"There's this guy, he's a love, takes publicity shots around town. Those were freebies." She bent and disappeared from view for an instant. A cabinet opened and closed, then Carla stood up holding a half-gallon of Dewar's. "I've got no J&B. I only just met you, next time I'll . . ."

"You got any pictures of the two C.C.'s?" Bino said.

She tried to fake it, her lips working thoughtfully as she poured. "The two . . .?"

"You know," Bino said, "Carla and Chris. The loving couple."

"I might have some old shots in an album in the closet," she said. She set the bottle down, making no move to screw the cap back on, her expression showing dread, her eyes betraying her knowledge of what was about to come.

"Who handled you guys' divorce, Carla?"

She rediscovered the drinks, brought one to him, then sat on the couch and curled one leg up underneath. Thigh muscle tensed under satin stretch material. "Some lawyer, I don't really remember."

"Well, do you remember the year?"

She lifted her drink to her lips and sipped, regarding him over the rim of her glass. She swallowed. "Why the questions?" Calmer now, more matter-of-fact.

Her stereo was an old-fashioned console, dark wood carved to match the bar. He carried his drink over and looked through her cassettes. She had a few rock albums, some easy-listening stuff, but most of the tapes showed handwritten labels. He selected one marked "Golden Nugget, February 7, 1988." "You mind?" he said.

She shrugged. "Be my guest."

He turned on the power and inserted the cassette. Classy combo music preceded a male-female vocal. "That's What Friends Are For," the song that Dionne Warwick, backed by Stevie Wonder and a host of others, had made into a megahit. Bino liked Carla's rendition more than the original. He lowered the volume. "That your husband?"

"Yes. *Was* my . . ." Her gaze lowered. "Yes," she said.

He returned to his chair. "You don't remember the name of the lawyer? It could be important someday, if someone wants to contest something. You never know."

Her chin tilted angrily. "Why don't you quit dodging around?"

He blinked. "Why should I? *You've* been dodging around."

She glanced at the ceiling. Condensed moisture dripped from her glass onto her white puffed sleeve. She didn't seem to notice. "Wait here," she said, then got up quickly and left the room. She returned in a moment carrying a shoebox, which she dropped in Bino's lap. Something in the box rattled. Carla retrieved her Scotch, then testily resumed her seat on the sofa. "They're in mothballs. You satisfied?"

Bino set his drink on the floor and lifted the lid of the box. Inside was a velvet palm-size jewelry case sitting on top of some newspaper clippings and more photos. He lifted the case and opened it. The engagement stone was a carat-and-a-half blue-tinted sparkler, the wedding and engagement bands matching beveled gold. "You-all must've done pretty well moneywise on your gigs," Bino said. On the stereo Carla and Chris blended their voices in the finale. Smooth, strong, and enough to raise goose bumps. Bino pictured Donnie and Marie a few years back when they'd stunned a Super Bowl crowd into pin-drop silence with their rendition of the national anthem.

"The drug trade was better," Carla said.

"It always is."

"Till the bust in San Francisco," she said. She studied him, her gaze now steady, her mouth relaxed. "How much do you already know?" she asked.

He leaned back, closed the jewelry case, set the shoebox on the floor, and closed the lid. He picked up his Scotch and sipped. The digital numbers on the face of her stereo now showed ten to four. In another hour it would be summer dawn. "Some," he said. "What did Goldman promise you?"

"A release for Chris, with the San Francisco judge's approval. Which he's already showed me in a letter. Termination of my own probation." She studied her lap. "I did six months inside."

"Lexington, Kentucky?" Bino said. "One of the female joints."

"Pleasonton, California. They had men, too."

Bino nodded. "Sure, a coed pen. Another brilliant federal idea, put the boys and girls together and then tell them not to touch. Works about as well as everything else they do." He swallowed. The Scotch burned a bit going down. "If you got six months, that would make old Chris worth at least fifteen years."

Her mouth puckered sadly. "Twenty. Of which he has to do a shade under seventeen, unless I can help him get out. There's no federal parole."

"Don't I know it," Bino said. "And that's about status quo, on a husband-and-wife arrest. Six months for you, twenty years for him. If you're going to walk on the shady side, be female. That's what I tell my clients."

"I can't help my gender, Bino."

"He can't help his, either."

She took a big glug and swallowed hard. "I can't do anything about it if I've made you hate me. I didn't try to do that."

The song now playing was "Goin' to Jackson," a number Nancy Sinatra had done years ago with a country basso whose name Bino couldn't recall. Might have been Johnny Cash, he wasn't sure. The two C.C.'s were a knockout act. "You didn't?" Bino said. "I like to know when women are married. Gives me a choice, at least."

"*Dammit . . .*"

"You a plant?" Bino said. "Or did you meet Rusty and Rhonda by accident?" He grinned. "The two R's."

Carla adjusted her position on the sofa and hooked one arm over the back. Her breasts pressed out against satin fabric. "That much I told you was the truth. I knew them around the clubs at first. I came home one night, just about this time in fact, to find Mr. Goldman and two FBI agents sitting on the couch. I nearly fainted."

"And he had a big old dossier on you," Bino said.

"Right."

Bino leaned forward and rested his forearms on his thighs. "He wasn't bluffing, Carla. If you'd shot him the finger, told him to get lost or something, your probation was history."

"Oh, he told me that up front. Said he could have me back in Pleasonton in forty-eight hours if he wanted."

"He could, too," Bino said. "So when Rhonda and Rusty split, he used your place as a free safe house for her, and you to slip him information about whether she was being a good little cooperator. How long she live with you?"

Her mouth quivered. "You know about that."

"Yep. Found it out today."

"About four months. Rusty was siphoning her some money, to keep her quiet. Mr. Goldman told her to play along."

"Through a stockbroker and a guy named Kinder."

She nodded. "It wasn't a real fun four months for me. I couldn't stand Rhonda. She was nothing but a whore."

Bino snickered, then felt guilty.

Carla's gaze smoldered. "Think what you want about me. At least I never spread my legs on Mr. Goldman's cue."

"Sure, you didn't," Bino said. "You thought I was Tom Cruise. Made you quiver just to be in the room with me. I'm just dumb-lucky I didn't tell you everything I was doing to defend Tommy Clinger. Eventually I probably would have, and you could really have filled old Marv in. Jesus Christ, what did they do? Have a guy in Arthur's giving you the high sign and pointing at me?"

"Listen," she said, then sighed and said, "I wasn't faking it with you, and that night I wasn't putting you on. I am nearsighted, can't see worth flip, and I thought you were the judge. It was the next day when Mr. Goldman called me about you. They . . . had someone taking pictures and got us on film."

"Not at my apartment, I hope."

"Nothing that revealing," Carla said. "Just some shots of us at the table in Arthur's. One as we were leaving in your car. Those are the only pictures I've seen. I don't think there are any more."

"I guess Goldman wanted to tie me in to the conspiracy," Bino said. "Hell, I'm lucky he's not indicting me."

"That's what he wanted to know at first," she said. "Whether you were involved."

"Sure. And then rigged you up to take me to Houston with you."

She hugged herself. "No, that was my idea. It wasn't all a fake."

Bino's chin lifted, then dropped. "Come on, Carla. I guess it was your idea to act like it was big news to you that Edgar Bryson was a judge."

She looked at her knees. "No. That was Mr. Goldman's idea."

"Jesus, you change your story so much, I don't know what to believe."

She met his gaze. "Try me, then. What do you want to know?"

"Okay. For starters, which one of you lovely young ladies had the assignment of getting Bryson to talk?"

"Rhonda was the one. Bryson is nothing but a horny old bastard, and while she was in bed with him he told her lots of things. I told you, I'm no whore. You can believe that, or you can go to hell."

"Which she repeated to you?" Bino said.

"Kinda sorta," Carla said. She remorsefully lowered her chin. "She volunteered. I didn't ask."

Bino's expression softened. "Oh, Carla, the way Goldman plays you people. He'd coach her exactly what to tell you. When she gets on the stand to testify against Bryson, you can back her up. It's called corroboration, babe. Only with Rhonda dead, what she told you becomes hearsay. Your testimony's no longer worth two cents to Goldman."

"He says it still is."

"I don't know how. About the only thing he could use you for, after Rhonda died, was to pump me for information. You'd be his pipeline to the defense. Where'd he want you to hide the bug, Carla, seeing as how you were buck naked most of the time? Under the pillow?"

"Stop it." Tears welled in her eyes. "I don't sleep with anybody unless I want. Since I've been married, you're the only one."

Bino glanced at the stereo. "You got a tape of the 'March of the Sweet Potato Queen'? Jesus Christ, Carla."

"Chris has been locked up nearly five years," Carla said. "I did six months, just like I told you, and I've been on probation four and a half years myself. Not once in all that time, until you."

Bino scratched his forehead above his eye. "At this point it doesn't matter whether I believe you or not."

"It matters to me," Carla said.

Bino studied her, the lovely slanted eyes and buttermilk skin, narrow waist, taut muscular thighs. It would be a real ego-builder to believe her, sure it would. Something he'd always wonder about.

"One thing bothers me," Bino said. "What the hell was Rhonda doing running off to Houston?"

Carla showed genuine shock. "You don't know?"

Bino frowned. "Know what?"

She got up, crossed over, and leaned on the bar. Next to Dodie Peterson, perhaps, she had the most gorgeous fanny Bino had ever seen. She regarded him over her shoulder. "Rhonda never went to Houston," she said.

Bino's teeth clicked together. "Huh?"

She pointed toward the rear of the house. "Rhonda stayed in the spare bedroom back there, and Mr. Goldman had the room wired from A to Z, for when the judge came over. Mr. Goldman didn't want to chance meeting Rhonda in person, he'd have me get the tapes and bring them to him. Some kind of legal rigamarole."

"It's called 'chain of custody,' " Bino said. "Without somebody to testify who-all's had possession of the tapes, from the time they were made, Goldman can't get them into evidence. He'd have Rhonda get on the stand and say she made the tapes, then have you say you carried them from her to Goldman. Bores juries to death, but it's something they have to do."

"That last night I got home from the club around four in

the morning." Carla retreated from the bar, sat on the floor Indian style, and leaned her elbow on the coffee table. She looked up at him. "God," she said. Her lower lip quivered.

Bino watched her, not saying anything.

She raised her gaze. "It had been raining to beat hell, and had just let up to a sprinkle sort of, but it was still thundering and lightning like I don't know what. Made the whole thing even more horrible. I still have nightmares. God, she was . . ."

Cold anger built up, low in Bino's chest and working its way up through his neck as realization dawned. "*You* found her," Bino said.

She nodded, and her look of fear left no doubt that she was telling it just like it was. "Her car . . . her white Cadillac, you know? It was parked, about the same place your Lincoln is, at the curb. Slanted funny, with the rear wheels sticking out. I put on my raincoat and went over to look inside. God, I wished I'd never seen it. She was . . ." Carla covered her face.

"I saw the autopsy report," Bino said. "What did Goldman tell you to do?"

She lowered her hands. Her mouth twisted as she raised an eyebrow.

"Goldman," Bino said. "He told you to call him at once if anything went wrong, didn't he?"

"How did you know that?" she said.

"Carla," he said, "if I had a dollar for every time Goldman's . . . just leave it that I know how he operates, okay? What did he tell you to do?"

"Nothing," Carla said. "He said he'd take care of it."

"What about the police?"

"He told me not to call them. That he'd take care of it."

Bino pounded his forehead with the heel of his hand, twice. "Rusty was tooling his clients around. He put out the word he was looking for Rhonda, when all the time he knew right where to find her. Bryson had to know about the hit. Or maybe he even helped arrange the damn thing." His expression softened as he looked at Carla. "For your sake, I hope you've got your arrangement with Goldman in writing, babe. I hate to be the bringer of tidings, but old Marv's been known to crawfish when things don't go just right."

"He's already had Chris transferred from California to Texas," she said. "He's out in the Mansfield Jail. I've . . . been to see him today." She tugged on her earlobe. "I was fibbing when I said I tried to call you. I was worried about facing Chris, after what happened with you. Now I don't know if I can look either of you in the eye."

Bino watched her. "If he's going ahead with the deal he made you, you must have heard Bryson say something in person."

She shook her head. "I never did. But Mr. Goldman wants Bryson to think I did."

Bino frowned.

"Mr. Goldman says he likes for his quarry to sweat," Carla said.

"Jesus Christ, he used that word? His *quarry?*"

She nodded.

"What an asshole," Bino said.

"He says that he's let Bryson know I'm still around as a potential witness against him."

Bino's forehead tightened. "How'd he do that?"

"Through another judge," Carla said. "A woman . . ."

"Old Hazel," Bino said. "Goldman would. The old heifer could drop enough hints at coffee, in judges' meetings and whatnot, that Bryson would be on pins and needles." He rose. "I'm going to call somebody."

Her mouth softened in surprise. "Who?"

"A county cop I know, and maybe a D.A. The cop's name is Hardy Cole. I doubt the county can do anything about what Goldman's pulled up to now, but at least I want them to know there's been a murder in their jurisdiction that the feds neglected to clue them in about. Hardy will want to hear about this bad enough that he won't mind me waking him up. I don't care what time it is."

He crossed over to the phone where it sat on a low table beside the stereo. The two C.C.'s were now crooning "Take It to the Limit" in chill-bump unison. Bino would like to have caught the act in person. He picked up the receiver, then paused with his fingers over the digital keyboard. He wasn't getting any dial tone. He jiggled the disconnect switch. Nothing. He turned and said to Carla, "You paid your phone bill?"

She rose from the floor, looking concerned. "Sure. I just made a call this afternoon. Why, is there . . .?"

Bino was looking out the front window, the shade pulled halfway down, light from the living room casting a parallelogram on ragged Bermuda grass. He replaced the phone in its cradle. "Douse the lights, Carla," he said. "Right now."

As the lights went out and the windows darkened, Mancil Adriani massaged the back of his neck. They'd taken their time about it, huh? The white-haired bozo must be dumber than he looked, shooting the shit with the broad instead of hauling her off to the sack to begin with. Broad that looked like that one, the white-haired bozo must be dumber than hell.

He pulled on surgical gloves, snapping the latex up around his wrists, picked up the Beretta from the seat and checked the clip, then reached in the glove compartment for the padded silencer. After fitting the silencer onto the pistol's muzzle, he stretched his arm over the seat for the three rolls of adhesive tape and six feet of nylon rope on the backseat floorboard. He shoved the tape in his back pocket, looped the rope over his shoulder, then got out and crossed the lawn, headed for the vacant eastern side of the duplex.

Adriani knew the eastern half was unoccupied for the same reason that he knew every foot of the space in which the cute little bimbo lived: He'd been waiting for several hours and had been inside and made a walk-through. He hated doing things half-assed, without knowing in advance every single move he was going to make. The man downtown had convinced him that this job had to be done right now, this minute, and the hurried survey he'd made of the kill zone would have to do. If this turned out to be the final screwup, Adriani thought, he couldn't blame anybody but himself, doing business without knowing he was fucking with a lawyer to begin with. If he got past this job in one piece, these Dallas people had seen the last of Mancil Adriani; he'd already made up his mind that he'd even forgo the rest of his money. To hell with the cheese, Adriani thought, I want out of the fucking trap.

Moving swiftly and noiselessly on foam-soled suede loafers, Adriani moved at a half-crouch into the shadow of the house. He hurried along parallel to the duplex's eastern wall, vaulted the thigh-high fence into the backyard, and paused to catch his breath. He needed to do some jogging or something. He kept his mouth closed, inhaling and exhaling through his nose until the rising and falling of his chest slowed, listening to the steady *chirrup, chirrup* of crickets and casting his gaze over unmowed Bermuda with Johnson grass stalks waving in the wind. Beyond the back cyclone fence, light shone here and there from windows up and down the alley.

Adriani called up a mental image of the layout inside the duplex. When he entered the bedroom, he had to be silent. He imagined with a grin what it would be like, the dumb white-haired bozo in midstroke, his ass raised to drive one home as Adriani put one bullet through the side of the bozo's head and then walked up to shoot the woman. Calm now, his pulse a steady seventy beats a second, Adriani strolled past the vacant half of the duplex and paused. He stepped forward, wriggled in between the six-foot juniper bush and the wall, and placed the latex-covered fingers of one hand beneath the edge of the bedroom window. The screen which he'd removed earlier was propped against the backyard hydrant, six feet from where he stood. Just two hours before, standing inside the bedroom, Adriani had pumped several drops of WD-40 lubricating oil in between the window and the frame on both sides. He applied slight fingertip pressure; the window slid soundlessly upward a good six inches. He adjusted the rope around his shoulder, tensed himself, shoved the window all the way up, and hoisted himself up to sit on the sill. He slid back the bolt on the .380 with a near-inaudible click, then leaned backward inside the bedroom. Filmy drapes parted to admit his body; he twisted at the waist and thrust the silencer toward the bed. Sure of his direction, the bed exactly four paces ahead and the top of the mattress exactly twenty-one inches above the floor, Adriani squeezed the trigger.

The gun bucked in his grasp, the sound a quick, spitting

hiss, the bullet whining through the darkness and thudding into the far wall. Adriani lowered the barrel a couple of inches and fired off three more shots; two of the shells thumped the mattress and the third whanged into the wall. Puzzled, Adriani lowered himself inside to the floor and walked over to the four-poster queen-size. The bed was empty. There was a mirrored dresser on his left. As Adriani turned, a single ray glinted from the Beretta's muzzle. Somewhere inside the house water gushed.

Shower, Adriani thought. Well, ain't that sweet? The bozo's soaping her down. He pictured the hallway leading from the bedroom to the front of the house; six strides would take him from the window to the door. He retreated to just inside the sill and took confident steps, one, two, three, and his fingers contacted the wooden doorframe on the exact count of six. So far, so good. The door was open; the distance down the corridor to the bathroom was seven baby steps. May I? Adriani thought. He grinned. "May I" was a game which Adriani used to play with the other kids while the dons and their old ladies watched, thinking it was cute, the old dons having just murdered people the night before and now watching the little dumplings play "May I." You forgot to say "May I," you were fucked. He took the seven steps down the corridor, carefully sidestepping the one squeaky board on step number four. At the count of seven he turned to his left. A two-inch stripe of artificial light showed near his toes. Beyond the closed door a jet of water bombarded a silicone curtain.

Adriani raised the .380 to ear level, reached with his free hand to turn the handle, and shoved the door quickly open. In he went, one long step, down in a crouch, the pistol tight in his hand, his left hand clamped onto his wrist. He fired three times, snake-hiss volleys. The bullets punctured the rose-patterned curtain in a right-to-left pattern. The curtain billowed inward, then puffed back out under the relentless beating of the nozzle spray. Adriani stepped forward and slid the curtain aside with a rasp of hangers. Water splashed on green-tiled walls. Three of the tiles were missing dollar-size chunks, the bullets rolling harmlessly at the bottom of the tub. Adriani turned off the water. The faucet dripped monotonously. At the front of the house a door opened.

Adriani moved rapidly, no need for silence now, went back into the hall and toward the front of the house. He felt rather than saw the corridor widen into the living room, sensed the sofa three paces in front of him, the kitchen six strides to his left. The air-conditioning sprang to life as warm outside air blew on his cheeks. He squinted. Visible through the open front doorway, the three-quarter moon illuminated the ragged lawn. From far away a starter chugged and an engine sprang to life.

Adriani muttered, "Fuck me." Around the sofa he charged, his footsteps pounding on carpeted hardwood. He banged the screen door open and thundered onto the porch. In the driveway on his left, headlamps beamed. The red Mustang squealed backward into the street. Adriani snapped off one wild shot as the Mustang reversed its direction and sped away. Now he was sprinting across the lawn, gasping for breath, each step jarring him. The white Lincoln Town Car still was parked by the curb, and Adriani skirted the Lincoln's nose as he crossed the street to his own rented Ford and dived in behind the wheel. He dropped his gun on the seat and turned the key; the engine caught at once and raced. Adriani floored the accelerator, the Ford fishtailing and burning rubber. He held the steering wheel in a death grip as the Mustang's taillights brightened, and then dimmed as the little car bounced through an intersection.

Suddenly the Mustang screeched to a halt and stood stock-still in the middle of the street. Adriani slammed on his own brakes, frowning as he stopped with his front bumper just feet from the Mustang's rear end. He couldn't figure out what the fuck was going on, the broad running off like that and then suddenly stopping. It's a trap, Adriani thought, it's got to be, the white-haired bozo hiding in the Lincoln as Adriani had run by, now coming in pursuit, the broad in front, the Lincoln in back, and Mancil Adriani as the meat in the sandwich. He snatched up the Beretta as he swiveled his head to look behind him.

And recoiled in pain and shock as something heavy smashed into the side of his head, the white-haired bozo right there in the Fairlane's backseat, scant inches away, his breath blowing on Adriani's face. The scent of aftershave wafted up his nostrils as he tried to raise the pistol, his fingers suddenly numb as the club now slammed into his forehead, the gun dropping from his grasp as he collapsed against the door. His forehead throbbed and blood ran down his face. His vision blurred. Maybe go to sleep, Adriani thought, catch a little sack time.

As he watched in a daze, the white-haired bozo scooped up the Beretta and pointed the muzzle at Adriani's nose. He's going to shoot me if he's got any sense, Adriani thought. Dumb as he is, though, he might not kill me. Adriani waited patiently for the bozo to make his move.

The guy grinned at him, white teeth flashing in the moonlight, holding the pistol close, reaching out his free hand to display the club. Adriani blinked. Christ, a statue, a broad in a Farmer's Daughter dress, holding a lumpy pumpkin over her head.

"It's the Sweet Potato Queen," the bozo said. "Maybe you ought to be a candidate, you figure? Put a dress on you, asshole, you might even win."

25

BINO LIKED THE OUTFIT, ESPECIALLY THE LAVENDER COTTON polo with the button-down collar, and wondered where the guy had his laundry done. The clothes were pressed to perfection, the creases to die for. When Bino had herded him inside at gunpoint, the stocky man had asked for a rag or something to keep blood from dripping on his shirt and pants. Carla had furnished one of her throwaways, a pink fuzzy beach towel which was tattered around the edges. Since his initial request, the guy hadn't spoken a word.

Bino now said to Hardy Cole, "Mancil here's got a lot he could tell you, if you could get him to talk."

Mancil Adriani's heavy-lidded eyes twitched slightly. It was the fourth time Bino had called him by name, having first referred to the card he'd gotten from Dante Tirelli, the tightening of the guy's expression saying that, yeah, he was the man.

"It'd be nice," Hardy Cole said, "if we could get him to tell us whether or not he wants a lawyer. Or a doctor. Or a hamburger. I'm wondering if maybe he's deaf and dumb." The county detective was lean and angular and, Bino had always suspected, just about as tough as he looked. Cole was seated on the couch beside Adriani, and the two were handcuffed together, right wrist to left. Hardy wore tan rumpled cotton pants, grimy white socks, and black lace-up shoes. Carla had used a neighbor's phone to call Cole while Bino kept the prisoner company. According to her, Cole had been pretty rude at first, getting a call in the middle of the night, but once she'd filled him in Hardy had hotfooted it on over. Carla was curled up in an easy chair. Bino sat in the other padded chair with his ankle propped up on his knee, his shin pointing off at a right angle. It was a couple of minutes after five. Visible through the window, the blue-black sky faded slowly to gray.

"I doubt he'll give you any trouble," Bino said. "Old Mancil knows the ropes, if anybody does." This time Adriani stayed deadpan, apparently accustomed to Bino's use of his name and not interested in acknowledging his identity or copping out to blowing his nose. Bino fished out his lone pack of filtered Camels, only three smokes remaining in the crumpled package. "You want a cigarette?"

Adriani scowled. "Don't smoke. And if you're going to light up, go outside, huh?" He carefully laid the towel across his lap. The blood smears had dried to reddish brown, the gashes on his forehead clotting and scabbing over.

"He can talk," Cole said. "Wonders ain't ceased."

"He broke in," Bino said, "while I was interviewing the young lady on behalf of a client."

Cole glanced at Carla, his look more of a leer actually, taking in the snug pants and the bolero top with puffed sleeves. Carla suppressed a yawn and laid her cheek back against the cushioned chair. "Hope you were getting the right answers," Cole said.

"He's good for Rhonda Benson's murder," Bino said, poking the cigarettes into his breast pocket. "A whole bunch more, too. Our friend here's a federal protected witness."

Cole snorted. "Protected from what? Look, Bino, it's nice

that you know all this about the guy. You got any proof? All I do is read the paper, but I thought Rhonda Benson's husband was the murder suspect. Plus, unless I'm forgetting something, this all happened down in Houston. Not one of my favorite locations, plus I got no more authority in Harris County than you got in Bumfuck, Egypt." He glanced once more at Carla. "Excuse the language, miss." Carla gently closed her eyes.

"The murder happened in Dallas," Bino said. "That much she"—pointing at Carla—"can give you. We're going to have proof of some other things before long. Aren't we, Mancil?" Adriani watched the far corner of the room, where the ceiling and walls joined, and didn't say anything. "For now, Hardy," Bino said, "what we need is for you to keep him isolated."

"Jesus Christ," Cole said. "You ever hear of jail crowding? You want a reservation, call a year in advance like Disney World."

"It's why I wanted you instead of some beat cop," Bino said. "You got influence."

"With the D.A., maybe, even the police department. With the jail captain, nobody's got influence. It's first come, first served down there."

"Tell them he needs to be in protective custody," Bino said. "Tell them he's gay, that usually works. Say there's a big bull after his ass for fooling with one of the queens."

Adriani sneered.

"I might could do something for a night or two," Cole said. "Beyond that, I doubt it."

"I think tonight's all I need, Hardy," Bino said.

"You know what I got to charge him with as it is?" Cole said. "Burglary. Aggravated, yeah, 'cause he had a gun, but so what?"

The corners of Adriani's mouth turned up.

"He knows that," Bino said. "I'll bet old Mancil here knows the law better than I do. All these ex-con assholes do. Don't they, Mancil?"

Adriani's mouth relaxed.

"Here's what I'm wanting," Bino said. "Keep him in isolation, call Mac Strange as soon as it gets late enough he won't blow a gasket over you waking him up."

"Mac don't work on Sunday," Cole said.

"He's a county prosecutor, isn't he? Through rain and snow and all that? You don't work on Sunday, either, Hardy, but I notice you're sitting there. This is something Mac's going to want as bad as you do."

"I'll call him," Hardy said. "What do I say, other than that I've got this guy?"

"Tell him I'll meet you and him down at the jail as soon as I've had time to get a couple of hours' sleep and shower and whatnot. Say eleven o'clock. I've got some ideas kicking around in connection with Mr. Adriani here."

"I'll do that much," Cole said, standing. "Come on, Droopy." He undid the cuff from his wrist and motioned for the prisoner to get up. There was a holstered service revolver clipped to Cole's belt.

"Mancil," Bino said. "His name's Mancil."

"Whatever," Cole said. He pointed a finger down and drew a circle in the air. Adriani turned his back and extended his wrists so that Cole could cuff his hands behind him. "Going to jail don't seem to bother him much," Cole said.

"Walk in the park for this boy," Bino said. "Come on, I'll follow you out to your car."

Carla caught up with Bino as he stepped down from the porch, Cole ten yards ahead escorting the prisoner across the lawn with a hand on the inside of his forearm. Carla said, "I need to talk to you."

Bino turned and lifted his eyebrows.

She folded her arms and looked down. "Look, I'll admit I'm not exactly Braveheart Bertha. After this, I don't want to stay here alone."

Bino looked down at her, the upturned oval face, the slanted eyes showing real concern. "Don't take this wrong, Carla," Bino finally said, "but I'm beat, and I've got a couple of things to do. So if you're scared, call one of your neighbors.

Personally, I'm sure you're okay with this guy locked up. At least for now. So try to relax. Spend some time polishing your trophy, there's probably a few dents in the sweet potato. Better yet, if you need company, call Goldman. Maybe old Marv would let you stay at his place, you think?"

Bino studied the list of phone numbers he'd made on a sheet of notebook paper, handed a Xerox of the page over to Mac Strange. "This list should go down as 'Who's Who,' " Bino said.

There were times when Mac Strange was a pretty funny guy, having a few pops at Joe Miller's Bar with Bino and some of the other lawyers, but this wasn't one of the times. His face was drawn and tired-looking. He wore a baggy nylon jogging suit, navy blue with yellow stripes down the legs, and the paunch sticking out against the fabric said that the garb was strictly for show. Mac was soft and round, had receding gray hair and a double chin. He was seated on a conference table, and now gestured toward the one-way mirror. "If I call these guys," Strange said, "are they going to tell me something about our friend in there? He's sure not going to tell us anything."

Bino looked through the glass as well, at Mancil Adriani sitting inside the interview room with his arms folded. He wore a tan jumpsuit with DALLAS COUNTY JAIL stenciled between his shoulder blades. The jumpsuit was rumpled to beat hell, and Bino suspected that the guy's glum expression had more to do with the wrinkled clothes than the charges against him. Right now Adriani was looking at eight to ten months for burglary and damn well knew it. Bino said, "I don't think anybody on this list would give you the time of day, Mac."

"That's sure nice to know. We've kept a man in isolation for five hours and stiffed him for a phone call. We've told him the jail phones are out of order, which is bullshit a defense lawyer will get his cookies over. Not only do I think we've blown the burglary case, Mr. Adriani in there can sue the shit out of us and probably collect. How 'bout it, Hardy? You get anything out of him?"

Cole was rocked back on the hind legs of a folding chair, still dressed in cotton pants and black shoes. The detective had a heavy five o'clock shadow. "I got out of him that he don't like our jail laundry much. The only thing he's asked for is an iron to press his jumpsuit. Don't even act like he wants a lawyer."

"Oh, he'll want one," Bino said. "Only it'll be a certain lawyer, likely a guy from Houston. Protected witnesses got a list of lawyers the FBI furnishes 'em." He was freshly shaved and wore ragged running shorts along with an AMERICAN BAR ASSOCIATION—NATIONAL CONVENTION '89 T-shirt. His rump was propped against the edge of the table on which Mac Strange sat.

"I'll tell you something," Cole said, jerking a thumb toward the one-way glass. "That's one tough son of a bitch in there. Almost every one of 'em, they want some kind of deal, but not this guy. Acts like he doesn't care what we do."

"I doubt he does," Bino said. "A little time every once in a while, that's just a cost of doing business. I think these phone numbers might change his mind."

Strange studied the numbers. "How so?"

"I'll demonstrate," Bino said, "while the three of us and Mr. Adriani have a little talk."

One corner of Strange's mouth tugged to the side. "That's out of line, having a civilian question the prisoner."

"No more than you're already out of line with this guy," Bino said. "Come on."

Cole and Strange exchanged glances. "He's got a point," Cole finally said.

The three men walked around to a metal door with a deadbolt lock. Cole jingled a ring of keys at his hip, undid the bolt, held the door, and stood aside. Bino followed Strange into the interview room, Adriani's thick brows moving closer together as he eyed the two, Bino catching his own reflection on the inner side of the one-way mirror. Strange sat across a low table from the prisoner. Bino parked his rump on the table and leaned in. "Mancil," Bino said, "how you doing?"

Adriani tugged at the sleeve of his jumpsuit. "Guy's got no

pride in here. Gimme a month in the laundry I'll have the whole population looking good."

"You iron your own clothes?" Bino said.

"Yeah, don't trust nobody else to."

"They look good, those chinos and that polo shirt. You mind if I wear the shirt while you're away?"

Adriani propped a knee against the edge of the table. "I ain't going to be gone long enough you'd get much use out of it."

Cole moved up beside the table and leaned against the wall. "He's got it figured out, don't he?"

Adriani looked away, watching his reflection in the mirror.

"Yeah, too smart for you guys," Bino said. "Thing is, Mancil, I don't think you're going anyplace at all. What I was wondering, maybe you could leave me the pants and shirt in your will."

"I plan on living a long time, bro."

"I'm not your bro, Mancil," Bino said. "But I am good news for you. We talked it over this morning, the young lady and me, and I'm not sure you're the guy that broke in last night."

Now it was Mac Strange's turn to scowl. "What're you talking? You captured the guy."

"I captured *a* guy, Mac. I'm not sure it's this one."

"God amighty, you get me down here . . ." Strange halted in midsentence as Hardy Cole nudged his arm. Cole winked at Strange. Strange relaxed and watched Bino.

Bino favored Adriani with a big wide grin. "See how easy it is? If we can't identify you you're home free. Be out walking the street this afternoon. I felt so bad about falsely accusing you, Mancil, I even made a list of friends that'll be interested to hear you're okay." He slid a second Xerox of his list over in front of the prisoner. Bino hoped his scribbling was legible. Dante Tirelli had talked a mile a minute on the phone while Bino wrote like mad.

Adriani snatched up the page and read. His mouth slacked. He dropped the sheet on the table and said, "Fuck you."

"Now is that any way to talk to a guy that's trying to help

you?" Bino said. "All those Philadelphia people on the list, every single one wanted to know where you'd been. Said you hadn't been around the neighborhood lately. Let's see, I got your Houston phone number, and you're living in a place rented as Charles Dorrell."

Adriani pointed a finger. "You son of a bitch."

"A lot of folks think that. But I get concerned for people. In fact, this one guy, let's see . . ." Bino bent near the table and pointed to a name on the list. "That guy, Jimmy Ditulio. Told me you'd know him as Jimmy Dit. Old friend of yours, right?"

Adriani blinked. "You told Jimmy Dit where I was?"

Bino slapped Adriani on the back in gleeful good cheer. "Sure did. And you know what? He was so excited about you getting out soon, he wanted me to let him know exactly when you'd be leaving the jail. Said he'd put somebody on a plane. Must be a welcoming committee, huh?"

Adriani rubbed his back where Bino had slapped him. He gritted his teeth.

Bino's eyes widened. "I say something wrong? Gee, I didn't mean to." Mac Strange grinned at Hardy Cole, who scratched his nose and grinned at Adriani. "Well, you'll feel better once you're out," Bino said. "Come on, Mac, you got to get the processing started on this man's release." He got up and headed for the exit.

Adriani stood. "I ain't copping to no capital beef."

Bino turned. Cole and Strange watched.

Adriani put hands on hips. "No aggravated. A non-aggravated life in Texas, that's parolable in eight years."

"You been studying up," Bino said. He waved a hand in the general direction of Strange and Cole. "What, you got something to say to these guys?"

"We got a deal on the time, you get a steno in here," Adriani said. "And get me an iron. Jesus Christ, these clothes are bugging me to death."

26

ON THE MONDAY MORNING AFTER THE WEEKEND IN WHICH HE'D nearly been killed, Bino Phillips got up whistling and put on a suit. He selected a Rusty Benson courtroom special, a robin's egg blue lightweight cotton, and spiffed up his outfit with a patterned Christian Dior shirt and snow white tie. Just before leaving his apartment, he turned sideways to examine himself in the mirror and winked at his reflection. Easter Parade, Bino thought, here I come.

He continued to whistle a C&W tune which had been running through his head, but whose title he couldn't recall, as he walked briskly through the patio and did a little hop-skip-step through the breezeway into the parking lot. He felt better than he had in months. Yesterday he'd sat in on Mac and Hardy's session with Adriani for a little more than two hours, then had gone home, hit the sack around five in the afternoon, and hadn't come up for air until the sun was shining brightly through his bedroom window.

He got in and started his engine, moved the a/c lever onto the MAX position, and pointed the Linc's nose downtown in the mercilessly climbing July temperature. The heat wave was likely to continue into late August with no significant rain until fall. Normally his driving temperament followed the weather pattern, but his spirits had soared to the point that he wouldn't let small things bother him. At the on-ramp to Dallas North Tollway, a woman in a Nissan cut in front of him. He gave her a grand go-ahead wave and grinned from ear to ear.

He parked across the street from the office and crossed at the light, swinging along amid honking horns and city bus exhaust fumes, inhaling deeply and imagining that the horns were music and the exhaust odor expensive perfume. Once across the street he hung a left, leisurely strolling a block and a half to the west and entering One Main Place through revolving doors. He rode an elevator up to the twenty-eighth floor, pausing to allow a young lady to exit the car in front of him, then continued to whistle softly under his breath as he went down the corridor, entered the offices of Wick, Hamill & Co., and had a seat in the waiting room. He crossed his legs and smiled at the receptionist.

The girl behind the massive oval desk, punching lighted buttons and routing calls, had full cheeks and a pouty-sexy mouth along with enormous breasts which touched the switchboard keys when she bent over just the slightest. Her smile showed interest. "Hi, I'm Bobbi. You wanted to see . . .?"

"Larry Murphy." Bino rummaged through the magazines and selected a *Golf Digest*. On the cover, John Daly completed a massive backswing with the toe of the club practically touching the ground. "If he's tied up, I'll wait." Bino thumbed through the pages, found an article on chipping by Ben Crenshaw, and began to read.

Bobbi touched the tiny mike suspended in front of her mouth. "And you are . . .?"

Bino hesitated. Murphy shouldn't worry about an old college buddy dropping by. "Bino Phillips," he finally said.

She nodded, pressed a button, announced Bino's presence, and went on about her business. She had a lit Virginia Slim balanced on an ashtray, and Bino thought that was unusual. Most firms these days prohibited smoking, and Bino decided that this young lady must have some pull in the organization. He wondered why.

In a couple of minutes Larry Murphy entered from a door behind the receptionist's desk. Christ, Bino thought, everybody I run into these days looks like a halfback. Murphy wore a tapered shirt, navy slacks, and gray lizardskin boots. He thumbed his gray polka-dot tie, then stepped forward and extended his hand. "Dream come true," Murphy said. "Come in this house, ole *podnuh*."

Bino stood and accepted the handshake. Back in the old days, when Murphy had been SAE Fraternity president and had been running for some student body office or the other, pressing flesh with the guy had been something akin to arm wrestling. Things hadn't changed. Murphy gripped Bino's knuckles in a real bone crusher, Bino's grin frozen in place, the white-haired lawyer determined not to let Murphy know he was hurting. Murphy finally released. Bino dropped his throbbing hand to his side and said, "Hi, Larry."

"Say, you won't believe . . . come on, come on back." Murphy gestured and led the way into the inner offices. Bino followed, taking in rows of desks with new-recruit brokers on phones, squinting at printouts while talking a mile a minute to customers. Hot items, straight off the press. As he walked, Murphy said, "You won't believe this, but a guy was just asking about you the other day. Got your picture on my wall, in fact. Small world."

Bino didn't answer. Murphy ducked through a doorway and sat behind a desk the size of a handball court. Bino sank down in a visitor's chair, feeling leather-covered cushioning give, looking past Murphy at the haze-surrounded tower on top of the old Mercantile Building. Murphy hadn't been lying about the picture. Bino would like to forget his lone Byron Nelson Classic Pro-Am appearance, during which he'd lost a half dozen balls in water and woods while Mickey Mantle's tee shots made the gallery *oh* and *ah* and Lee Trevino kept 'em in giggling stitches. He'd forgotten Larry Murphy's presence in the group.

"You couldn'a picked a better day," Murphy said, leaning

back. "Got something new, specially designed for guys with fluctuating income. It's a back-in option that—"

"I've got nothing to invest, Larry," Bino said.

"Nobody thinks they do, but hey, just a little every month, you'd be surprised what it'll amount to."

Bino placed his elbows on the armrests and touched his fingertips together. "Things must be slow, you're not shooting for the home run. Just a little a month, that's what you guys are pushing now?"

"It's no secret, podnuh," Murphy said. "Damn Ann Richards. We get some good Republican influence, it'll be a hot time in the old town tonight again. Until then . . ." He shrugged, palms up.

"Times being tough," Bino said, "that why you're doing business with Pete Kinder?"

Murphy's confident expression sagged, a fleeting instant of panic replaced at once by the used-car salesman's grin. "Old Pete? Boy's had some tough times. He came in here, he was in good shape, a long time before that trouble with the feds. Wick, Hamill doesn't do business with him any more. They get flaky, we cull 'em out."

"Well, he ought to be back on the top of your list, then," Bino said. "They dropped his charges last week."

"Hey, podnuh, that's good to hear. Never like to see a man in trouble."

"Especially as long as it's not you, huh?"

Murphy scowled. "What's up, Bino? I don't see you for years, now you're in here asking me all this . . ."

"I'm representing a cop."

Murphy waved a hand like he was batting mosquitoes. "Police, schoolteachers, now, that's a group I don't mess with. Not enough money in it to . . ." He snapped his fingers. "All those cops taking bribes. That what you're talking about?"

"My guy didn't take any," Bino said. "But basically, yeah."

"Puts a black mark on the whole system," Murphy said, "those guys putting their hands out."

"Oh? How 'bout stockbrokers? What's that do to the system?"

Murphy tried faking it. "We're into moving money, there's a lot of temptation. What, you're wanting to know about some broker mixed up in something? Sure, podnuh, if I know anything I'll—"

"Well, how about crooked lawyers, then?" Bino said. "Rusty Benson, that ring a bell?"

"Sure, the guy on television," Murphy said. "Jailed in Houston, his wife's dead and they think he—"

"Cut the bullshit, Larry." Bino checked his watch. "You don't have much time."

Murphy's pointed chin quivered. "How come I don't?"

The intercom buzzed. His eyes narrowed, his gaze still on Bino, Murphy picked up the receiver. "Yeah?" He listened, then said, "I'm tied up right now, Bobbi. Tell him to wait." He brushed the back of his hand across his forehead. "He's going to have to wait, it's all I can tell you." He hung up, looking pale.

"I knew I should have gotten here earlier," Bino said.

Murphy chewed his lower lip.

"I was shooting for nine-thirty," Bino said. "But I overslept. Court opens at nine, and that's the soonest he could come up with a warrant. Figuring a few minutes to get down here from the Crowley Courts Building, the ride up on the elevator . . ."

"What the hell's going on here?" Murphy said.

Bino jerked a thumb toward the exit. "The guy in your waiting room. Hardy Cole, right?"

Murphy lowered his gaze and squeezed his hands together.

"Your buddy from Houston had a little trouble night before last, Larry," Bino said. "Had a wreck with a sweet potato, believe it or not. Talked to a county stenographer for, hell, just hours yesterday afternoon. Need I say more? You'd better hurry it up, Larry. Hardy's not going to wait, and your receptionist's boobs won't slow him down for more than a minute or two."

The lips turned up, revealing perfect dental work as the centerpiece in a look of complete desperation. "I need a lawyer. Christ."

"Don't look at me, I already got a client in all this mess. On top of which I don't make a practice of representing snitches, which is what you're going to have to be to get your chestnuts out of the fire." Bino bent from the waist and leaned closer. "I figure I got less than a minute, Larry, so listen up. For now they've got only you, since you're the only one your hit man had any dealings with. You want to give up the party you were acting for, you can make a helluva deal.

"I know who it is," Bino said, "since he's the only one with enough stroke to find a federally protected witness who's doing a few murders on the side. You'll have to tie in Kinder and tell them all about the investment laundering for Rusty and his buddies. But it won't be hard. You sing the right song, you might even make it back to civilization in time for the next financial upswing. Say, maybe, two thousand and five? The way the economy's going, it might just take that long."

Murphy choked and reached for a glass of water. At that instant the door burst open and Hardy Cole came in, wearing slacks and a plaid sport coat, and dangling a pair of handcuffs. Cole said, "Mr. Murphy? You're under . . ." He spotted Bino. "Jesus Christ, you're every fucking where," Cole said.

Bino stood. "Just doing my civic duty, making your job easier. I think Mr. Murphy knows what to do now, Hardy. Just do me a favor, huh? Don't go busting into federal court until I get there to watch. I think I deserve a ringside seat, don't you?" He took a long step toward the door, then paused and turned. Murphy was standing, the tail of his tapered shirt pulling out of his waistband and hanging down. Bino pointed at the wall. "Say, Larry," he said. "As long as you're not going to be needing it for a while, I'd like to have that Pro-Am picture, if it's all the same to you."

27

THE WALK OVER TO GOLDMAN'S OFFICE IN THE EARLE CABELL
Federal Building wasn't a long one, and Bino covered the
distance in a hurry. Perfectly timing his arrival was a
must. Tomorrow the grand jury would meet, which meant
that Goldman would reserve most of his day for witness re-
hearsal. That's what Bino was counting on. In order for him to
be effective, he needed an audience.

He exited the elevator on the third floor and walked past
the receptionist with his head down. Years of battling Goldman in court had taught him that when visiting old Marv in
person, announcing oneself was a mistake. Going through
channels in a bureaucracy guaranteed at least a half hour of
cooling one's heels, even when Goldman was anxious to see
his visitor. If old Marv *didn't* want to talk to whoever had come
calling, the wait could string out for hours and hours.

Bino went quickly through the maze of corridors, nod-

ding briskly at passersby as if he was just one of the boys, and
arrived outside Goldman's office without any trouble. There
was no name on the door, only a room number on a white
pasteboard sign. Bino went in. Goldman's reception area consisted of a couch, two stuffed chairs, and a secretarial desk minus a secretary. According to Dodie Peterson's rumor mill,
Goldman was such a wild man that he couldn't keep help on
the payroll, and Bino had no doubt that the story was true. He
tiptoed to the edge of the secretarial desk and leaned over to
peer around the doorjamb into the inner chamber.

A quick glance told him that he'd struck pay dirt. Rusty
Benson's square jawline was visible, as were the ferret profile
and sweaty underarms of Detective Captain Terry Nolby. Bino
couldn't see Goldman—a file cabinet was directly in his line of
vision—but the U.S. prosecutor was doing all of the talking.
Bino inhaled and strode on in, dragging the secretary's chair
behind him. "Hi, guys," he said, grinning around. "Am I late?"

In addition to Nolby and Rusty Benson, two FBI agents
had chairs leaned back, taking notes. Goldman, behind his
desk in a short-sleeve white shirt and black tie, was squeezing
a hard rubber ball. His forearm muscles knotted under
smooth skin. His mouth hung open. He finally said, "This
meeting's private."

"Rusty," Bino said, ignoring Goldman. "You forgot to tell
me you were checking out of the Harris County Hotel, old
buddy. These guys must have picked up your tab. How's the
safe house?"

Rusty wore a formfitting blue golf shirt and white jeans
along with blue suede loafers. He studied his knees and didn't
answer.

Goldman pointed. "There's the door, buddy."

Bino glanced over his shoulder. "So it is. What, I'm inter-
rupting?"

"You want to see me, make an appointment." Goldman
squeezed the ball until his neck muscles stood out from the effort.

"Oh, this won't take long," Bino said. "I thought I'd save
you some time." He gave the back of Terry Nolby's neck a one-

handed affectionate squeeze. "How's my man Terry?" Bino said. Nolby shook off the hand and faced the front.

"Nobody in here's going to talk to you," Goldman said. He frowned. "Save me some time from what?"

"*You're* talking to me, Marv," Bino said. "I thought I'd save you some grand jury time. Your judge is going to be in state custody before you can get him indicted."

Goldman had his legal pad spread out, and had been taking his own notes. He covered his work with his forearm. "What judge?"

"Hey, Marv, you don't have to play 'em close to the vest with me," Bino said. "Old Prayin' Edgar. You'll have a tough time prosecuting anything so tame as a bribery case, with Bryson up on capital murder charges."

Goldman lost his cool, leaning forward. "Who'd *he* kill?"

Bino looked in turn at Goldman, Rusty, and Nolby, then said to the FBI agent nearest him, "These three guys beat all I've ever seen. How 'bout you, agent, you ever seen anything to match 'em?"

The agent, a blond on the rookie side of thirty, looked at his partner, an older man with a graying mustache. Both agents shrugged.

"Really, I can understand the way old Terry Nolby here's acting," Bino said. "He's been getting it under the table for so long, sending a fellow officer down the tube is just another payoff deal to him. But Marv, now, this is a treat. He's got Rusty Benson ready to testify against a judge in return for getting a state murder charge dropped. The thing is, they couldn't have convicted Rusty anyhow. Could they, Marv?"

Goldman scratched his chin. "A conviction's always a possibility in trial. You know that."

"Not when the state doesn't even have any evidence to put on," Bino said. "And you want to hear the really funny part? This is about the only thing Rusty's clean on. He didn't have anything to do with Rhonda's death, Marv. Fooled you."

Goldman did a double take in Rusty's direction. Rusty looked out the window.

Bino stood and jammed his hands into his pants pockets,

really beginning to enjoy himself, feeling for all the world like Hercule Poirot. "Now that doesn't mean Rusty wouldn't have done it if he could have. He would've killed Rhonda in a heartbeat to keep her quiet about what he'd been up to. But he still had ears out for information on Rhonda's whereabouts while she was sitting down there in that canal. Since he didn't even know where she was, he couldn't have killed her." He slapped Rusty on the back. "Why, old Rusty here's such a horse's ass, he's willing to become a snitch against the judge when he knows damn well he can't get convicted on the murder. What were you looking at, Rusty, six months in Harris County waiting for bail to get set? That's all, and you know it. Your testimony comes too cheap, pal, you should have held out for snitch money."

"What makes you so sure I couldn't have gotten hung, even if I didn't do it?" Rusty said. "Because I had such a great lawyer?"

"Hell, Rusty, anybody could have gotten the no-bail order overturned. It didn't take somebody with my talent. As long as they had you down in Harris County, they could turn you any way they wanted to. Me, too." He jerked a thumb at Goldman. "You don't think old Marv died laughing that night they locked me up? Made his year. The problem is, though, Rusty, Rhonda didn't get herself killed in Houston. The murder happened right here in good old Big D. Now, ain't that a kick?"

Now Rusty threw a wide-eyed look at Goldman. Goldman folded his arms and said, "I'd watch myself, Bino, if I was you. Dammit, I was afraid that girl . . ."

Bino's jaw thrust forward. "Watch myself how, Marv? Come on. As for Carla Carnes, before you decide to really screw her around, you'd better hear me out."

Goldman puckered his mouth. "You might be painting yourself into a corner, running your mouth."

Bino lifted his coattails and put his hands on his waist. "Come to think about it, maybe I am. It's my corner, though, so let me paint." He turned to Rusty. "Your buddy Mr. Goldman had the body moved. Sounds implausible unless you really know old Marv." Now he looked at the FBI agents. "Was that you guys' job, moving the body two hundred and fifty miles and dumping it in that canal, and then calling up the Houston people to pinpoint the location for 'em? Somebody on the federal payroll did it."

The two agents looked at each other and grinned. Goldman slammed his desk drawer.

"The whole thing, Rusty," Bino said, "was to get you out of Dallas County's jurisdiction. In Dallas, Goldman knew you were the nuts to make bail, but down there in Houston the county will play ball any way the feds want them to. He had it figured right, too, Rusty. You folded like an accordion.

"But Rusty didn't kill Rhonda, Marv. The judge himself did it. Figured out that all the things he'd been saying in the throes of orgasm could get him in trouble. Which was why Rusty was pimping for his own wife anyway, to get something on the old boy. Jesus Christ, you people make me sick to my stomach."

Goldman ignored the compliment; the federal prosecutor was the only guy Bino knew who actually thrived on insults. "The judge couldn't've," Goldman said. "We had guys on him."

"Oh, shit, Goldman," Bino said, "he *hired* it done. So now you've pulled all this for nothing. The state's going to get your judge before you can lay a hand on him, and you're not going to have anybody left to prosecute."

"The hell I'm not," Goldman said. "There's still your cop friend. Clinger."

Bino sat back down. "Haven't you been listening? You're going to drop the charges against Tommy, which you were already planning to do, but there's going to be no substitute indictment. Tommy walks, which he should have all along."

Now Nolby sat up and took notice.

"And what is it," Goldman said, "that's going to force me to do all this?"

Bino grinned. "Carla Carnes."

"*That* bimbo?" Goldman said.

"Watch it with the insults," Bino said. "She's the one with the key to your heart. You almost got her killed, you know, having old Hazel pop off about her so Bryson would come unglued. He did, too, and Carla's mad enough over it to stop dating you. I've been blowing all this smoke, but I've sure as hell got no proof you did all this. Carla does, though. She's the one that found Rhonda and turned the situation over to you."

Goldman looked at the ceiling. "Christ, the people you have to deal with in law enforcement."

"Yeah," Bino said, "including you. Take it from me, Marv, you're going to do two things. You're going to drop the charges against Tommy, and you're going to keep your deal with Carla Carnes, including putting her hubby on the street. You crawfish on either of those deals, the newspapers and television are going to have a field day. 'MARV MOVES BODY,' how's that for a headline?"

"What makes you so sure," Goldman said, "that the state can put anything on Bryson? Assuming we can't, aside from the payoffs."

"Because the state's got Bryson's contract killer, Marv. He's the one getting the good deal out of all this, the hit man. Oh." Bino pointed a finger. "One more thing, the thing that's really going to do your plans in. You ready?"

"You're doing the talking, my bunny-haired friend."

Bino touched the top of his head. "Bunny-haired friend. Hey, that's pretty good. He's a federal protected witness, Marv."

"Who is? We didn't promise to put either of these guys in the program. I don't think they'll be in any danger."

Bino paused, stumped for an instant, then said, "I'm not talking about Rusty or Nolby, Marv. The contract killer. He's the one, been doing one hit right after another all the time you nice federal folks were protecting him."

Goldman sank down in his chair. His complexion went slightly green.

"That's how the judge knew about the guy, Marv, through the witness program. Now, you want all that out for public consumption?"

Goldman looked down. "How do I know it's true?"

"It's true, okay, and you'll verify that the second I walk out that door." Bino settled down. "If you use your head, though,

Marv, you might be able to salvage a little something out of this."

"Oh?" Goldman said. "How's that? According to you, we're out in left field on the entire investigation."

"You could go back to square one," Bino said, "and prosecute this guy"—he pointed at Nolby—"and this guy"—now pointing at Rusty—"who are the two bad dudes in the first place. You can get both of them on the payoffs, and that'll get you something for all your trouble. All you got to do with Nolby is have the whores, pimps, and whatnot finger Nolby instead of Tommy Clinger. And, if you live up to your deal with her, Carla Carnes can give you Rusty, hands down. Oh, yeah, there's a state prosecutor Rusty's been funneling money to, a guy named Arnold Bright. That'll give you only three guys to prosecute instead of the three hundred or so you were planning to, but hey, any port in a storm. Ever think of doing a straight prosecution, Marv, without a bunch of hocus-pocus?"

Goldman perked up, looking interested.

Now Terry Nolby spoke up. "Wait a—" he croaked, then cleared his throat and said, "Wait a minute. I got a deal."

Rusty glumly regarded the floor. "I thought I did, too."

"I'll have to look at the file," Goldman said, "to see how firm those deals are."

"Goddammit," Nolby said, rising. "I need to see my lawyer."

"Hell, *he's* your lawyer," Bino said, indicating Rusty. "Talk to him."

Goldman smiled and yanked on his goatee. "You guys aren't under arrest, so you aren't entitled to Miranda warnings. Not yet."

"Wait a minute," Rusty said. "The stuff we've already told you. You're not planning to use that. It's protected under the deal."

Goldman looked at the FBI agents. "You guys know about any deal with these two?"

One agent shrugged. "Not me."

The other agent massaged both sides of his nose. "Me, neither."

Rusty looked at Nolby. Nolby looked at Rusty. Both men's

jaws dropped. Goldman grinned at them. "What deal?" Gold-man said.

Bino stood. "With my client out of the soup, none of the rest of this is any of my business. If you guys'll excuse me, I've got someplace to go."

"What makes you so sure," Goldman said, "that the state can beat me to the punch on indicting the judge?"

Bino checked his watch. "Because your grand jury doesn't meet until tomorrow. You'd have to bring charges in the next fifteen minutes, Marv. Otherwise you're fucked, I'd have to say."

The three Mountainites didn't seem to have moved, stern faces set in granite, the woman between the men, seated on a bench outside the U.S. District courtroom. Their glares were directed to an adjacent bench, on which sat Larry Murphy along with Hardy Cole and Mac Strange. Murphy studied his lizard boots. His lips trembled. Cole returned the Moun-tainites' stares while Mac Strange read the newspaper. As Bino approached, Cole nudged Strange and said something from the side of his mouth. The Mountainites looked ready to pray Hardy straight into Hell.

Bino stopped before the cultists, briefly wondering where the guys bought their stovepipe hats, and pointed toward the other bench. "Those guys aren't telling dirty jokes, are they?" Bino said. The Mountainites now included Bino in their ven-omous glares. He grinned, went over and said to Cole, "If they've really got a pipeline to the Man Upstairs, you've had it. Thanks for waiting." He did a double take at Murphy. "Larry joined the force or something?" Murphy continued to trem-ble and watched the far wall.

Cole stood. "Naw, saves me some time. I got two guys to book, I see no need to make two trips to the jail. Old Larry here's my pal, anyway, he's not going to give me any trouble." He glanced at the courtroom. "Besides, I want Bryson to see him." He reached in his inside breast pocket, produced a war-rant, and read it over.

Mac Strange got up and folded the newspaper under his arm. "You kept us long enough, Bino. You ready?" He looked at the Mountainites. "Or you got some more praying to do?"

The scene was like an old-time revival meeting, Mountainites in full Quaker dress jamming the courtroom pews and lining the walls. Bino had never seen Big Preacher Daniel in person before, but now understood why the Preacher was the leader of the flock. He had the shoulders of a Mack truck, and over his beard his eyes gleamed like Christ's. Or Manson's, Bino wasn't sure. Big Preacher dwarfed his lawyers, a couple of guys named Eidson and Smart, both of whom Bino knew. The attorneys were average-size men, but alongside Big Preacher Daniel looked like a couple of midgets. As Cole, Bino, Strange, and Murphy trooped in, the Preacher surveyed the newcomers as if passing judgment, then returned his attention to the front of the courtroom. Lawyer Eidson recognized Bino and waggled his fingers. Bino smiled hello. He stopped near the railing gate behind Larry Murphy, with Cole and Strange bringing up the rear. In the media section, a *Dallas Morning News* reporter nudged a young lady from the Associated Press and pointed. Both reporters stared.

There was an FBI agent on the witness stand, answering questions from a slim female prosecutor. The prosecutor wore a straight gray dress. There was a rustling in the courtroom as the entourage marched down the aisle. The Assistant U.S.D.A. stopped in midquestion and turned. She looked more than a little annoyed.

Bryson was on the bench, his head cocked attentively, his thick white hair perfectly combed. He snapped his head around at the commotion and glared, first at Mac Strange, then at Hardy Cole, and finally at Bino. Finally the judge's gaze fell on Larry Murphy.

Bryson's face sagged as if made of Play-Doh. His cheeks collapsed; the bags under his eyes drooped even further. He removed his glasses and massaged his eyelids. Then he returned his attention to the witnesses, as if by carrying the tes-

timony along he could make his troubles disappear. The
judge boomed, "You were asking, Miss Hill?"

The prosecutor stayed rooted in her tracks. The witness
adjusted the lapels on his coat.

"Miss Hill?" Bryson repeated.

Cole looked at Strange, who nodded. Then Hardy went
through the gate and approached the bench, dragging handcuffs from his back pocket as he moved along.

Bryson favored the county cop with a challenging stare.
"What is this?" the judge said.

Cole remained deadpan. "Edgar Bryson, you are under
arrest for the murder-for-hire of Rhonda Benson. You have
the right to remain silent. Anything you say—"

Bryson put on his glasses and blinked owlishly.

"—can and will be used against you in a court of law. You
have the right to an attorney. If you cannot afford an attorney,
the court—"

Bryson looked around as if asking for help.

"—will appoint you one." Cole raised the handcuffs and
rattled them. "Let's go, Judge. This is one time I hate doing
this. And believe me, I don't hate it very often."

Bryson uttered an audible sob as Cole came around behind the bench. Cole drew the judge's hands behind him to
apply the cuffs. Bryson stammered, "My . . . robe. Maybe I
should . . ."

Cole stepped back. "Up to you, Your Honor."

Bryson stiffened. "I'll wear it."

"Might not go good for you," Cole said, "when the other
prisoners see you in that outfit."

"I said I'd wear it, officer." Bryson lifted his chin and
thrust his hands out behind him.

Cole shrugged, then rasped the bracelets onto Bryson's
wrists one after the other. He then led the judge around the
bench, through the bullpen area, and stood aside with the
gate open. Bryson locked gazes with Larry Murphy for an instant, then looked at the floor. As he passed Bino, Bryson
snapped, "Are you part of this charade, Mr. Phillips?"

Bino looked at Bryson's feet, then slowly up until he and

Bryson were eye to eye. "I guess I am, Judge," Bino said. "And I'll tell you something, you can can the theatrics. I represent some pretty bad guys, Your Honor, but I am what I am, and I don't pretend to be anything else. You and your religious bull- shit . . . well, don't expect any sympathy from me, is all I can tell you."

Cole led Bryson away with Mac Strange and Larry Mur- phy falling in step behind. As the foursome exited the court- room, one of the Mountainites, a short balding guy, stood in the aisle. "The Reverend Brother Preacher is saved, brothers and sisters," he shouted. "Hallelujah."

In the silence that followed, Bino remained in the aisle near the celebrationer. Big Preacher Daniel stood at the de- fense table as if he'd just witnessed the Second Coming. Bino walked over to the happy flock member and looked down at the guy.

"Well, the salvation is probably temporary," Bino said. "But for now, yeah. Amen, brother, pour it on."

28

FOUR DAYS LATER BINO HAD AN APPEARANCE IN FRONT OF JUDGE Hazel Burke Sanderson, to plead out a counterfeiter named Inky Briscoe. There wasn't much to the hearing, Briscoe having suffered a federal raid while in the process of loading three bushel baskets of still-damp twenties into the rear of a van. Since his client had done three previous falls, Bino had very little to do in explaining the plea bargain process. Inky knew the ropes quite well, thank you. Bino found it distracting that during the judge's pre-plea spiel, his client was murmuring the words in a whisper right along with old Hazel. To compound the problem, when she said, "Are you pleading guilty because you are guilty and for no other reason?" Inky snickered out loud. This brought both lawyer and client a glare from the bench which could melt tooth enamel. Bino shrugged at old Hazel, palms up, as if to say, "He's the counterfeiter, I'm not," then regretted his action as

Judge Sanderson's face turned ripe purple.

After old Hazel had accepted the guilty plea and set sentencing for six weeks hence, Bino turned to Inky Briscoe and extended his hand. "Sorry it couldn't turn out better, Ink. You may be looking at as much as a dime."

Briscoe, a short round man with a permanent squint, gave Bino a firm grip. "Nothin' to that," Briscoe said. "But, how 'bout doin' me a favor?"

"If I can," Bino said.

"I got the word from the marshals," Briscoe said, "that they're shippin' me to Big Spring. The warden up there's an old buddy of mine, so how 'bout callin' him up. Tell him old Inky's comin' down. That way he'll hold me a job in the cable factory, okay?"

Bino agreed, and Inky toddled off between two marshals, happy as a clam. Sometimes Bino wondered if guys like Inky Briscoe didn't have the best of things. He smiled at Judge Sanderson—who snugged her Martha Washingtons up on her nose and ignored him—then strolled through the gate, up the aisle, and left the courtroom.

The arrest of a federal judge on murder charges had occupied the headlines for several days, and Goldman's convening of a special grand jury to investigate corruption in the police department, the D.A.'s office, and the judicial system had drawn only moderate coverage. That Marv wasn't grabbing all the attention pleased Bino and, he thought, was just as the situation should be for a change. On the afternoon of Edgar Bryson's arrest, the feds had taken Rusty Benson, Terry Nolby, and Assistant D.A. Arnold Bright into custody, which Bino further thought was exactly where the three guys belonged. The grand jury witnesses Goldman had subpoenaed were pimps and whores, some of whom Bino knew. He supposed that Carla Carnes would put in an appearance as well, but she wasn't under subpoena. Bino figured that Goldman had kept his deal with her and that Carla would show up without any prompting. Big Preacher Daniel's trial had been set off a couple of months, and the rumor was that old Hazel was going to be the Preacher's new judge. God versus Godzilla,

Bino thought. He nodded to a couple of lawyers he knew in the hallway, and strolled on toward the elevators, glad that Tommy and Molly Clinger had been on cloud nine all week, and that he'd been able to help them. Bino suspected that Terry Nolby's job was Tommy's for the asking. Whether or not Tommy wanted to remain a career policeman after what he'd been through was up to him.

Bino halted as a perky and familiar female voice said from behind him, "Hold it there, hoss."

He turned. Carla bustled in his direction wearing a conservative charcoal suit and medium-heeled pumps, and she had a young man in tow. He was clear-eyed with a photogenic smile and dazzling dental work, and had shoulder-length brown hair, washed and brushed as though ready for an onstage appearance. Bino felt a twinge of apprehension.

Carla stopped and did a pirouette. "How 'bout it? Witness for the prosecution, huh?" she said. "Bino, meet Chris." She grabbed the young man's arm and tugged him over.

The guy extended his hand. "Hi. Carla's—"

Bino exerted a medium grip. "Glad to—"

"—told me all about you," the second C.C. finished.

Bino swallowed hard. "She has?"

Carla stepped quickly in between the two. "I told him all about, how you helped. You know, with Mr. Goldman and all?" Unseen by Chris, she threw Bino a saucy wink.

"Glad to know who my friends are," Chris said brightly. "And, man. Am I glad to be out."

"Yeah," Bino said. "They turned you loose in a hurry."

Carla hugged Chris around the waist. "I told Mr. Goldman like you said, that I wasn't appearing before any old grand jury until I had my husband beside me. Worked like a charm."

Bino was puzzled. "Like I . . .?"

"Like you said," Carla said firmly. She grabbed Chris's hand and tugged him away down the hallway. "Showtime in five minutes," she said, "or whatever they call this testimony stuff. See you, hoss. Be sure and catch the act sometime."

Bino watched them go, Carla's fanny bouncing from side

to side, the couple's arms about each other. He wondered if Carla had been telling him the truth, that he was the only one. He supposed he'd never know.

"Catch the act? Count on it," Bino said to himself.

He took the afternoon off, tooling the Linc out the tollway to Vapors North, sitting with his feet propped up on the kitchen table and watching Cecil drift aimlessly for a while, finally dropping a minnow in the Oscar's tank and looking on as Cecil ran the darting little bugger down. He then retreated to his bedroom, put on a sunflowered boxer-style bathing suit, snatched up a plastic bottle of Bullfrog sunblock and this month's *Golf Digest,* then sat down on the edge of the bed to call his office. He got the answering machine, supposed that Dodie had run over to the courthouse on some errand or other, and left her a message.

Fifteen minutes later, his chest, stomach, and legs coated with Bullfrog, Bino hopped up and down in the shallow end of the pool and then launched himself headlong onto an inflated raft. Then he turned over and backstroked his way to the edge, grabbed up his magazine and a pair of Cool-Ray sunglasses, and floated aimlessly to the center of the pool. He scanned an article, wondering if the hand action which Paul Azinger described would help him fade the ball. In a few minutes his fingers relaxed, the *Golf Digest* fluttered down open across his chest, and Bino emitted a series of snores.

There he stood in the eighteenth fairway at Augusta National, tossing up some blades of grass to test the wind, the hushed mob jamming both sides of the fairway and encircling the green one-eighty in front of him. The leader board showed a tie for the lead: Phillips −12, Zoeller −12. Ten yards behind him stood Fuzzy Zoeller himself, grinning a challenge, hands on hips. Bino glanced at the green to see Zoeller's white ball perched ten feet above the hole. He gritted his teeth and asked his caddy for his five-iron. Club in hand, Bino assumed his stance and made a perfect swing. The ball flew straight at the pin, drifting, spinning, and . . .

A sheet of water cascaded over him. He opened one eye as a well-formed leg kicked another spray in his direction. He sat up.

Dodie sat on the edge wearing short white shorts and a Harvard University T-shirt. Beside her was a covered pot. She picked it up. "It's a ham," she said. "Where's your apartment key?"

He looked up, the sun still high in the sky and beating down on him. Sweat ran down his neck. "Who's minding the office, Dode?"

"It can mind itself, for all I care. I haven't taken off in—"

His magazine slid into the water. "Hold on, I know you've been working hard. I just wondered—"

"—three months. I'll need some rolls, something for a salad. After we eat we can take in a movie or something." She held out her hand. "The key."

He pointed to his towel, rolled up on a wooden chaise longue. "In there," he said.

She stood holding the pot, water beading on her calf. She was barefoot, feet spread. "It'll be ready in an hour, in case you want to shower first." She walked toward the chaise longue, bent at the waist, and held the pot on her hip while she rummaged for his apartment key.

He rolled off the raft and stood in waist-deep, rippling blue water. "Did you say a movie?"

She looked at him over her shoulder. "That's what I said. *The Fugitive,* if you haven't seen it." She had the key now and stepped toward his apartment.

"Tonight?" he yelled.

"Yep." She kept walking.

He jumped up and down and cupped his hands around his mouth. "Wait a minute. What about this Robert guy?"

She stopped, stuck out one hip, and grinned at him. "Who the hell is Robert?" Dodie said.